We asked readers wh

Danielle Steel

'Danielle's books always make me feel **strong, inspired and happy** – truly a page-turning experience' *Liz*

'She has a remarkable ability to write different stories at an **amazing pace**. Every time I pick up a book, I know that I'm going to be taken through **highs and lows**' *Gillian*

'I feel like I've **travelled the world** through her descriptions of the places in her books' *Ann*

'Every book **gets you hooked** from page one' *Julie*

'Danielle Steel takes me to another place with her masterful story-telling . . . **Absolute reading pleasure** from the first page to the very last' *Holly*

'I have **drawn immense strength** from the characters in many of her books' *Sarika*

'I love how she puts **her whole heart** into her writing' *Corina*

'I just love getting lost in her books. I can **stay up all night reading one** just to know how it ends' *Kimmy*

'Danielle is such **an inspirational writer** whose experiences are carried into the books. When I read each book, I feel as though **I am there with the characters** . . . They have got me through some very tough times and I would be lost if I didn't have one of her books in my hand' *Katie*

'Danielle Steel's books are **the perfect escape** from reality. Every time I read her books, I'm transported to another place, ready for a new adventure' *Kelly Ann*

'I have been reading Danielle Steel books for fifty years or more and have kept every one – she is **my favourite author**' *Christine*

'**Gripping** reads that you **can't put down**' *Joanne*

'Her stories are **beautiful** and **gut-wrenching** and **totally unforgettable**. She has to be one of the best in the world' *Linda*

NEVER TOO LATE

Danielle Steel has been hailed as one of the world's most popular authors, with a billion copies of her novels sold. Her recent international bestsellers include *Triangle*, *Joy* and *Resurrection*. She is also the author of *His Bright Light*, the story of her son Nick Traina's life and death; *A Gift of Hope*, a memoir of her work with the homeless; and the children's books *Pretty Minnie in Paris* and *Pretty Minnie in Hollywood*. Danielle divides her time between Paris and her home in northern California.

By Danielle Steel

Triangle • Joy • Resurrection • Only the Brave • Never Too Late • Upside Down • The Ball at Versaill
Second Act • Happiness • Palazzo • The Wedding Planner • Worthy Opponents • Without a Trac
The Whittiers • The High Notes • The Challenge • Suspects • Beautiful • High Stakes
Invisible • Flying Angels • The Butler • Complications • Nine Lives • Finding Ashley
The Affair • Neighbours • All That Glitters • Royal • Daddy's Girls • The Wedding Dress
The Numbers Game • Moral Compass • Spy • Child's Play • The Dark Side • Lost and Found
Blessing in Disguise • Silent Night • Turning Point • Beauchamp Hall • In His Father's Footsteps
The Good Fight • The Cast • Accidental Heroes • Fall from Grace • Past Perfect
Fairytale • The Right Time • The Duchess • Against All Odds • Dangerous Games
The Mistress • The Award • Rushing Waters • Magic • The Apartment
Property of a Noblewoman • Blue • Precious Gifts • Undercover • Country
Prodigal Son • Pegasus • A Perfect Life • Power Play • Winners • First Sight
Until the End of Time • The Sins of the Mother • Friends Forever • Betrayal
Hotel Vendôme • Happy Birthday • 44 Charles Street • Legacy • Family Ties
Big Girl • Southern Lights • Matters of the Heart • One Day at a Time
A Good Woman • Rogue • Honor Thyself • Amazing Grace • Bungalow 2
Sisters • H.R.H. • Coming Out • The House • Toxic Bachelors • Miracle
Impossible • Echoes • Second Chance • Ransom • Safe Harbour • Johnny Angel
Dating Game • Answered Prayers • Sunset in St. Tropez • The Cottage • The Kiss
Leap of Faith • Lone Eagle • Journey • The House on Hope Street
The Wedding • Irresistible Forces • Granny Dan • Bittersweet
Mirror Image • The Klone and I • The Long Road Home • The Ghost
Special Delivery • The Ranch • Silent Honor • Malice • Five Days in Paris
Lightning • Wings • The Gift • Accident • Vanished • Mixed Blessings
Jewels • No Greater Love • Heartbeat • Message from Nam • Daddy • Star
Zoya • Kaleidoscope • Fine Things • Wanderlust • Secrets • Family Album
Full Circle • Changes • Thurston House • Crossings • Once in a Lifetime
A Perfect Stranger • Remembrance • Palomino • Love: *Poems* • The Ring
Loving • To Love Again • Summer's End • Season of Passion • The Promise
Now and Forever • Passion's Promise • Going Home

Non-Fiction
Expect a Miracle
Pure Joy: *The Dogs We Love*
A Gift of Hope: *Helping the Homeless*
His Bright Light: *The Story of Nick Traina*

For Children
Pretty Minnie in Hollywood
Pretty Minnie in Paris

Danielle Steel

NEVER TOO LATE

PAN BOOKS

First published 2024 by Delacorte Press
an imprint of Random House
a division of Penguin Random House LLC, New York

First published in the UK 2024 by Macmillan

This paperback edition first published 2024 by Pan Books
an imprint of Pan Macmillan
The Smithson, 6 Briset Street, London EC1M 5NR
EU representative: Macmillan Publishers Ireland Limited, 1st Floor,
The Liffey Trust Centre, 117–126 Sheriff Street Upper,
Dublin 1, D01 YC43
Associated companies throughout the world
www.panmacmillan.com

ISBN 978-1-5290-8560-0

1 3 5 7 9 8 6 4 2

A CIP catalogue record for this book is available from the British Library.

Typeset in Charter ITC by Palimpsest Book Production Ltd, Falkirk, Stirlingshire
Printed and bound by CPI Group (UK) Ltd, Croydon, CR0 4YY

Visit **www.panmacmillan.com** to read more about all our books
and to buy them. You will also find features, author interviews and
news of any author events, and you can sign up for e-newsletters
so that you're always first to hear about our new releases.

To my beloved children,
Beatrix, Trevor, Todd, Nick,
Samantha, Victoria, Vanessa,
Maxx, and Zara,

May all your dreams always come true,
and bring you joy, love, and satisfaction.
May you always be safe and loved,
with all my heart and love,
always and forever.

Mom/d.s.

NEVER TOO LATE

Chapter 1

Kezia Cooper Hobson flew from San Francisco to New York in first class, with four big suitcases that held the last of her things she was bringing to New York. Everything had been sent ahead weeks before, her clothes, all her mementos, her papers and personal treasures. Her furniture and art were due to arrive at the end of August. She'd been living at the Ritz-Carlton in San Francisco for the last month, while she concluded the sale of both her Pacific Heights home and her share of the venture capital firm she had inherited from her husband, Andrew Hobson, when he had died of Covid-19 five years before, after a business trip to China. Twenty years older than Kezia, he was seventy-five at the time, vital, healthy, active, handsome, successful, and youthful for his age. The virus had hit him hard and he was dead in five days. He was a wonderful person from a wholesome Midwestern background. He had gone west to Stanford for college and business school, established his groundbreaking business in San Francisco, and remained there.

Andrew Hobson had been one of the legends of early venture capital and one of its innovators in high-tech and biotech investments.

The firm he had founded originally with two partners had been bought by a newer, larger venture capital firm, since Andrew's partners had been older than he and were now well into their eighties. The life had gone out of Weintraub, Mills, and Hobson once Andrew was gone, with his incredible energy and constant daring new ideas. One of his partners was ill now, the other eager to retire, and the offer they received for the firm had come at the right time. Kezia had been active on the board since Andrew's death.

Originally from a small town in Vermont, the only child of a widowed and dedicated country doctor, Kezia had shared a thrilling life with Andrew. She had met him at a high-tech medical conference she went to in San Francisco, and married him not long after that, when she was thirty-five. The twenty years they had been married had been extraordinary, and profoundly happy. He had shown and taught and shared things with her that she would never have experienced otherwise. San Francisco had been the perfect small city to bring up their two daughters, with an agreeable cultural life and active business life for him of major international proportions with important investments in Asia, and good schools for their two girls. But once widowed at fifty-five, she found the city small and lifeless and limited. It was a lonely life for her. Everyone in her social circle was married, many of the men to younger women, much younger than Kezia by then. Her girls, Kate and Felicity, had gone east to college and never moved back to San Francisco. They loved living in New York, so Kezia traveled there frequently, to see them. She was bored with the opera and ballet boards she had served on for years. It all felt different as a widow. She felt like the odd man out with her married friends, and the city was just too small and provincial to provide an interesting life for her as a single woman. She could see herself growing old, with nothing changing in her life for the next forty years or more.

In exchange for the golden life Andrew had given her, she felt an obligation to remain involved with his company and sit on the board, but the offer to buy the company that came along unexpectedly was a blessing for Andrew's partners, and for Kezia. It forced her to re-evaluate her life and decide how she wanted to spend the rest of it, and where. It was time to let go of the past and move on. She would be turning sixty in the fall, even if she didn't look it, and it felt like the right time to make a bold move and re-enter the world, at fifty-nine.

Once she'd made the decision, her house sold quickly, and with two daughters in New York, it was the obvious place for her to go, and it would give her the life she needed and wanted after twenty-five years in San Francisco, the last five of them without Andrew. San Francisco had stopped making sense for her once he was gone. He had added life to it for her.

One of her daughters had a booming career and life in the city, the other lived in the West Village and some of the time in a house close to the Vermont town where she and her mother had been born. Kate was trying to write a book. She spent enough time in New York that Kezia knew she'd see more of her if she lived there herself than she would visiting her from San Francisco.

Kezia was excited about the move. Her whole focus was turned to what lay ahead for her.

She was still beautiful at fifty-nine, and easily looked ten years younger than she was. She was tall and slim, with a lithe, youthful, trim figure and strikingly pretty face, with blonde hair and deep blue eyes. She felt profoundly revitalized and renewed by the move to New York. San Francisco was just too small and too sleepy and now that she was no longer married to Andrew, even though she was a powerful force on the board of the company, people forgot about her. She wasn't by any means ready to give up her life yet, and quietly close her doors and sit at home. New York had all the life, vitality, and energy she craved, and with her daughters there, it made total sense. She was sorry she hadn't made the leap sooner. She was in great spirits on the flight on the way there.

It was the last week in June, and the weather was warm. The airport was teeming when she arrived on a Friday afternoon. She already knew that both her daughters were out of town for the weekend. Her younger daughter, Felicity, was working in Paris for two weeks, at Paris Fashion Week. At twenty-three, she had become a stunningly successful model and had been on magazine covers all over the world for the past three years. She had been eighteen when her father died, and she went to college at USC in L.A., as he would have wanted her to. But she had never been a strong student, and she dropped out after two years, when she was discovered by the head of a major New York modeling agency. Within the first six months she was on the covers of *Vogue, Harper's Bazaar, Elle,* and *L'Officiel,* and was known all over the world as the most exciting new face to come along in years. Felicity was responsible about her career. She took it seriously, and worked hard, and Kezia was proud of her success. Felicity had bought her own apartment in Tribeca

5

from her earnings a year before, at twenty-two, and led a glamorous life that would have turned most women's heads. She had learned to spot the men who pursued most models and were just looking for entertainment or arm candy, or simply wanted to be able to say they'd gone out with her. She had a tendency to go out with older men. Her boyfriend for the last year, Blake White, led a fashionable jet-set life at thirty-nine, and had a big job as a wealth management consultant at Goldman Sachs for some very illustrious clients. He was from a prosperous family himself, knew many important people as clients and friends, and loved going out with beautiful young women. But he also saw something deeper and different in Felicity, something that he hadn't come across before. In spite of her success and the money her father left her, she had sound values, strong family ties, and a good mind, and was more sensible than most women her age. Her own success hadn't turned her head. She was upbeat and fun to be with. Blake had been married before, to a socialite he had grown up with. He was divorced and had a six-year-old son, Alex, who spent alternate weekends with them, and would be with Blake for the month of August.

Felicity enjoyed spending time with Alex, and he loved her. She treated him more as a big sister would, rather than taking on a motherly role, which Blake also liked about her. She had no hidden agenda, considered herself too young to marry anyone, and had no desire to have children of her own anytime soon. After years of dating women since his divorce who were hell-bent on getting Blake to marry them, being with Felicity was refreshing, happy, fun, and a huge relief. She didn't try to court Alex in order to woo his father; she just had a good time with him. She was in love with Blake, but she loved her career too. She considered herself fortunate that her career had taken off and provided her a big income and great opportunities over the past three years. Blake loved being with her. He considered it ironic that the one woman he had taken seriously since his divorce didn't want to get married, and viewed herself as too young to consider it for at least another ten years.

Kezia knew that Felicity had been in Paris for fittings all week, at the various houses she would be "walking" for in the fashion shows. Both Chanel and Dior had hired her as one of their star models, and she was spending the weekend in Saint-Tropez at the house of friends of Blake's. He had flown over to be with her and see her in the haute couture shows the following week. Kezia couldn't wait for her to see the new apartment when she got back. She had gone all out with a real showplace in New York.

The apartment Kezia had bought was half of the penthouse floor in a relatively new sixty-story building on Fifty-fifth Street between Fifth and Madison Avenues. It was two floors taller than any other building near it, and she had a hundred-and-eighty-degree view of the city. She had been ordering furniture and draperies with a New York decorator for the past few months, and it was going to be sublimely comfortable and elegant. She had put some of the old furniture in a storage unit to keep for the girls. She had sold a lot of it, and sent only her favorite pieces to New York. It was a new world, a new life, a new home. She had kept most of the art because she loved it.

Kezia had rented the bare-bones basics from a staging company her decorator had recommended, so that she'd have a bed, several dressers, and a chair in her bedroom, two couches in her enormous living room, some comfortable chairs in case she had guests, a big coffee table, and a large dining table and chairs in the kitchen. She didn't need more than that until her furniture arrived at the end of August.

She had made no summer plans. She was looking forward to two months in New York, exploring new shops and restaurants and obscure museums. Her daughters were horrified that she was staying in the city, and Kezia insisted she didn't mind the heat or the tourists. She was going to make the city her own before the summer was over. Felicity had rented a house in Southampton for June, July, and August, and she and Blake would commute for work when necessary and were planning to entertain there. Alex would be with them in August. Felicity wanted her mother to come visit. She was always warm and welcoming, and mother and daughter had fun together, usually spontaneous adventures or evenings on the spur of the moment when Felicity was free.

Kate, Kezia's older daughter, was more complicated, and always had been. She was just as beautiful and striking as her younger sister, but everything about her was more serious and more intense. She had dark brown hair and big brown eyes, and delicate features. She was smaller than Felicity, who was tall and looked a great deal like Kezia, with blonde hair and blue eyes. Kate's beginnings were very different from Felicity's, and yet she had been just as fortunate, possibly even more so.

Kezia's mother had died of breast cancer when Kezia was three, and she had no memory of her, although her father spoke of her constantly in glowing terms. She had been a nurse and worked with him. Kezia had grown up in a tiny town in Vermont as the daughter of the local general practitioner, and he had shared with her his dedication to medicine, which was his passion. Her childhood had been a happy one, and Thornton Cooper was a loving, attentive father. Kezia had stayed close to home and attended the University of Vermont, as a science major, and entered nursing school in Boston after she graduated, to become a nurse practitioner and work with her father, which was her lifelong dream, and his. Shortly after she began the nurse practitioner program, she had discovered that she was pregnant, by a boy she'd had a romance with that summer, Reed Phillips. But neither of them had intended for it to be long-term. It was a hot summer romance they both knew couldn't last. She was going to nursing school, and he was a medical student at Dartmouth and was starting his internship in L.A. He had a summer job at a small country inn in Vermont, where he met Kezia.

Discovering that she was pregnant when she got to Boston after the summer was not good news for either of them. She liked Reed, but there was no hope of a future for them. They were headed in different directions, on opposite coasts. When she called to tell him she was pregnant, he came to see her. He was three years older than Kezia, steeped in his medical studies, and planning to move to L.A. for his internship. He liked Kezia a lot but he wasn't in love with her, nor she with him. There was no room in his life for a wife and a baby, and he made that clear. His life's dream was to go to Africa and work with Doctors Without Borders. His and Kezia's career goals were similar in medicine, but their paths were not destined to intersect in the future. She planned to work in a small Vermont rural town with her father, and Reed wanted a life a world away in underdeveloped countries.

Reed was very direct that he could not participate in the life of a baby. He would help her support it if necessary, but he was not going to engage in fatherhood with her. It was the last thing he wanted, and he didn't want to mislead her. Kezia spoke to her father after she'd spoken to Reed, told him what had happened, and offered to drop out of the nursing program. She had a partial scholarship, and her father was paying the rest. Her father was, as he always had been, loving and compassionate and generous with her. The baby was due at the end of the spring semester. He insisted that she stick with her studies, have the baby over the summer, and leave the baby with him in the fall and go back to school. He and a local girl would care for the baby during the week, and Kezia would come home on weekends from Boston to take care of her child. It would be arduous for both of them, but he was more than willing to do it. He would have done anything for her. Miraculously, it all went according to plan. Reed, the baby's father, stayed true to form too.

When the baby was born, Kezia named her after her mother, Kate Morgan Cooper. Reed was starting his internship in L.A. by then, and never came to Vermont to see the baby. He had sent Kezia relinquishment forms as soon as the baby was born. He wanted no responsibility for her. He offered to pay support, in spite of surrendering all parental rights, and Kezia refused. She didn't want money from him if he wanted no involvement with the child. They signed the papers when Kate was less than a month old, and he left her life without ever entering it. Until she was twelve, the only parents Kate knew were her mother and grandfather in the small town where Kezia had grown up.

It was a happy, carefree life. From time to time, when she was younger, Kate wanted to know why other children had a father and she didn't, and Kezia simply said that it had worked out that way. She explained that Kate's father was a doctor, he worked in Africa, and they couldn't be together. It was enough information for her as a young child. She spared Kate the additional information later that he had married a South African physician who also worked for Doctors Without Borders. Kezia had heard it by chance when she met someone who had gone to medical school with him. Kezia never heard from Reed again after he signed the relinquishment papers. Just as he had told her, he wanted a clean break. Kezia had wanted her baby anyway, doubly so to make it up to her for not having a father. And Kezia's father had been wonderful to both of them.

Kate had an easy, healthy childhood, adored by her mother and grandfather, and Kezia loved working as the nurse practitioner in her father's practice. No one in their little rural town had sparked Kezia's romantic interest, few wanted to date or marry a woman with a child, and some were bothered that she hadn't been married to Kate's father. It was a small, gossipy town.

It was Kezia's father who had suggested that she go to the medical conference in San Francisco, to learn about some of the new technologies. She'd been hesitant at first, and had resisted, but he insisted it would be good for her to get away. He took Kate camping that weekend. She was twelve, and loved camping and fishing with her grandfather. It was the only life she'd ever known. She had a serious, introverted nature, kept a journal, and loved to write. She wanted to be a writer and was always creating stories or scribbling in her journal. She said that one day, she'd write a book.

"If that's what you want to do, you will," her grandfather told her. "That's how I felt about being a doctor." Medicine held no fascination for Kate.

At the medical conference in San Francisco, by sheer chance, Kezia met Andrew Hobson, who had invested heavily in several of the technologies that were being introduced. He had come to see the presentations, since he lived in San Francisco. He took her to dinner, and to lunch before she left. She was somewhat dazed by having met him. He was incredibly impressive and the kindest man she'd ever met. He was a widower without children, twenty years older than Kezia. And for the next six months, he flew to Vermont as often as he could to spend time with her and Kate. He and

Thornton, Kezia's father, became good friends, and were not so far apart in age. They were both good men who respected each other.

Six months after they met, almost to the day, Andrew and Kezia were married in the small church in her hometown. She hated to leave her father; it was a wrenching decision for her. She knew it would be hard for him without her, but he wanted her happiness more than his own, which was the kind of person he was, and why everyone loved him. He wanted a better life for her than their small rural town could offer. Andrew Hobson was presenting her with a rare opportunity. And they loved each other.

Kate and Kezia moved to San Francisco with Andrew. He bought a big enough house for them to have more children, and he solemnly asked to adopt Kate within a few months of their marriage. He treated Kate as his own child right from the beginning. When Kezia and Andrew's baby girl was born two years later, they named her Felicity. He never differentiated between the two girls and treated them equally. The estate he left reflected that, and he divided his bequests equally between Kezia, his wife, and his two daughters, Kate and Felicity, with equal trusts for both girls.

Kate was fourteen when Felicity was born. She had treated her almost like her own baby, holding her, changing her, feeding her, like a live doll she had waited for all her life.

But as Kate entered her twenties and Felicity got older, Kezia could see that Kate was starting to view Felicity differently, as the intruder who had come to steal the limelight from her and rob her of her parents' time and attention.

Felicity was an enchanting, happy child, easy to love and spend time with. She had a sunny, open, uncomplicated nature, and Kate had a dark, brooding side to her which got more intense as she got older. Kezia wondered at times if Kate's biological father had a similar personality, but she hadn't known him well enough to be able to tell. Their relationship had been short-lived over a summer. When Kate turned twenty-one, Kezia shared the details of her history with her, thinking it only fair to do so. She told her about the summer romance that had been the origin of her birth, and the father who had chosen to relinquish her. She made it clear that it hadn't been Kezia's decision. It had been his.

The truth had come as a blow to Kate, even though he had given her up without ever seeing her. It wasn't that she didn't measure up, Kezia tried to explain, it was that *he* didn't. He didn't feel ready to be a father, no matter how lovable Kate was, and Kezia assured her she had been the joy of her life and of her grandfather's.

Sadly, the year after Kezia and Andrew married, Kezia's father had been diagnosed with leukemia and died in three short months. Kezia had been able to spend his last month with him, and Kate had come to say goodbye before he died. It had been an immeasurable loss to them both. But Andrew was close at hand to comfort them. And Felicity had been conceived shortly after Kezia's father's death, which had given her some consolation.

Kate had been depressed for months after she learned about the circumstances of her birth. She had thought about writing her biological father a letter, asking him to explain to her, in his own words, why he had given her up, but she never had. She wrote more than ever then, and her stories were always dark and sad. As she got older, she had a perspective on life that was always about loss and rejection, without taking into account how Andrew had embraced her fully, to balance it, from the moment he adopted her, and even before. Reed Phillips, her birth father, remained a mystery in her life and a dark specter, which in Kate's mind overshadowed Andrew's unconditional love, as well as her grandfather's.

Kate had a series of unhappy love affairs in her twenties, always with men who rejected her for one reason or another, as though she was trying to reenact the circumstances of her birth and have it come out differently. But it never did.

She was thirty-two when Andrew died, and she inherited a large amount of money immediately, because of her age. Felicity was eighteen when her father died, and had to wait until she was twenty-five, thirty, and thirty-five in order for the trust to disburse her inheritance. Kate received two-thirds of it immediately, since at thirty-two she was deemed to be a responsible age, according to the terms of Andrew's will. In spite of her inheritance, Kate lived relatively frugally, and bought a small house in Vermont, barely more than a cabin, a few miles from where her grandfather had been revered, and where she had spent her first twelve years. Kate was always in mourning for something, a broken romance, her father, or her grandfather. She was always looking back over her shoulder at the past. Felicity, in contrast, looked toward the future with excitement, and saw bright horizons all around her. There were no ghosts in her life, unlike Kate's.

"Obviously," Kate said sarcastically to her mother about it one day, "her father didn't refuse to see her and give her away."

"Andrew *chose* to be your father," Kezia pointed out to her. "He met you, and loved you, and made you his daughter, entirely equal to Felicity from the time she was born. He never saw you as second best, so why should you?"

"Because that's what I was," Kate insisted. "A reject."

"Reed Phillips was the loser, for what he missed. Not you." Andrew was a thousand times the man Reed had been. Kezia never pointed out that her adoptive father's love had come with a huge financial gift that would give her freedom for the rest of her life, and the ability to do whatever she wanted, which was hardly negligible, but it didn't seem to matter to Kate. Her birth father's rejection meant more to her than Andrew's love and her inheritance. It was how she looked at life. She always saw what was missing, rather than the blessings she had. It was the exact opposite of Felicity's view of life. She was free and unfettered, whereas Kate was always haunted by the ghosts of the past, including those she'd never met.

Kate had continued to write throughout her life, always journaling, and her latest romantic partner of the last four years, Jack Turner, was a struggling writer who seemed to enjoy the struggle more than the writing. In that way, he was well suited to Kate, although Kezia found him tiresome, always expounding about something, and pompous. Kate had met him at a writing workshop. He had been an English teacher at a prestigious boarding school and had given it up to become a tutor and try to write a novel. He hadn't so far, but Kate was convinced he had real talent. He had grown up in Boston and gone to Boston University. He had published short stories, and taught creative writing at one of the many writers' workshops he attended that flourished in Vermont. He was from a family of teachers. His father taught English literature at Harvard, but Kezia thought Jack lacked ambition and was less sure than Kate about his talent. He was good-looking but not exceptional on any front, with graying brown hair and brown eyes.

Now thirty-seven, Kate had been with Jack for four years and time was slipping past her. She had started a novel when Andrew died, five years before, but hadn't finished it, and still spent her summers in Vermont, going to writing workshops with Jack. He was forty-two years old, and never mentioned marriage. His own parents had divorced when he was young. He and Kate talked more about their unwritten novels than any plans for the future. Their life was eternally on hold, waiting for the great American novels to spring forth on their own. And conveniently for him, Jack had moved in with her three years before, after they had dated for a year. He had given up his fifth-floor walkup studio apartment in a shabby building on the Bowery, and Kate discreetly supported him, by tacit agreement. The subject seemed indelicate to bring up, and Kate could afford it, which seemed to Kezia a poor reason to be supporting him. Jack didn't make enough to live on. Kate insisted he was brilliant, but her mother wasn't so sure. His talent seemed to be latching on to the right people and making a living of it. Kate didn't seem to be madly in love with him, but their outlook on life was similar. He was good-looking, bright enough, and well brought up. The relationship was comfortable, but he was more of a habit than a passion. Kezia was no longer sure that Kate would ever marry and have children, but if she did, Kezia hoped it would not be with Jack. Kate was still nursing the deep inner wound of having been rejected by her birth father.

She was cautious with the money Andrew had left her and didn't live extravagantly. Her cabin in Vermont was barely big enough for the two of them, and her apartment in the West Village was a comfortable loft, but everything in it was secondhand and looked like she'd found it on the street.

By contrast, Felicity's big sunny apartment in Tribeca overlooking the Hudson was spectacular, and very chic. She and Blake went back and forth between her apartment and his equally nice one, a few blocks away.

Kezia often wondered why Kate continued the relationship with Jack. It seemed so unproductive and unrewarding, but it appeared to meet a need for her, for companionship, and for being with someone who was always struggling, as she was, to find herself. Kezia didn't have much faith in Jack at forty-two, but she still had hope for Kate at thirty-seven. She liked to tell herself that her older daughter was a late bloomer, but that was seeming less and less likely as the years went by. She had never met the right man. It was easier to be with someone like Jack, who hadn't made a success of his life, than with someone who had and made her feel inadequate. It was always easier to blame someone else. And with what Andrew had left her, Kate could spend the rest of her life trying to write the great American novel, and it didn't really matter if she never did.

In Felicity's case, she hadn't even come into her inheritance yet, and lived lavishly on what she made as a model. Kate was always critical of that, and said the money she earned was obscene, since it was a job that didn't require a brain. But it required flair and style, energy, persistence, and a positive outlook on life, and Felicity had them all, along with her beauty. The simple truth was that Felicity was happy and Kate wasn't, which made Kezia's heart ache for her. But the only one who could change that was Kate.

Kezia had hired a car and driver to take her into the city from Kennedy Airport. He had come with a van, and managed to get her four big bags in, and she smiled as she watched the outskirts of Manhattan slide by.

"This is home now," she reminded herself with a smile, content in the back seat. She was wearing jeans and a T-shirt, with a well-cut black blazer and loafers, and carried an Hermès Kelly bag. She had a natural chic. Her hair was pulled back in a long blonde ponytail, and some loose strands flew in the breeze that came in the open window. She was excited to see her new apartment again. She had been working from photographs and floor plans while she bought new furniture and ordered rugs. She was eager to see how it would all come together, but she had two months to wait for that. In the meantime, she didn't mind living in the sparsely furnished apartment with rented furniture. She didn't care if she lived with orange crates for two months.

She couldn't wait to show the apartment to the girls. Neither of them had seen it. She had bought it on a quick weekend trip to New York when it had become available, and the New York realtor she had been working with called her and told her to grab it before someone else did. It was a prestigious address, a great location, and one of the two best apartments in the building. When she bought it, Kate had been in Vermont for another writing workshop, and Felicity had been in Milan for Gucci. Kezia felt like she was jumping off the high dive when she saw it on her own and said she'd take it. It meant starting a whole new life. It was the perfect antidote to turning sixty. She still couldn't believe she was that old. She didn't look it or feel it. Some people retired at sixty, but she hadn't worked since she was thirty-five, when she'd married Andrew and given up nursing. She still missed it sometimes, but that was part of another life. Out of sentiment and nostalgia for her father, she still kept her nursing license up to date, but she hadn't practiced in twenty-five years. It seemed like an eternity, and it was.

It was early evening when the car pulled up to her new address. Fifth Avenue was crowded and so were the side streets. It was fun to be surrounded by all the noise and activity. She wouldn't hear it on the sixtieth floor. Her view stretched to both rivers and included the Empire State Building. The realtor had mentioned a number of famous people who lived in the building. Two senators and a congresswoman, a famous writer, and several actors. Notably Sam Stewart, the Oscar-winning actor, had the other half of the penthouse floor. They each had their own express elevator so they never had to see each other or other residents, or wait for the elevator. They had total privacy. A hedge separated his terrace from hers. The realtor had assured her that he was a notoriously quiet neighbor, and he was away on location most of the time.

Kezia remembered that his wife had died in a helicopter accident while filming a movie two years before. She was an equally famous actress, and they had been a legendarily happy Hollywood couple with a solid marriage, which ended in tragedy. Since Kezia and Sam Stewart had separate elevators, she would never see him, although she had seen most of his movies. He was a man of immense talent, strikingly handsome, and the realtor referred to him as a recluse, so at least he wouldn't be giving parties on his half of the terrace, which she would be able to hear even though she couldn't see him. The realtor said he was known to have a fabulous art collection, although the realtor had never seen it, since she hadn't sold him the apartment. He wasn't one of her clients.

The building manager had an envelope with the keys in it for Kezia, with a note. Her rented furniture had been delivered the day before. She had hired a cleaning service, until she found a housekeeper, since she had nothing of value in the apartment. She was intending to cook for herself or buy takeout food, or order in. She was perfectly content to be alone in the apartment for the summer, without anyone to fuss over her. She liked being independent after having been alone for five years.

She had been sad to let her employees go in San Francisco when she sold the house. Some of them had been with her for her entire marriage, and the five years since, but all of them had lives and families in San Francisco, and they didn't want to leave, which was fine with her. It would be a completely fresh start.

The elevator shot upstairs, with a porter pushing her bags on a trolley. There were concierges, security men, and doormen in the building, a gym, a pool, a roof garden, and a dry cleaner. The door to the apartment opened easily, and the alarm wasn't on. She tipped the porter, he left, and she went out on her terrace and looked south, toward downtown to where her daughters lived, and where the Twin Towers of the World Trade Center had been before 9/11. The sun was setting to her right, in a blaze of flame. The windows of other buildings below her sparkled like diamonds. It was a perfect welcome to her new life in New York. It looked exciting and beautiful, and she stood there smiling, and sat down on one of the rented deck chairs, feeling joy well up inside her. It was one of those rare moments when everything comes together and feels just right. It couldn't have been better. It was perfect. Welcome to New York, she whispered to herself. She loved it.

Chapter 2

Kezia slept late on Saturday morning. It was a gorgeous day when she woke up. The weather was getting warmer and she poured herself a cup of coffee from the Nespresso machine the realtor had left her, along with a few basics, some plates, cups and glasses, cutlery, a frying pan, and a saucepan from IKEA. She walked out onto her terrace and sat down on one of the deck chairs. It felt almost like flying, being that high up. She closed her eyes in the sun for a minute, still in her nightgown. It was hard to imagine that this was home now. It felt more like a summer adventure, probably because none of her things had arrived, so there were no familiar objects to ground her and relate to. Everything around her was new, and the apartment was empty. The rooms were so large that the minimal amount of furniture she had rented looked lost in the open spaces. With no art on the long white walls, the apartment looked even bigger. She knew the place would seem to shrink at least a little once all her things were in it.

She showered and put on faded jeans and sandals and a starched white shirt from one of her suitcases, sped down to the lobby in her private elevator, and headed east to Second Avenue, where she knew there were grocery stores and a hardware store with some of the things she needed. Shopping kept her busy for two hours, and she had everything delivered. Then she walked back to Madison and wandered uptown to look at all the fancy designer stores, and when she got to Seventy-ninth Street, she headed to the park. It was crowded on a Saturday. Children were playing ball, couples were lying on blankets on the grass, people were riding bicycles and skateboarding. New York always had a feeling of celebration to her. It was the weekend before the Fourth of July, which would officially be the launch of the summer season. Memorial Day had gotten things started a month before, but now the weather was fully cooperating. Kezia could easily imagine that the beaches were already crowded. It was going to be a hot summer, and Felicity was going to enjoy her house in Southampton when she got back from Paris.

Kezia sat down on a bench and observed the action for

a while, smiling at the sight of the children crowding around an ice cream truck. It reminded her of when Felicity was little and Kate was a teenager and took such pride in her. Kate hadn't gotten jealous of Felicity until later, but once she did, it had never gone away. She resented every lucky break her younger sister got, and there had been many. In recent years, Felicity's success made Kate feel even worse about the book she wasn't writing and kept promising to. Felicity just forged ahead, and opportunities rained down on her. She always seemed to meet one great man after another, while Kate got stuck with the bad ones, and then stayed with them. Felicity's positive outlook on life and her unabashed youth seemed to attract blessings in her life. People couldn't wait to shower her with golden opportunities. Kate always felt like the uninvited dark fairy at Sleeping Beauty's christening, the one who put a spell on the infant princess. Kate hadn't resorted to spells yet, but she was harshly and very vocally critical of her younger sister, which never bothered Felicity. She just went on to the next victory, magazine cover, and handsome boyfriend. And remarkably, she never held Kate's criticism against her. She was extremely tolerant of her older sister, and good-natured about it.

After she had watched the action around her for an hour, and enjoyed sitting in the sun, Kezia walked slowly down through Central Park toward her apartment, so she'd get there in time for her groceries to be delivered.

Kezia enjoyed looking in the store windows as she made her way down Fifth Avenue, and got home just before the delivery arrived. She put everything away neatly in the cupboards, and sat on her terrace for the rest of the afternoon. She thought she heard some activity on the other side of the hedge that bordered her half of the terrace. She heard some watering going on with the hose and decided it must be the gardener. She had no idea whether or not her famous actor neighbor was in residence and wondered if she'd ever see him.

She watched a movie and went to bed early that night. It was an old favorite. She didn't feel lonely in the apartment. Everything was so fresh and clean and new. The walls had been painted exactly the colors she wanted, a creamy warm ivory in the living room and the palest sunny butter yellow in her bedroom. She thought that would be cheerful on dark winter days. She had put a lot of thought into the apartment once she'd decided to make the leap and move.

Kate woke her up early on Sunday morning. Kezia squinted as she looked at the clock, and saw that it was a few minutes after eight when the phone rang. Kate was an early riser and thought the rest of the world should be too.

"Are you awake?" she said into the phone, sounding busy and energetic, as Kezia rolled over on her back and looked at the ceiling, holding the phone.

"I am now. How was your workshop?" Kezia wondered how many she'd taken by now. Surely dozens, maybe hundreds.

"Great. We have the closing breakfast this morning, and then we're coming back to the city. I should be back in town around six."

"Do you want to come see the apartment?" Kezia smiled at the prospect. Although Kate wasn't an easy person, she was still her daughter and Kezia loved her, and she hadn't seen her in over a month, since her last trip to New York to see her decorator.

"That's why I'm calling," Kate said tartly.

"Great, come by whenever you get to the city. I'll be here. Will Jack be with you?"

"Actually, no. He's going to drop me off. He's working on a short story he started here, and he wants to finish it while the comments from the class are fresh in his mind. I'll take an Uber home."

"Come whenever you want. I'm not going anywhere today." It was another glorious sunny day, and Kezia wanted to lie on her terrace and get a tan. She had arrived pale from San Francisco, due to the cold weather and summer fog.

"See you later, Mom."

Kezia puttered around the apartment, setting up minor things, like a magnifying mirror in her bathroom. There was one being built into the dressing table she was having made, but she had two months ahead without one. She had bought some more minor kitchen equipment the day before. A blender, a toaster, some kitchen cutlery, a simple set of white plates, and glasses. There was a built-in microwave. And she had bought no-slip mats for the shower and bathtub, and silly things she didn't have in the brand-new apartment.

She had a late lunch and fell asleep reading in the sun. She was wearing pink denim shorts and a T-shirt when the doorman called her at six-thirty to tell her that a Miss Kate Hobson was there to see her, and she had him send her up. Kate rang the doorbell even before her mother could get there. Kezia opened the door with a big smile and put her arms around her daughter to hug her. Kate was always a little stiff, unlike Felicity, who was like hugging a big puppy and always squeezed her mother tight. Kate disentangled herself quickly from her mother's arms and looked around. She had long straight dark brown hair, and her brown eyes took in every detail of the entrance hall and then the vast living room. You could see the view of the city as soon as they walked into the room.

"Wow, dizzying," she said. "That's quite a view, Mom. It's

a good thing Jack didn't come with me. He has vertigo and he's afraid of heights." Jack had a lot of neurotic quirks which Kezia found irritating and Kate found endearing. She was surprisingly tolerant, though less so with her family.

"It's more like being in a plane than at the top of a building," Kezia commented, and offered Kate a glass of wine, which she accepted, and took a tour of the apartment with her mother, while Kezia explained what she had planned for every room. It was obvious how excited she was about it.

"Well, you certainly didn't hold back, did you? Do you really want all this space?" Kate looked mildly disapproving. She was always careful about what she spent, and critical of others who weren't, although she could afford a great deal more. She lived in jeans, old NYU sweatshirts, and army surplus, and felt virtuous about it. Her loft in the West Village was in a slightly shabby unrenovated building.

"It was a rare opportunity," Kezia echoed the realtor. "And I love it. I feel like I'm up in the sky. Come look at the terrace." Kate followed her outside, and they sat on the deck chairs to drink their wine.

"It's very pretty," Kate conceded as she sipped hers.

She didn't say anything for a few minutes, and looked into her glass of wine and then at her mother when she spoke. Kezia noticed that she was wearing the expression she usually used when she was about to do battle. But there was nothing to argue about. It was just a casual Sunday night visit to see her mother's new apartment. "I'm glad I saw it. I wanted to come and see you before I left. I'm leaving on Tuesday."

"I'm glad you came too. Are you going back to Vermont? Another workshop?" They were back-to-back all during the summer months, most of them in New England. They were like summer camps for adults, or would-be writers, most of whom, like Kate and Jack, never wrote anything of consequence, or published.

"No," Kate said with a belligerent tone her mother still didn't understand. "I'm going to Africa."

"Africa?" Kezia was surprised. "For a writing workshop there, or just a trip?" Kate wasn't usually a big traveler, she hated to fly, and that was a long trip for her to be making. Felicity flew around the world all the time for work. Kate didn't.

"Jack has a cousin in Johannesburg. He wants to see him, and then we're going to one of the more remote areas on kind of a special mission."

It was so unlike her that Kezia was even more intrigued. "Do you have friends there?" Kate shook her head and didn't speak for a minute.

"I have a new shrink," she said, looking pensively into her

glass again, and then back at her mother. "She thinks I need to meet my father, since I never had closure with him." She couldn't have had closure. He had relinquished his parental rights when she was a month old. And Andrew had adopted her when she was twelve. Reed Phillips, her natural father, had never been part of her life, by his own choice. "She thinks it will either open a door for me, or finally give me the release I need to move on." He had given her up thirty-seven years before. It sounded a little crazy to Kezia, but she didn't say it. She knew that Kate had been tormented by her history and the specter of her father since she was twenty-one, when Kezia told her about him. "She thinks my writing will stay blocked until I see him and ask him myself what I need to know."

"Do you know where he is?" Kezia looked stunned. She wouldn't have had any idea where to find him, nor did she want to. But Kate had always wondered about him, and why he had given her up. She had never found her mother's explanation adequate, and she was sure there was more to it than that, some dark secret Kezia was keeping from her. Her father's reasoning had actually been very straightforward. He didn't want to be tied down to a woman or a child at that time in his life. And he didn't want to get married. He wanted to pursue his dreams at any price. And he had. Kate would have been too much baggage and was precisely what he *didn't* want, a child he'd have to think about, and a woman he'd have to alter his plans for.

Kate nodded in answer to her question. "I found him through Doctors Without Borders. It was easy. He owns and runs a small hospital in a remote area of Mozambique. I can drive there from Johannesburg." Kezia was stunned.

"Did you contact him?" Kezia's voice sounded chillier than she intended, but the mention of Kate's father was an unwelcome surprise. She never thought about him anymore. She had no reason to. And it upset her that Kate did.

"I sent him an email and he answered me right away. I said I wanted to meet him and talk to him. He invited us to come and stay. I'm not going to stay long. I just want to talk to him face to face, not on Skype or FaceTime. I want to sit across from him and say what I have to say and hear what he responds. His email was very nice. He's married to a South African doctor who works at the hospital with him, and they have a son. He's in medical school in England, so I won't get to meet him. If everything goes okay, I might stop and see my half brother on the way back." It sounded like a family reunion, and Kezia wasn't pleased to hear her refer to a "half brother". Kate's curiosity about her father had always seemed disloyal to Kezia, after everything Andrew had done for her, and how kind he was. She had been able not to have a job and to indulge her writing passion for fifteen years now, ever since she'd finished college at Columbia. Andrew had always been supportive and encouraging, and after he died, and Kate received the first part of her inheritance, she'd been able to continue writing without having to get a job. She had only had minor part-time jobs until then.

Reed had never done a thing for his daughter, not even send her a birthday or Christmas card, which wasn't surprising, since he had given up his right to her. But he hadn't even been curious enough about Kate to reach out to her and meet her. She had never given up the fantasy of him. Now she was going halfway around the world to see him.

"How long will you be gone?" Kezia asked her without editorial comment, but Kate knew how Kezia felt about Reed. She wanted nothing to do with him. But Kate did. She at least wanted to meet him face to face once. If he was a jerk, she didn't have to see him again. If it was a disaster, she could leave. Her shrink had reminded her of that when Kate said she was going. Her shrink had also said she was proud of her for taking action and not procrastinating, which was what she usually did, faced with any big decision. This was a first. She'd waited a long time for this, and once she made the decision, she didn't want to put it off. She had asked Jack to go with her. She was paying for the trip. He made a little money selling his short stories and essays, and he had the money he made tutoring, but he barely made enough to live on, and Kate made up the difference. He certainly couldn't pay for trips. Kezia didn't ask. She could guess the answer, and Kate was old enough to handle her money however she wanted. Kezia just thought it was a shame that she was wasting years with such a deadbeat, and she was sure Andrew wouldn't have approved. He had worked hard for his success. Jack seemed to contribute absolutely nothing that improved Kate's life, from what Kezia could see. She had never been able to understand his charm. He was bright, but without any real ambition. He talked about the book he was going to write one day, just as Kate did, but neither of them seemed to be doing anything about it, except going to writing workshops and wasting their time. It was a sensitive subject between Kate and her mother, and her birth father was another one. He wasn't a deadbeat, but he hadn't been a father to her either. At least he had followed his dreams and gone to Africa as he'd planned. Kezia wondered if he had any regrets about giving up a child, which was what Kate wanted to find out, once and for all. Going to see him would be the bravest thing she'd ever done. She wanted to know from him why he'd given her up.

"I'll be back in about a week, Mom," Kate said quietly. "We're going to see Jack's cousin in Johannesburg on the way there and stay with the Phillipses for as long as seems right. It's nice of Jack to come with me, I'm kind of nervous about it." She looked young and vulnerable when she said it, and Kezia felt sorry for her, and wondered if it was a good idea. What if he rejected her again, or was mean to her, or his wife resented her showing up? Kezia knew better than anyone that under Kate's prickly exterior, she was sensitive and easily wounded, which was why she attacked first, so she could hurt others before they could hurt her. It didn't make her easier to be with, but at least it explained it. Her barbs weren't as random as they appeared. They were imma-ture self-defense.

"Was this your idea or the shrink's?" her mother asked her.

"What difference does it make?" Kate asked, with a quick hostile glance that was typical of her.

"I'm just curious. Has it really bothered you that much for all these years?" It seemed so sad to Kezia, and such a waste of time, for Kate to go halfway around the world to see a man who had cut her out of his life nearly forty years before. Even if he regretted it now, so what? What good would it do her? It wouldn't give them back the years they'd missed or make him into a father now.

"Sometimes it does bother me," Kate admitted. "Not always. I don't think about him all the time. I just want to

39

see him, even if only once. You know who your father was, what kind of man. I don't." Put that way, it made some kind of sense, even to Kezia, but not enough. Maybe if he lived in Pittsburgh or Chicago, but not Africa. It was a hell of a long way to go on a quest about his motives thirty-seven years before. He had stated them clearly then, and apparently he'd followed through on his plans to practice medicine in Africa. He would be sixty-three now, and a very different man than he'd been when Kate was born. He had an entire life behind him now, a history, a wife, and a son. Kate had a half brother. It all seemed so remote to Kezia, and very unreal.

"My writing has been blocked lately, more than usual, and my shrink thinks that's what's bothering me, unresolved issues from my past. I know what I want to write, I can hear it in my head, but I can't get it down on the page. Jack thinks it's a good idea too." He would. He had nothing else to do and it was a free trip.

"I hope it gives you the answers you're looking for," Kezia said quietly.

"I know you think I'm crazy to do it, and that Andrew should have been enough for me. I loved him, but he wasn't my father, no matter how much money he left me. I feel guilty spending it, because I wasn't his daughter. Felicity is. I was just an add-on, and he probably did it for you."

"He did it because he loved you," Kezia said. "Why can't you accept that?"

"I don't know. That's what I want to find out."

"Then maybe you have to do it," Kezia said with a sigh. Kate always had to take the difficult road, to punish herself and others. She couldn't just embrace who she was and what she had. Kezia wondered if perhaps after she'd met Reed, she'd stop wasting her time with men like Jack Turner. In that case, it might actually be worthwhile.

Kate stayed for another half hour, and then she left, having told her mother what she was going to do. That was why she had come, not to see the apartment.

"I was hoping you'd come to dinner on the Fourth of July and watch the fireworks with me, if you were in town," Kezia said before Kate left.

"I bet they'll be fantastic from here. Sorry to miss it." Kate had more important things to do, and Felicity was going to be in Paris after the shows and at the Hotel du Cap for the weekend with Blake and some of his jet-set friends. Felicity definitely led a golden life. The two sisters couldn't be more different. Kezia hugged Kate when she left and thought about the trip she was about to embark on. It was a pilgrimage of sorts, and all Kezia could do was hope that she found what she was looking for, not just for her writing, but for her life. If she did, she might enjoy it more, and allow herself to find a man who was worthy of her, which Jack didn't seem to be, nor had any of the men who came before him. They were always losers of one sort or another, which was how Kate saw herself too.

Felicity called her from Paris on Monday morning, and Kezia was happy to hear from her. She told her about Kate's trip.

"That's weird," Felicity said, with all the insight of her twenty-three years.

"It is, but it's always bothered her that her father gave her up and she's never met him. The rejection of a parent is a big deal."

"She had Dad, once you married him," Felicity said.

"That's what I always tell her, but she never feels she had a right to him. She feels like you were his real daughter, and she's the fake. It's complicated," Kezia said. Felicity rarely looked below the surface. "How was Saint-Tropez?"

"A lot of fun. We both knew a lot of people there. We're going to Cap d'Antibes after the shows. Are you sure you don't want to use the house I rented in Southampton this weekend?" she offered again.

"I'm going to watch the fireworks from my terrace in the city. I'd love to go out there with you when you get home," Kezia said. She didn't want to use her daughter's space without her. She was respectful of them as adults.

42

They talked for a few more minutes and then Felicity had to go. She was walking in the Dior show that evening, and she had to be there in half an hour for makeup and hair, and a final run-through before the show. She took it all in stride and was a real pro. Kezia loved watching her in the fashion shows. She was so self-confident and in control. Kezia wished that Kate had some of that confidence. Maybe she would after she went to Africa and met Reed Phillips. Who knows, maybe her shrink was right, and meeting him was what she needed to allow her to put old ghosts to rest. She hoped so. To Kate, the glass was always half empty, and to Felicity, half full. She always found something to be happy about. She enjoyed her life, and was in the right career lane for now, although she couldn't model forever. But she was at the peak of her career for the moment, and she and Blake White seemed well suited, despite the considerable difference in their age. At twenty-three, sixteen years was a big difference.

Kezia worried about both her children, although they were adults now. But Felicity gave her a lot less to worry about. She had been an easy, happy child, and had carried her optimism and joie de vivre into adulthood.

Kezia spoke to Kate again that evening, the night before she left for her trip on Tuesday. She was busy getting ready, and had to buy some things for the time she'd spend in

Mozambique. She hadn't had time to come uptown again to see her mother, and said she was too busy for Kezia to come downtown to visit her. Kezia suspected that Kate was avoiding her but didn't make an issue of it. And she was only leaving for a week.

Kate sent her a text on her way to the airport. She was excited about going to Africa and was sure she was going to unlock the doors of the mysteries in her life so far. She wasn't sure what she wanted from Reed Phillips when she met him, some form of acknowledgment, an apology maybe, an admission that he had made a terrible mistake abandoning her as a baby and had regretted it all his life. That was at the outside range of what she hoped for. And on a more human scale, she hoped he was a nice person, and that she would be happy to have met him, and glad to be his daughter. He had sounded warm and welcoming in their emails, and he said he was eager to show her around his hospital. If she was impressed by what he was doing for the locals, she thought she might make a donation when she left and could make a difference. If nothing else, if the trip went well, maybe it would unblock her writing, and she could write the book she had struggled with for so long. She hoped her shrink was right and that meeting her birth father was what she needed to turn her life around and get moving forward.

Jack was telling Kate about his cousin Chad in

Johannesburg as the plane took off, and how much she was going to like him. He worked at a bank and was supposedly a great guy and a lot of fun, even if he did like his single malt whiskey a bit too much. He was two years older than Jack and, at forty-four, he had never married, and was currently between girlfriends.

The whole trip sounded like a big adventure, and as she turned to look at Jack, she wondered if he'd ever ask her to marry him. He always said that he couldn't marry her, or anyone, until he could afford to support a wife and children, which had begun to seem less and less likely. They had their writing in common, and he was company when she was feeling unsure of her ability to ever write a book. He kept the demons of loneliness away, which always seemed like enough for now. She didn't like to look far into the future. It was enough to get through each day without anything really bad happening.

As New York shrank beneath them, Kate closed her eyes and tried to envision what it would be like to meet her father. She had seen a photograph of him on the internet. He was a tall, pleasant-looking man with thinning white hair, and a small white-haired woman beside him. She couldn't imagine her mother with him, but that didn't matter now. This wasn't about her mother or her sister. They were so much alike, and she was always the outsider. Maybe she would find that she was like her father. At thirty-seven, Kate wanted to find a person she had something in common with, someone who was like her, even with all her fears and insecurities. She always felt different when she was with her sister or her mother. All she wanted now was to find her father, and maybe be like him. After that, she would write the book she had always hoped to write. Jack was still talking about his cousin, with a glass of wine in his hand, when she drifted off to sleep, dreaming of her long-lost father.

Chapter 3

The same day Kate's plane took off for Johannesburg in the morning, a plane from Houston landed at Kennedy Airport. It was crammed full of low-fare travelers. The plane was full, and the passengers rushed toward baggage claim, or pulled their rolling bags along, heading for the exits. There was a group of eight young men traveling together, wearing big Stetsons, some wearing cowboy boots, others in sneakers, and some in military boots. They were wearing jeans with jackets that looked like army surplus. They were in their twenties, and had an air of confidence about them. They were good-humored and playful, even boisterous, pushing and shoving each other and teasing, and hooted at a group of girls who flirted with them. They acted as though they owned the world, and piled into two taxi vans, with four in each cab. They were wearing backpacks and were strong and young and full of mischief. They'd all been drinking on the plane, but they weren't drunk. They were high on the excitement of being in New York.

They agreed to meet in Times Square. Three of them said they'd never been to New York. Two of them said they wanted to find women. They looked like hicks in the big city, but they weren't shy or intimidated. Their excitement was contagious as the cabs took off toward Manhattan.

They were off on their big adventure. The trip had been planned for two years and they had come three days early for some fun. They intended to enjoy it fully and savor the delights of the city, the women, the bars, the sights, the sounds, and the smells. They had come to New York for a break they'd never forget, and had waited a long time for it.

They hooted at each other out the cab windows as both vans left the curb, headed toward the city, and disappeared into the traffic. Eight cowboys from Houston heading for the time of their life. They had three days to play and do everything they wanted, and they were going to enjoy every second and not waste a minute. And after that, they had work to do. One of them lit a joint, and the driver smiled and didn't say a word.

They smiled at each other as they passed the joint around. It was strong. The weed came to Houston straight from Mexico. It was easy to get in Texas, top quality. They'd been told not to risk flying with drugs and getting caught, but there had been no K9 dogs on duty at the Houston airport to detect it, and it was easier to bring it with them than try to find it in New York. It was part of the fun of their days off. They needed relief from the pressure of their assignments. Each of them was an expert in their field, although you wouldn't know it to look at them. They just looked like a bunch of high-spirited young men, a sports club of some kind, a bunch of cowboys from Texas.

They were already laughing from the joint before they reached Manhattan. They were ready to take on the city. It was going to be the best three days of their lives.

Kezia got a text from Kate late Tuesday night as soon as she arrived. It was Wednesday morning in Johannesburg. They had landed safely. Jack's cousin Chad had picked them up at the airport, but they hadn't had time to visit the city yet. They were going to spend two days with his cousin. Chad had taken time off from the bank to be with them, and on Friday morning, they were planning to leave Johannesburg at dawn for the long drive to Mozambique, through Kruger National Park, and arrive at Reed's hospital by dinnertime. Kezia was eager to hear more about that part of the trip.

There was a brief parade down Fifth Avenue on the Fourth of July, which blocked all the traffic while it lasted. Kezia stayed comfortably in her penthouse. She had nowhere to go. Everything was closed for the holiday, and she wanted to avoid the crowds milling around the streets during and after the parade. With her daughters away, there was no one she wanted to see. She hadn't contacted any of her New York friends yet, and she was sure that everyone she knew was away anyway. She had been in New York for exactly a week, had settled into her new apartment, and already felt at home there. It was kind of fun living with wide-open spaces and few possessions.

Her San Francisco home had been beautifully decorated, filled with valuable art and treasures she and Andrew had collected on their travels, and she had shipped many of them to New York. She had exciting plans to turn the penthouse into a showplace and entertain there. But until it all came together, she was enjoying the huge rooms, with just a few pieces of furniture. She had rented the bare minimum, and she had a feeling of freedom being there. She wanted everything about this apartment to be new and different from her old home. Being there was a rebirth of sorts. She had reinvented herself with the move to New York, and the apartment was a big part of it.

She watched part of a TV series she liked that night, and helped herself to a glass of wine. She didn't usually drink alone, but it felt like a festive night, and she was waiting for the fireworks to start once it was dark enough. People all over the city were waiting on their rooftops. She was sure the display was going to be spectacular. She expected nothing less in New York.

At nine, she walked out on her terrace, and lay down on one of the deck chairs under a starry sky. It was a warm night and she was wearing a T-shirt and jeans. There was some landscaping on the terrace, but she was planning to add more. The thick hedge was about nine feet tall and divided the terrace between the two penthouse owners. She couldn't see over it or through it, and it seemed very dense. She thought she heard a noise on the other side as she sat down, but decided she had imagined it. There had been no sign of life from the other apartment in the week since she'd arrived. Sam Stewart was obviously not in residence, and she was alone on the penthouse floor, sixty floors up in the New York sky. She felt as though she could reach up and touch the stars as she lay there, waiting for the fireworks to start over the East River. They began half an hour after she sat down.

They started right off the bat with three gigantic balls of red, white, and blue, followed by a humongous ball of what looked like falling stars. There were five great bursts in a row, and then what sounded like a sonic boom to her right. She turned to see an orange ball to the west. She wasn't sure if it was a second display starting in another location, as the fireworks continued to her left. She was watching both shows as she saw a huge spiral of black smoke rise above the orange ball that hadn't faded yet, and she wasn't sure what it was. Just then two more sonic booms went off one right after another, one in front of her and then a second orange ball appeared straight ahead and a third one far down Manhattan, and it suddenly occurred to her that they weren't fireworks. They looked like explosions, but that didn't seem possible as the multicolored shower of lights continued over the East River.

Kezia wasn't sure what she was seeing, but a chill of fear ran down her spine, and a distant memory came to mind of twenty-four years before on a fateful September day when the Twin Towers of the World Trade Center were hit by two jet planes. It wasn't possible, but the orange balls grew bigger, surrounded by more smoke, and a few minutes later, the firework show stopped, and she heard a shout from the other side of the hedge. Someone shouted "Oh my God" as she watched in horror and the orange explosions seemed to rise up in the sky. There were three of them. She knew someone else was watching them too. Below, she could see other people on roofs, some gesticulating wildly, and she could feel fear race through her body. Then there were the sounds of sirens everywhere. The thought went instantly through her mind.

What if this was a missile attack? What if there was a war? She wanted to run into the living room to turn on the TV, but she felt frozen to the spot and couldn't move.

"Hey!" a voice called out to her from the other side of the hedge. "Are you watching this?"

It took her a few seconds to find her voice. "I am. What is it? Is it some kind of nuclear attack?" she called back.

"I don't know. Some sort of explosions." And then there was silence as they both watched the orange balls grow. The closest one seemed in the vicinity of the Empire State Building, twenty blocks south of them. It was all lit up in red, white, and blue, and as they watched, the lights went out, and they both realized at the same time that one of the explosions was there.

"Oh my God." Kezia said it this time, and she was shaking when the voice spoke again.

"I don't know if I can move this thing. Can I come through?" She saw the branches of the hedge shaking as someone pushed from the other side. It only moved about a foot, and she saw a man standing in the opening in a blue shirt, with his shirttails out, and jeans. He had dark hair, and was tall, and she recognized him in the dark. It was Sam Stewart, and she looked at him in surprise.

"I didn't know you were here." She didn't know what else to say.

"I've been here for a few weeks," he said, glancing toward the Empire State Building. There was smoke billowing from it now, which obscured part of the building.

"What do you think happened?" she said, watching it too.

"I think someone planted a bomb, a lot of them." Kezia suddenly wondered if there would be more, if their building would be bombed too.

"Do you think we should leave the building?" she asked, and he shook his head.

"Do you want to come over here and see what they're saying on TV?" he asked, and she nodded and followed him through the opening in the hedge. The sliding glass window to his living room was open, and she stepped inside as he grabbed a remote and turned on a huge television screen that covered most of one wall. It looked like a movie theater in his living room. They both stood staring at the screen divided in three, as an anchorman hurriedly described what was happening, and banners raced across the screen with the latest bulletins. The images showed the Empire State Building, with a ball of flame at the center of it, while the second screen showed a cluster of buildings, three of which were on fire.

"What is that?" Kezia asked him. It didn't look familiar to her.

"I think it's Hudson Yards." The text racing at the bottom of the screen confirmed it. It was a recently built vast expanse of beautiful modern buildings that covered five blocks near the Hudson River on the West Side. It was the pride of New York's newest architecture, built half a dozen years before, over sunken railroad tracks. There were several more deafening explosions, in stereo, both on the screen and coming from outdoors.

The third image of flaming destruction was of the new World Trade Center that had been built to replace the old Twin Towers. The reporter on screen said it was assumed to be a terrorist attack, and buildings all around those that were burning were being evacuated. People poured into the streets, crying, screaming, running to escape, as hordes of firefighters, police, and first responders fought their way into the buildings to rescue anyone they could. It was 9/11 all over again, times three. The damage was less extensive than that after the planes had hit the buildings on 9/11, but it was nonetheless impressive. The explosions had severely damaged the buildings, and flames were devouring what was left. Bombs had been detonated in all three locations.

The announcer said that no terrorist group had claimed responsibility so far. The police commissioner came on the screen a few minutes later, urging people not to panic, to stay in their homes if they lived far from the blazes, and not to attempt to come to the scenes, but everyone in proximity to the explosions should leave their homes, wear masks if they had them, exit their buildings, and proceed as quickly as they could as far away from the burning buildings as possible. The smoke was thick and intense, and Kezia and Sam could smell it wafting in from their terrace. It smelled like the whole city was on fire. They could hear sirens shrieking through the night as they were dispatched to all three locations.

Without thinking, Kezia sat down on a black leather couch as she stared at the enormous screen, and Sam Stewart handed her a glass of water. She took a sip, set it down, and thanked him.

"I'm Sam," he said with a serious face, staring at her with his deep blue eyes. She could see him more clearly now inside. He hadn't shaved in several days.

"Kezia. I live next door. I'm your new neighbor."

"I guessed," he said with a small smile. "Either that or you broke in to watch the fireworks. Jesus, I never thought something like this could happen again." It was twenty-four years later, but the images of 9/11 were still vivid in his mind. He'd had an apartment downtown then, not far from the Twin Towers. There had been ash and rubble everywhere, and body parts. He had sold the apartment and moved uptown afterward, and had lived at the Dakota until the new tower was built where he and Kezia both now lived. "My son was nine years old when 9/11 hit. He never forgot, nor did I. My wife was in California, and I took my son uptown to a friend's house. I thought we were going to be attacked again. I kept waiting for it to happen, but it never did."

"Do you think there will be more explosions tonight?" she asked him.

"I don't know. It depends on who did it. I wonder if this is happening in other cities, or if it's just New York." They said on TV that there was concern on the West Coast and in Chicago that it would happen there at nine or ten their time, when their firework shows were scheduled to start, which would be any minute in Chicago and midnight or later in California. The anchorman said that the office of Emergency Services, police, and bomb squads in other cities were combing their cities for bombs, and firework shows all over the U.S. had been canceled at a moment's notice.

What had already become apparent was that three iconic buildings had been hit, one the symbol of New York and the other two new buildings the city was proud of. Buildings with similar distinction were being carefully examined all over the country to detect bombs.

The TV showed scenes of injured people being put into ambulances at the scene, bodies being covered with tarps. News crews had begun to arrive and were being held back from the scene, not to add to the confusion. All of the city's hospitals were preparing to receive the victims. There was a heartbreaking scene of a fireman running with a child in his arms, burned and screaming as paramedics took her from him and put her in an ambulance. You could hear her screaming for her mother on the air.

"Oh my God, this is awful," Sam said as he ran a hand through his hair, and Kezia realized that she was shaking as the announcers explained that all off-duty medical personnel were being called to their hospitals. Thousands of victims were expected, and the blazes resulting from the explosions were burning out of control. The city was filled with smoke, and it was drifting across the rivers. "You feel so helpless, don't you?" Kezia and Sam didn't know each other, but they were watching the carnage together, which was an instant bond. "I wonder who the hell did this." It felt like a moment in history.

The Empire State Building was an office building, so the only people in the building would be tourists on the observation deck, and the World Trade Center was offices too. The bombers had wanted to destroy the buildings the city was most proud of. But Hudson Yards was a combination of offices and apartment buildings, hotels, and one of the biggest shopping malls in the world. It was a beautiful conglomeration of buildings that had taken thirteen years to build and had been a major feat of architecture. Sam could guess that most of the victims would be there. It was south and west of where he and Kezia were.

There were gruesome scenes on the news of all three locations, with hundreds of firefighters, police, and first responders on site. It looked like well-organized chaos as injured people and bodies were brought out as fast as the emergency workers could get to them, but Kezia could see that there were bodies under tarps all over the scene. They were removing them as quickly as they could.

She and Sam were still mesmerized and hardly spoke an hour later when the mayor and the police commissioner spoke and requested that any trained retired medical personnel go to the following hospitals and to the scenes. They listed the hospitals that needed help, and said that trained paramedics were needed too. Kezia frowned as she listened and looked at Sam.

"I'm a nurse practitioner. I've been retired for twenty-five years, but my license is current. Do you think I should go?"

"I don't think it matters how long you've been out of it. You don't forget skills like that. Do you want to go?" She nodded as they continued watching coverage of the scene at Hudson Yards. Two of the apartment buildings had been bombed, and an incredible number of people had been wounded and killed. Stretchers were lined up in the streets around it for blocks, and lying on the ground, waiting for ambulances, as nurses, doctors, and paramedics did what they could.

"I feel like I should, to do whatever I can," she said.

"I feel like that too, but at least you know what to do. I'll go with you if you want to go," he said, and she nodded. "This is like a very bad movie. I hate movies about disasters. They're always so true to life," he said, and she smiled. This was an odd way to meet a big star, but he didn't behave like a famous actor. He just reacted like any normal person would when faced with the tragedies they were seeing, and several times, she saw him wipe tears from his cheeks, as a body was covered, or a child was rescued, or mothers or fathers were screaming for their children. It was an unbelievably horrific scene, and Kezia stood up and looked at him.

"I think I'll go." It was eleven-thirty by then, and the scene looked worse as more and more bodies were brought out of the buildings at Hudson Yards. All the windows had blown out of the buildings from the heat of the flames. "You don't have to go with me. I'll try to find a cab, or I can walk, it's not that far. It's about twenty-five blocks from here," she said at a guess.

"You shouldn't go down there alone, and maybe they need another pair of hands. I can't just sit here and watch it on TV." It was how she felt, and she just hoped she wasn't too rusty to be useful, but even untrained civilians could help in a disaster of this magnitude. In other parts of the country, the entire nation was riveted to their TVs, with everyone wondering if their city would be next. But so far, it only seemed to have affected New York, according to the news.

"I'll go get dressed," she said, thinking about what she could work in. She headed toward his terrace, and glanced back over her shoulder as he watched her. "Put on something with long sleeves, and maybe some kind of jacket, and gloves if you've got them, and heavy shoes." He nodded at her.

"Thanks." And with that she disappeared and was back minutes later, with a Levi's jacket over her T-shirt, and hiking boots, and she had brought a pair of leather gloves. She was wearing a fanny pack around her waist with her ID, some money, her phone, and her keys, and she'd put a copy of her nursing license in it.

Kezia and Sam looked serious and were silent as they took his private elevator to the lobby. He had taken her advice and was wearing a camouflage jacket he wore on the set for early morning calls. "Where did you move here from?" he asked her as they got out of the elevator.

"San Francisco," she answered as they rushed across the lobby toward the main door. All of the building security was in the lobby, prepared for anything to happen. They nodded when they saw Sam and Kezia.

"San Francisco is a nice city," he said as they walked

outside. The smell of smoke was even stronger on the street. They were talking to keep from panicking. "I've worked there a few times. Born there?" He was curious about her, and he'd been surprised when she said she was a nurse. He had expected someone spoiled and sophisticated to buy the penthouse apartment next to his. She looked like a real person, and he was impressed that she wanted to help and wasn't afraid to go to the scene.

"I'm from Vermont originally. I lived in San Francisco for twenty-five years. It was time for a change." Talking about normal life helped keep her calm, to keep from thinking of the enormity of what was happening. It was huge. And what if there were more explosions later? Or across the entire country? She was happy both her daughters were out of town and out of the country.

"I moved here from L.A. for the same reason," Sam said, as tense as she was. "Twenty-five years ago. I bought this apartment two years ago. I was living in New York when 9/11 happened. And now here I am again. My son lives downtown, but he's away for the weekend with his girlfriend, thank God," he said as he saw a cab and whistled for it, and it made a sharp turn to pick them up.

"I have two daughters who live here too. They're both away," Kezia said. She was planning to call them and tell them she was okay. It was still early in France, but Kezia didn't have a number for Kate in Africa. She would be with her father by now, and probably had no cellphone service. She was going to send Kate a text. She took her phone out in the cab and found that she had no service. The line on her cellphone was dead. She told Sam, he checked his and it was dead too. He told the driver where they wanted to go, and he said he couldn't get near it. He figured he could probably get within ten blocks and after that, they'd have to walk.

"That's fine," Sam said, and commented on their cellphones not working.

"I wonder what government or maniacs from what country are going to turn out to be responsible for this," he said with a muscle tense in his jaw. He kept thinking of the children they had seen on screen, and the body bags stacking up. "And what's the point of something like this, whatever they're pissed about? I hate shit like this. It's so senseless, and all it does is injure and kill the innocent."

The cab driver got them within a dozen blocks of the main entrance to Hudson Yards, Sam gave him a big tip, and he did a double take when he got a good look at Sam.

"You're . . ." he said in amazement.

"Yeah. Thanks for getting us here in record time," Sam said seriously.

"I'm sorry I can't take you all the way."

"This is good enough." They set off on foot heading due west, and then south through Chelsea. The smell of smoke was overpowering. Kezia had masks in her pocket but they didn't need them yet. The streets were choked with emergency vehicles, but no one stopped them. People were running and shouting. There was a police cordon when they were a block away, and an Emergency Medical Service worker told them that only officials and medical personnel could go beyond it.

"I'm a nurse," Kezia said calmly.

"Are you part of a team in there?" The worker pointed toward the burning buildings on the other side of the roadblock.

"I just came to help," she said. "Where should I go?"

"We've got two stations set up two blocks down, and we're taking volunteers." He pointed in the right direction, and Sam looked at him seriously.

"I just came to help too."

"Go with her," the EMS worker said, and answered a call on his radio. They wanted to know where the new ambulances were.

Kezia and Sam covered the two blocks in a few minutes, weaving through police cars and fire engines and a big station for the rescuers to drink water and catch their breath for a minute. Kezia threaded her way through the crowd to someone with a clipboard and a stethoscope around his neck who appeared to be in charge. His uniform said he was a paramedic, and Kezia told him she was a nurse practitioner. He didn't question her further and handed her an armband with a red cross on it, and gave one to Sam too. He didn't recognize him, which was a relief. Sam hadn't come to show off, only to help.

"I'm not in active practice," she told the paramedic with the clipboard. "I'm retired."

"We need you anyway," he said, and pointed her to a group of medical personnel who were waiting for the firefighters to bring more people out of the building. The heat in the area was overwhelming. When they got there, they assigned Kezia to a small group waiting for the severely wounded for triage. A second group was waiting for the walking wounded. Sam explained that he wasn't medical personnel, but he was willing to do anything to help.

"We need you too. I'm sorry, buddy, but we need help moving the body bags." Sam nodded, went where the paramedic pointed, and joined a group of civilian volunteers and OES workers. There were stacks of bodies in black zipped-up bags, and Sam got busy carrying them with another volunteer at the other end. They moved them as respectfully as they could to a location further away, where they wouldn't interfere with rescue operations. It was grim work. The whole event was shocking, and people were doing everything they could to help.

Sam didn't stop for three hours, and then paused for a few minutes to grab a bottle of water from the supply buckets at the volunteer station. He saw Kezia in the distance running alongside a gurney, holding an IV bag while they raced against time to save the man on that gurney. Sam didn't see her again until he went back for another bottle of water, as the sun was coming up. They had been there for over six hours, and the fires were still out of control. The heat and smoke were stifling. The bombs had been enhanced with additional explosives and the fire chief said they would burn for days. They had lost several firefighters that night, more than a thousand dead had been counted so far, two of the apartment buildings had come down, and half the mall and an enormous sculpture were burning. The firefighters were digging for people who were trapped and alive and had brought several out, severely burned.

"How's it going?" Sam asked Kezia when he saw her. She had soot smudged all over her face and she was wearing surgical gloves. Her own gloves had gotten lost in the shuffle somewhere and she didn't care.

"The burns we're seeing are awful, and the damage. The police are saying the bombs were full of debris to create maximum injuries. The wounds we're seeing are very military, like in wartime. It's the kids that always break my heart."

"Me too," Sam said with tears in his eyes. He had carried a number of small body bags that were featherlight. There were many they had no identities for. They would have to be identified later, by grieving parents, if they were still alive, or relatives or friends. The bodies were being taken to a warehouse the emergency services were using as a morgue further downtown. The OES and EMS workers said it was almost full, and they were going to use a second warehouse, probably several of them before it was all over.

The OES said they were very unusually built bombs, probably homemade, but with military expertise. They had brought in some army experts, and they said the effects were very similar to bombs the U.S. Army had used in Iraq. They wondered if there were some renegade army veterans who had gone over to the other side and become dissidents since coming back from the war. The bomb squads were gathering all the information they could while the fires burned.

Sam and Kezia went back to their tasks, and part of the mall collapsed an hour later. No one was in it, but the financial losses were going to be astronomical. The damage being done that night was approaching billions of dollars and couldn't even be properly assessed yet. The final construction phase of Hudson Yards had only been completed a few months before. The loss of human life was in the thousands.

Sam and Kezia worked until nine o'clock that morning, and Sam was finally told he could go home, and was thanked for his help. He was filthy, his face covered with soot and grime, and he had cried more than once that night. He went to look for Kezia once they released him. He had worked for nine hours at backbreaking work. It took him half an hour to find Kezia, but he didn't want to leave without seeing her and letting her know he was going home. He found her on the curb, sitting for the first time in hours. All the living victims found so far had been removed to hospitals by then. Those who were unhurt had gone to stay with relatives or friends. A few had gone to hotels uptown. At least no other explosions had occurred. The city was a shambles, and the mayor had declared a state of emergency. He ordered all businesses closed, including shops and restaurants, there were to be no public gatherings, and everyone was ordered to stay off the streets, in case there was another rash of bombs that day. If there were, it would bring the city to its knees even more than it already was.

Kezia looked up when she saw Sam. He looked grief-stricken. The injuries and loss of human life were heart-breaking and had touched him deeply.

"Are you going to stay?" he asked her, and she looked at

the EMS worker she had been reporting to for the last few hours. People were being moved around and used according to their abilities. It had felt good using even some of her old nursing skills. It all came back to her. She had been assigned to some of the most critically injured.

"You can go, Kezia," the EMS worker said gently. She was an older woman, an ER nurse from NYU hospital, who was on vacation and had come in when she saw the news on TV. "You've been on your feet all night. We've got it covered for now."

"I can go home and clean up, and come back later if you want," Kezia offered.

"I'll give you a number to call, and you can check back. I think they're still pulling people out downtown. We should have most of the area cleared by tonight," the EMS worker told her. They would still be searching for live buried victims for at least another twenty-four to forty-eight hours. After that it would be bodies.

Everything had run very efficiently, with the Fire Department, the OES, the EMS, teams sent by several hospitals, and the volunteers like Sam, who had been useful, freeing up trained personnel to take care of medical issues. The EMS worker wrote the number down on a piece of paper. It was a hotline for volunteers. Kezia stuck it in her pocket and looked at Sam.

"I'll go home with you." She knew she had reached her limit and needed to recharge her batteries and sleep for an hour or two before she came back to do another shift. He looked just as tired as they walked out of the area and headed home. Most of the emergency vehicles were still there, and they had to walk ten blocks before they found a cab. Kezia knew she could walk home if she had to, but she was bone tired. Sam looked it too. He looked as though he'd had a hard night, and she said so admiringly.

"Not as hard as the victims. It kills me when innocent people get hurt like that. I hope they catch the bastards who did it."

"Yeah, me too," Kezia said in a tired voice and looked at her watch. She wanted to contact her girls in Africa and France. She wrote Kate a quick text, which sent, but there were still no circuits to call France. She couldn't get a signal. She commented on it to Sam.

"Maybe they knocked the towers down too. Are you calling locally?" She shook her head.

"No, Africa and France."

He looked surprised. "Where are your daughters?"

"One is in the south of France, the other's in Mozambique, Africa."

"On safari?"

"No, visiting a relative. And I can't get hold of either one."

"The lines will clear up soon, this isn't 9/11 after all," he reassured her.

"It sure looked like it last night," Kezia said in a tired voice, and leaned her head back against the seat.

"You were running around like crazy every time I saw you," he said, impressed.

"So were you." She had seen him with the body bags all night. It was backbreaking work, and hard to stomach, as well as grueling emotionally. "Thank you for coming with me."

"I'd have gone even if you didn't," he said. "I'm glad we both did. I don't know about you, but most of us lead such useless lives. What I do is like playtime compared to something like this. It's embarrassing. At least last night, I could do something to help. What made you give up nursing?" he asked, curious about her. "You look like you're good at it."

"I loved it. My father was a country doctor. I worked with him for several years until I married and moved to San Francisco. My husband supported me, and we traveled a lot. My working as a nurse didn't fit with our life."

"Was your husband a doctor?"

"No, but he was on the board of some big medical companies, pharmaceuticals, and other things."

"You're divorced?"

"Widowed," she said simply.

Danielle Steel

"That's its own special kind of hell, isn't it? If you had a good marriage," he said quietly.

"We did. He got Covid-19 on a trip to China at the beginning of the pandemic. He was gone in five days."

"I remember that year distinctly. We actually had a nice time sheltering in place as a family. But it made hash of everyone's life for two years. And then it finally got less dangerous than it was in the beginning," he said.

"Viruses do that," she confirmed.

"When are your daughters coming back?" he asked.

"One of them next week, the one in France. The other one, in Africa, I'm not sure. Maybe a week. It helped me feel less useless, taking care of people last night. I'd forgotten what that's like."

"Would you ever go back to nursing?"

She thought about it for an instant before she responded. "It's been a long time. I think it's too late now, and I'd have to go back to school, to do it right. My girls would certainly be surprised."

"It's never too late to do what you love. I love what I do. It's very rewarding. I lost my wife too. I bought the penthouse after she died. I couldn't stand staying in our apartment. I kept looking for her every time I opened the door. I finally decided to move. It helped make my peace with it. I think now that people's lives happen the way they're meant to, timing and all."

"I wasn't ready to lose my husband," Kezia said. "It was so sudden. But we've managed without him. I still miss him. It's been five years. You get used to it."

"It's been two years for me, and I'm just figuring out how to live with it now. The first year was incredibly tough. Loss is a strange thing. They take a part of you with them, a big part." Kezia nodded agreement.

They had gotten to their building by then, said goodbye, and went upstairs, each in their own private elevator. Kezia almost stumbled into the door of her apartment. All she wanted to do was sleep for a few hours, and she'd go back later, if they needed more help.

When she let herself into her apartment, she walked out on her terrace for a minute and looked at the charred hull of the Empire State Building in broad daylight. It looked shocking. She heard a noise behind her, turned and saw Sam peering cautiously through the part of their hedge that he had moved the night before.

"Tell me if you go back. I'll go with you. I don't have your number. I didn't know if you'd want to give it to me," he said shyly.

She walked toward him, exhausted. "What's your number? I'll call you and then you'll have mine." He told her, and she performed the necessary maneuver.

They'd just been through an incredibly difficult night

together. It created a bond between them. They had seen life and death and terrible tragedy. "I just want to get some sleep, and then I'll go back if they want me."

"I think they will." He smiled at her. "It's been nice to meet you, Kezia."

"Thank you, Sam," she said, and walked back into her apartment, smiling. It was certainly an odd way to meet a famous movie star. But whenever she talked to him, she forgot all about who he was. And with that, she headed for her bedroom, and as soon as she lay down, she passed out before she even got undressed, with her boots on.

Chapter 4

By the time Kezia woke up at noon, stiff all over and still in her clothes from the night before, New York had been shut down, and so had the whole country. Cities nation-wide were braced for terrorist attacks like the one in New York. And as long as no one claimed responsibility for the attacks, no one had any idea who the enemy was, or if they intended to strike again. There had been no attacks in other cities.

She took a shower, put on a robe, and turned the news on while she made coffee. She hadn't realized the physical efforts she'd made, while running from one victim to the next, and helping to put some on stretchers while she offered comfort. Her body felt as if she'd run a marathon or had been beaten, and she was stunned to see on TV that every major city in the country was under lockdown, all airports were closed, the planes grounded. International flights scheduled to fly into the States had been canceled, and those that had been in the air when the multiple attacks happened were turned back across U.S. borders and had landed in Canada or Mexico, or returned to their countries of origin. Domestic flights had landed immediately at the nearest airport. No one was getting in or out of the country until the perpetrators were found and the responsible government or terrorist group was identified. The news reported that intelligence sources were following several leads, but no conclusions had been reached yet. And no one had come forward.

More than four thousand people had been killed in the three explosions, most of them at Hudson Yards when two enormous apartment buildings exploded, a third caught fire along with the shopping mall, trains were crushed beneath five blocks of the structures, and half of the huge mall was destroyed. Another three thousand people had been critically injured, and several hundred had suffered less severe injuries. Countless cars parked close to the bomb sites accounted for more victims. All the hospitals in the city were sharing more than their load of victims. Hundreds of medical and nonmedical personnel had come to assist the first responders and law enforcement. Medical workers had driven in from New Jersey and Connecticut to volunteer. The news anchor said that martial law was being considered. No final decision had been made yet, but residents of every major city, particularly those with iconic landmark structures, were being told to stay home, and all events honoring the national Independence Day weekend had been canceled. The entire military was at the ready for an attack of nuclear proportions. Since the military didn't know who had done it, all eventualities were being considered and prepared for. It was clearly carried out by foreign nationals, but no one knew which ones.

It was a sobering summary of the situation and what it could lead to. It was by far the worst and most destructive attack on American soil ever, and everyone was warned to be careful. Security measures had been set in motion to protect television and radio stations in the event of an enemy attack or military takeover by a hostile nation. Intelligence services and the Pentagon were hard at work to find out who was responsible. And the death toll was still climbing.

The news report showed a military presence visible in every major city to protect both monuments and people. Most bridges had been closed, federal buildings were under heavy guard, and state and national parks were closed to the public. A second attack was feared in the coming hours. The president and cabinet were meeting that morning, and the nation would be addressed from an underground safe room in an undisclosed location that night. America was braced for another deadly assault.

Kezia tried to reach Felicity again after she watched the news, and couldn't get through. The circuits were busy, but at least she was safer in France than in the United States. She was with Blake, and Kezia knew he'd take care of her. They couldn't fly back to the U.S. now, but she'd be safe with him in the south of France. And Kate was in Africa with Jack, out of communication anyway, so Kezia couldn't reach her either.

There were worse places for Felicity to be stuck than the Hotel du Cap in the south of France, the most luxurious hotel in the world. Kezia wasn't worried about her. She didn't like not being able to reach either of her daughters to reassure them that she was okay, but it couldn't be helped. Kezia couldn't do anything about it. They were cut off from the rest of the world.

She sent both girls texts and emails, hoping they'd get through eventually, reassuring them that she was fine, which was the best she could do for now. They were both sensible adults. She was sure they were worried about her.

In France, Felicity had called her mother again and again, and couldn't get through. The United States appeared to be cut off, with its borders closed and sealed tight, and there was no access by phone for the moment. The phone lines were overloaded.

Blake came back to the bedroom from the living room of their suite.

"Did you get through to your mom?" he asked her, and she shook her head with tears in her eyes. She looked very young as he put his arms around her. "I'm sure she's okay. The city's locked down. She'll stay home. And this is probably the worst of it, like 9/11."

"What if they bomb New York, or there's a war and we can't get home?"

"I don't think that's going to happen. And we'll be able to get through and you can talk to your mom in a day or two."

She hoped he was right. "Did you get through to Jen?" Blake's ex-wife, Jen, and his son, Alex, were in the Hamptons with friends for the Fourth of July weekend. He no longer wanted to be married to her, but she was sensible and responsible and a good mother. He knew his son was in good hands, and he was glad they were out of the city. And Jen's apartment was on the Upper East Side. They would be far from the damaged areas when they were able to go back to the city.

After the holiday, Jen was going to stay with her parents in Greenwich, Connecticut, for the month of July, with Alex. And Alex was coming to stay with Blake and Felicity in the

Hamptons for August. So he'd be out of the city, away from the damage and the tragedy in the aftermath of the attack.

Blake and his ex-wife were both good parents and he knew Alex would be safe with either one. They had managed to have a decent, respectful relationship despite the divorce. And she had no serious objections to Felicity so far. Jen had a boyfriend, so she didn't care what Blake did. It had been a relatively amicable divorce, and Blake was a good guy, and had been generous with her. He wanted more children, but Felicity was too young to even consider it. If he wanted her, he knew he'd have to wait.

He was the youngest of four, and his two brothers and one sister were all married and had kids, and he saw them and his parents frequently. He had gone to Yale, and Harvard Business School, and his father was in investments, as he was. His father was extremely successful. His brothers had good jobs too, and his sister stayed at home with her three kids, but she had a law degree she'd never used. They were a high-achieving but close family, and Felicity had met them all and liked them. His siblings all thought she was great but too young to take seriously, and it was a shame he hadn't met her ten years later. It seemed unlikely to them that the romance would last with a young woman her age, and she had every man she met at her feet. But she was faithful to Blake, and very much in love with him.

Blake had tried to call his family too, and couldn't get through to them either. He was less worried than Felicity. She was younger and close to her mother.

He comforted her gently and convinced her to go to the cabana with him. He knew the hotel well and came often, and she'd been there with him once before, after the Paris haute couture shows. Blake liked spending time in France and Italy. His family had a rambling vacation home in Maine, where he'd spent his boyhood summers, but he was more sophisticated than his older siblings, who were married with kids, and he preferred vacationing in Europe.

The setup at the Hotel du Cap was perfect for them. The cabanas were entirely private, and they could sun and spend the day there, where no one would recognize her or gawk at her. They could have lunch privately in the cabana and swim in the Mediterranean, or in the infinity pool. And they dined at the hotel at night. It was the most romantic hotel in the world.

He finally got Felicity to put her bikini on and they went to the cabana and lay in the sun. He tried to keep her from obsessing about what was happening in New York. The photos on the internet were terrifying, and he promised her that as soon as the planes started flying again, they'd go home. The friends they were supposed to meet had gotten stuck in New York, so they had time together alone.

She relaxed as they lay in the sun and talked. She always

felt safe with him. They were both strong with positive personalities. They enjoyed life. He was tall and blond and athletic, as she was. They were a beautiful couple.

They swam that afternoon and made love when they got back to the room at the end of the day.

It was still only noon in New York then, and Blake wondered what was happening, but he didn't say anything to Felicity about it. She was sleeping peacefully in his arms, and he let her sleep as he watched her, before they dressed for dinner in the hotel's elegant dining room.

As long as they were locked out of the United States, he couldn't think of a better place to be while they waited.

Sam sent Kezia a text, which she saw after she tried unsuccessfully to call Felicity. "Are you going back today?" he asked her. She called him after she read it.

"Hi, how are you feeling?" she asked him.

"I hate to admit it, I haven't done that much heavy exercise in years. I could hardly get out of bed this morning. I feel like an old man." But he wasn't—she had looked him up on Google and he was fifty-seven, two and a half years younger than she was. And he looked great. She laughed at what he said.

"You're not an old man, and I felt that way this morning too." The stress of the situation all night didn't help. They'd both had a few hours' sleep and it was early afternoon. Kezia had a number to call for the woman who was organizing the volunteers, and she said they'd be grateful for some help, but would understand if she didn't come down. They were still digging people out and finding people alive. When she said it, Kezia knew she wanted to go back to the bomb sites. She felt an inexorable pull she couldn't explain. She said as much to Sam, and he agreed.

They decided to meet in half an hour, and had been assigned to the World Trade Center downtown. It was shocking that the new building had been severely damaged, although it hadn't fallen down like the last ones. But there was a risk of collapse in all three locations. And if that happened, it would cause untold damage to the buildings around them, and claim more lives. Kezia hoped that wouldn't happen as she and Sam shared a cab heading downtown.

"Do you know any of the people in our building?" Sam asked her.

"No, I just arrived a week ago, and didn't know anyone there before."

"I knew several people before I moved in, which was how I heard about it. One of my favorite people lives there, Louise Smith."

"The photographer?" Kezia was impressed.

"Yes, and documentary filmmaker." He smiled. "I've known her for years."

"She must be very . . ." Kezia tried to find a polite word and couldn't, and Sam laughed.

"Old? In years, yes; in mind and energy, no. She's the youngest, most exciting woman I know. She's turning eighty-nine, and fully active. She's always traveling somewhere for a shoot, or a book, or to make a film. She's at every natural disaster, and every war. She knows every head of state. I'll introduce you to her if you like. If she has time!" Sam said, and Kezia smiled. For seventy years, Louise Smith had been taking photographs that were works of art. They sold for a fortune now, which didn't matter to Louise. "I met her when I first got to L.A. She was living there then, and then she moved back to New York. She flies all over the world constantly. She's given me some beautiful photographs. She took a photo of my son, John, when he was a little boy. She blew it up and gave it to me for Christmas. It's on the wall in my office." Kezia hadn't explored his apartment, so she hadn't seen it. Louise Smith had a unique style that was easy to recognize. She would have identified the photographer if she'd seen the photo of Sam's son.

"I've always wanted to buy one of her photographs. They have such an incredible range, from joyful to tragic. I especially love her photographs of children."

"I'll show you the one of Johnny. He was about four or five."

"How old is he now?" she asked him.

"Thirty-three."

"He's ten years older than my youngest, and four years younger than my oldest. That's a good age. You can be friends with them then, although I have an easier time with my younger daughter."

"The model who's in France right now?"

She nodded.

The city seemed to grow quieter and quieter as they rode downtown. There was no one on the streets, except for an occasional person walking a dog. And then they turned a corner, and they saw the building. The entire façade was black, the top had fallen in the explosion, and there was a gaping hole in its side, as though a giant monster from outer space had taken a bite out of it. As they drove around it, from a distance, they saw that the entire rear façade had been sheared off, and every office stood open and exposed. It was such wanton destruction it brought tears to Kezia's eyes. And if the attack had been planned for a weekday, during office hours, thousands more would have died.

The cab dropped them off at the police cordon on Murray Street, and Sam followed Kezia behind it. She asked where the volunteers were gathering and they were sent to a small tent set up by the EMS again, with people crowded into it, and a larger group congregating outside, come to help. She asked who was in charge and was directed to a young man in an NYU sweatshirt. Some of the students had come to volunteer. Sam and Kezia asked what they could do to help, and she explained that she was a nurse practitioner. The firefighters were still digging through the debris for survivors. Every once in a while there was a shout of excitement, as they found someone alive, and the paramedics rushed forward to help, but more often by now they were finding bodies. It was sixteen hours since the explosion, so there was still hope of finding some people alive. But the blast had been so powerful that most people in the vicinity had been killed. The survivors they found came out covered with ash and soot, and several of the firefighters got injured attempting complicated rescues. They had already gone through the parts of the building that were accessible, but many areas were too unsteady to enter. Most of the people they found had been walking near the building when it exploded. The memorial pool commemorating 9/11 was filled with debris, twisted steel, and mounds of ash.

The rescue work was less frantic than it had been at Hudson Yards the night before, and the area less crowded. The most gravely injured had been taken to hospitals the night before. Kezia comforted people as they waited to get into ambulances, and Sam helped the police hold people back, so they wouldn't interfere with the rescue work. It was sad just being there.

A reporter spotted Sam halfway through the afternoon and recognized him. She pushed through the police cordon and shoved a hand mike into his face, and he turned swiftly away. He had just watched a young woman's remains pulled from the mountains of rubble around the building.

"This isn't the time," he said gently to the reporter, who was persistent, and kept trying to goad him into an interview he wasn't willing to give. He finally slipped into the crowd and escaped her. Kezia had watched it happen and felt sorry for him.

"That must happen to you a lot," she said when she was standing next to him, and they were both drinking water and taking a brief break. Between the heat and the ash and the acrid smell of smoke, they were all constantly thirsty, and sick from what they were seeing.

"I try to be patient about it," he said, referring to the invasive reporter, "but sometimes it's just so wrong and they don't want to get it. I've only lost my temper a few times over the years, and I'm not proud of it." This was a hard time for anyone on the scene. There had been so much loss of life, and there were severed pieces of human flesh and limbs, which made him either cry or want to throw up. He didn't want a reporter in his face to register his emotions for the public. He was there as a private citizen and a man with a heart. Kezia respected him for it. He could have been at home, watching it on TV.

In slower moments when they took a break, the workers and volunteers all talked about who might have done it. Everyone agreed that it was political, and that the perpetrators were undoubtedly foreign, the attacks some statement of protest, or revenge for something that had been done to their country, or an act of religious zeal of some kind. Whatever slight had provoked the attacks, nothing justified the assault committed on innocent people, and even children, and the enormous loss of life the explosions had caused.

When they finally left the scene at eight that night, Sam and Kezia were quiet on the ride home. He was texting someone and she looked out the window, trying to push from her mind everything she had seen that day and the night before. It was unforgettable, no matter how hard she tried to focus on something else. And the injuries had been terrible from the kind of things the attackers loaded in the bombs, which was part of their special brand of terrorism.

Sam looked at Kezia as they got out of the cab. She looked tired and disheveled and her face was dirty. There was ash in her hair, and Sam surprised her as they walked into the lobby.

"I texted Louise Smith. She says she'd love to meet you."

"I'd love that," Kezia said with a tired smile. It had been nice spending the afternoon with him, crossing each other's paths occasionally but doing different jobs. She had been assigned to help the paramedics again, with smaller jobs this time. The big tasks were done by the first responders and EMS personnel officially working there, but the volunteers had been useful too. It seemed like very little to do, given the enormity of what had happened and what had to be done.

"Louise said to bring you up for a drink, if you want. She just got back too. She was at Hudson Yards all day, and she was at the Empire State Building last night. She was taking pictures. Do you want to meet her?"

"Now?" Kezia was surprised. "I'm filthy dirty and I look a mess." She had peeled her gloves off in the cab, and her hands were clean, but nothing else was. Even her jeans were smeared with the residue of the debris.

"She said exactly the same thing," he said to reassure her, and Kezia hesitated. She wanted to meet the legendary photographer and had always admired her, but it seemed like an odd time to meet her now. "I always figure seize the moment. Shall we do it?"

Kezia let herself be swept along. "Can I go upstairs and wash my face first and put on clean jeans? I'd be afraid to even sit down." She had blood and dirt all over her jeans.

"Sure. But no makeup and high heels," Sam warned her, and she smiled.

"Should I meet you there?"

"I'll come with you. I guess I could use a clean shirt and pair of jeans too." He hadn't noticed how dirty they both were. They rode up in their separate elevators. She scrubbed her face and hands and nails and brushed her hair when she got upstairs, put on clean jeans and sneakers and a clean T-shirt, and climbed through the hedge on her terrace to find Sam. She called his name to warn him she was there. He came out of his bedroom with his shirt off and fresh jeans on, and she noticed that he was in great shape for his age. He put a clean white T-shirt on while he talked to her. They looked like twins, and a lot cleaner than they had a few moments before.

"I'm glad you suggested that. My jeans left a pool of black grease and ash on my bathroom floor." And it was deep under his nails since he hadn't worn gloves that day.

"Are you sure we're not intruding, or I'm not?" she asked him hesitantly as they rode down in his private elevator.

"If she didn't want to see us, she wouldn't have invited us. She said she needs to see people, after everything she saw since yesterday." Sam and Kezia felt that way too. They needed normalcy and there was none.

The elevator stopped on the seventeenth floor, and Sam led the way. He had been there many times before. There were six apartments to a floor on that level, and Louise had two of them. She used one of them as her studio, he explained as he rang the doorbell. Kezia didn't know what to expect, although she'd seen photographs of Louise. A tall, very thin woman with long snow-white hair in a ponytail opened the door to them. She had a youthful look and body, but from the road map of wrinkles on her face, it was obvious that she was very old. She was wearing a black blouse and black jeans, with sturdy old vintage military boots that were well broken in. She wore no adornments and no jewelry. She had a beautiful face and a soulful expression in her sky-blue eyes, as though she had seen all the trouble in the world in her lifetime. And she had photographed it as well.

"Hello," Kezia said shyly, as Louise Smith stood back to let them in. She shook hands with Kezia, smiled at Sam, and then kissed him on the cheek.

"Someone's kicking our poor country around again," she said sadly. She had a British accent and Kezia remembered that she was English but had lived in America for a long time. "It's heartbreaking to see what they did to those buildings, and all the people they killed. How do things like this happen in America? This is supposed to be the Land of the Free. The world was a lot freer when I was a kid. Now everyone wants to kill someone, make a stink, complain about the country, or get pissed off at someone. It's not 'cool' to be happy anymore, or to be grateful for a great country. The pictures I took last night are some of the saddest I've ever taken. It's

such a statement about everything that's wrong in the world."
She led them into a big airy living room, full of primitive
African art, beautiful paintings, and some enormous enlarge-
ments of her photographs.

She pointed to the couch and they sat down. "Wine, scotch,
gin?" she offered, and they both picked wine. Louise had
scotch on the rocks. She was a serious drinker and an incredibly talented woman, and she had finished her work for the
day. There was a long vintage metal desk, and there were
some eight-by-ten prints lying on it. She picked them up and
handed them to Sam before she sat down, after she filled
their drink order and handed them their wine. "I developed
those last night when I got home." They were the faces of
people looking up at the ravaged Empire State Building,
looking like it was about to fall, but it hadn't. They were the
faces of fear, disbelief, disappointment, and tragedy. The
Empire State Building had been the symbol of New York since
1931, ninety-four years of a monument that was the symbol
of America, as well as New York, and now it was severely
damaged and might even have to be torn down. It would
have to be assessed for its safety and salvageability, but
Louise's photographs had captured the moment perfectly, on
the faces of women and men, young and old. The photos
were exquisite, and those taken at Hudson Yards were equally
so, with the injured victims littering the ground as first

responders knelt to help them and comforted those in extremis. Kezia's eyes filled with tears as she looked at them, and then looked at the artist who had taken them.

"They're incredible," Kezia said in a hoarse voice, and Louise smiled.

"I hate it when people think all I do are disasters, but the moments and the faces are so poignant. They tell a whole story of what the loss meant to them, and to us. Sam tells me you just moved to New York," Louise said to Kezia in a smooth, silky, almost sexy voice. Looking at her, one forgot her age. She was still a very attractive woman, and always had been. "This is quite an introduction to New York," Louise said apologetically.

"I'm just sorry it happened," Kezia said.

"You're a nurse?" Sam had told Louise about her when he called.

"I was. A nurse practitioner, that's like being a nurse plus. I've been a wife and mother for the past twenty-five years."

Louise looked surprised. "You gave up your calling?" Kezia nodded. "Was it your passion?"

"It was when I was working. I practiced with my father, who was a GP in a little town in Vermont. I loved it, and loved working with him. But then I married and moved to San Francisco. I haven't worked since."

"And your father went on practicing without you?" Louise

went right to the heart of the matter, in her photographs and in real life.

"He did. He encouraged me to make the move for a new life. I was thirty-five. Vermont was a dead end for me. He got sick a year after I left and died. Everybody in the county loved him. He taught me a lot when I worked with him."

"If you love nursing, you should go back to it. Sam says you were wonderful at Hudson Yards last night. What a tragedy this whole thing is. I hope they catch the people responsible. They shouldn't get away with it." It was twenty-four hours later and still no one had taken responsibility. "Do you have children?"

"Two daughters."

"I never had children. I was married for a short time. It wasn't for me. I need to be free, and children require you to give up your freedom. I'm too selfish to do that, and I enjoy my work too much." She smiled a mischievous smile and Sam laughed. She was a character, and he always enjoyed her company and admired her immense talent. "And I had a traumatic childhood myself. I was four when the war started in England. When I was six, my parents sent me to the countryside to get me out of the bombings in London. They died a few months later in the Blitz. I was ten when the war was over and spent eight years in an orphanage. I was awkward and outspoken, even then, so no one adopted me. At eighteen, I left the orphanage to get a job. I came to the States in 1953. I loved it, so I stayed and became an American. This is my country now. And now we're being bombed here. I take it very personally." She was direct and spoke her mind. She was strong and brave and seemed fearless, and had seen all the tragedies in life.

She showed them some more of the photographs she'd taken the night before. She had developed them herself in her own darkroom in the apartment next door. She loved working with old cameras and film. She had a Leica she cherished, which she showed Kezia. An hour later, Kezia and Sam went back upstairs after having a very pleasant time.

"What an amazing woman!" Kezia said to Sam.

"I love her," he said, and went back to his apartment via her terrace. They were both tired, and needed time alone to recover from all they'd seen.

There were ten CIA and FBI agents and a dozen top-level Homeland Security supervisors pressed into a small locked CIA office on the West Side, ten blocks from Sam and Kezia's building. It was a discreet gray stone building with a small sign that identified it as the ABC Import Company and a door that opened with a code. Once inside, there were countless electronic devices to identify anyone who entered.

The man at the front of the room, Joe Delano, was the most senior CIA agent present.

The twenty-two men standing and seated were the elite of the FBI, CIA, and Homeland Security, and had flown in for the meeting on Air Force planes a few hours before. They were studying a massive bulletin board with photographs covering almost every inch of it. Across the top of the bulletin board, in four rows, were the photographs of forty-six young men between the ages of nineteen and thirty-two. All of them were wearing military-style uniforms of various rank. Most of them were wholesome-looking. No facial hair, no piercings, no facial jewelry. "But lots of tattoos," one of the Homeland Security officers said, and someone laughed. All of them were based in Texas, in remote towns. And had weekly maneuvers.

"They have training camp every summer. They call themselves the Enforcers," Joe Delano said. "They started in Arkansas and Oklahoma, and the whole group moved to Texas three years ago. They had nine members initially, and they've increased their ranks to forty-five, with a leader. That makes forty-six. We believe that they worked this operation with three teams, with fifteen men on each team, including a leader, and the man who is their overall commander who masterminded the whole thing. They're anarchists. They want to bring the country down. They sent their advance team of explosives experts here a few days ago. They've been staying at a hotel in Times Square. Their leader, Filo Banks, runs his men like a small army. We educated most of them in Iraq and Afghanistan. They hate everything we stand for. We have an informant, who says they bought a lot of their material here and made most of the bombs themselves. More than half of them are expert explosives experts, forty of them have served in the army, two of them were Navy SEALs, and nineteen of them have been in prison, mostly in states other than Texas. Banks and our source hate each other. He wanted to be their leader. Banks double-crossed him and threw him out a year ago. So he came to us yesterday with the whole story. He says they brought an arsenal of weapons in from New Jersey, and most of the bombs in a stolen army truck. Most of them look like nice healthy guys from the sticks, just boys wanting to have fun. They're lethal and highly trained. One of them dragged his little brother into it. He's their computer whiz, and can hack into anything, and often does, just for the fun of it. They're fearless. Born killers. We believe our source. Our informant wants indemnity for charges he has pending in three states. We didn't believe him at first, but it all checks out." Two of the CIA agents exchanged a glance. Everyone in the room knew Joe Delano by reputation. He was a hard-looking man in a hard job, with military bearing.

"And are we going to give the informant indemnity?" a Homeland Security officer asked.

"We might," Joe said. "It depends on how solid the rest of the information turns out to be. What we have now appears to be accurate. He gave us all the names. They've been studying the targets for two years. They know every passage and air duct in the buildings they bombed. Some of them took jobs there briefly. They knew the security codes for entry. They want to bring the country down with a military coup. They were destroying the symbols of capitalism. It was meant to be an example of what they can do."

"By blowing up two major buildings and half of Chelsea?" one of the CIA agents said angrily.

"Banks had a brilliant record in the army, and then he went nuts in Iraq and started killing civilians. He wound up in a mental hospital and was discharged. He was taken prisoner in Afghanistan for three months and tortured. He's never been the same since, and when he was discharged he went back to Texas and recruited his own army. He's a tactical genius. He masterminded the July Fourth attacks. He wants to take over the government. July Fourth was just to get our attention and show us what he's capable of."

One of the CIA agents handed out folders to each of them then. "All the information you need on these guys is in the folders, along with your assignments." There was a female agent in the back of the room who had been observing the other agents, and she got a folder too. She was from internal affairs, and the second highest-ranking officer in the room, a retired army colonel.

"That's it for now," Joe said, and stood up, indicating that the meeting was over. Now they had to do their job. They had more than enough to go on, to learn who Banks and his men were, their habits and their histories. They had to find Banks and stop him. His goal was to blow up every monument in Washington, D.C., next, take over the government, and kill the president. Twenty-four hours after the explosions that had rocked New York, they knew who had done it, thanks to their informant. Along with the indemnity he'd asked for, he wanted witness protection, to be moved to another state, with a new identity. It was all possible if they got the green light. The secretary of defense and the White House had the final word. They had all the information.

"Are Banks and his men still in the area?" one of the FBI agents asked.

"We think so," Joe said. "They're lying low. They're in the city somewhere. We've put out the word to all our usual resources. Forty-six men are out there. Someone will slip or talk. If they find our informant, they'll kill him. He knows it. We have him under heavy guard in a hotel. We want Banks alive, whatever it takes. They're going back to Texas after this. Washington is their next target. We can't let that happen. They're working on it now. New York was just a practice round.

"Sometime in the next two days they're all going to disappear. Our job is to find Banks and his men before that happens. I want him and his men in twenty-four hours." Joe looked hard at them and then left the room, as the twenty-two agents looked at each other and opened the folders. Every one of them knew their jobs were on the line. They *had* to find Filo Banks and his forty-five-man army. The biggest shock was that they were Americans, not foreigners at all.

The Enforcers wanted to bring down the country. They had the skills, the knowledge, and the materials to do it. Their bombs were simple to build and effective, as they'd proven. They could kill thousands of people in any city they chose to.

They believed that once they took over the government, they would be able to enlist an army of like-minded people who hated the way the country was run too. Their informant had said they were planning to bomb the White House and the Capitol sometime in the next month. They were fueled by hatred and armed with the skills the army had taught them. They were damaged, twisted men, hell-bent on destroying their own country. Banks had trained as an engineer at MIT before enlisting. And the forty-five men were his pawns, and each of them had a score to settle with the government and the army. He had just proven that a small band of highly dangerous men could terrorize a city of millions. In Filo Banks's mind, this was only the beginning. A month from now, after Washington, he would control the whole country. He had to be found before he left the city. The race was on.

Chapter 5

Kate and Jack left Johannesburg early on Friday morning, as they had planned, in an RV with a driver. They were going to drive eleven hours through Kruger National Park to see the animals in the bush and cross the border into the Mozambique province of Gaza to the village of Tomanini, several kilometers from the district capital, Guijá. Reed Phillips's hospital was in Tomanini, which was tiny and extremely primitive. There was no electricity at all, the roads weren't paved, and Kate's father had warned her to expect rugged conditions. Her heart was pounding when she got in the car at six in the morning. She was thinking about the meeting with her father. The driver said that after the first few hours they'd be traveling over rough terrain. And she knew they'd be out of communication when they got there.

There was no cellphone service or Wi-Fi, only the radio at the hospital, which was all they needed most of the time. In emergencies, they would have to drive to Guijá, to have internet and more modern communications.

The drive from Johannesburg was beautiful, and the driver indicated points of interest along the way. Kruger National Park made the long drive worthwhile, seeing the animals in the wild, particularly zebras, who looked so elegant. The driver told them that no two zebras' stripes are alike—each zebra's stripes are individual to it, like human fingerprints. Once the travelers were in Mozambique, there were small villages tucked into the bush with a few thin cows and goats and some huts. The driver explained that there were still occasional tribal wars there, with people killed and injured. It was hard to imagine. Everything seemed so peaceful, and the locals looked friendly.

They stopped at a small store along the way with a gas pump and women in colorful clothing standing around. They sold some small handmade trinkets, snacks, and bottled water. Kate had brought sandwiches, which they shared with the driver, who accepted gratefully, as they kept driving. There was nowhere they wanted to stop. Kate was eager to arrive, preferably before nightfall. They were slowed down regularly by the bad roads.

Kate was thrilled by everything she saw, and Jack took

photographs with a new camera she had bought him. It was a long day, but there was so much to hold their attention along the way that the time flew. The road was rutted, narrow, and bumpy, so the drive took more than eleven hours, and they arrived at six o'clock. The driver knew the way, and drove into a dusty clearing, where there were children playing and a group of squatting women watching them as they laughed and talked.

They looked up as Kate got out of the car and Jack followed her. The hospital looked small to her, but it was clean and freshly painted, and there was a long row of tents behind it, and a small house. Kate was trying to take everything in. A small, sturdy-looking woman with short white hair, wearing a khaki jacket and shorts and heavy boots, came out of the hospital and approached them. She smiled as soon as she saw Kate, hastened toward her, and hugged her. Kate could guess who she was, as the woman directed the driver to take Kate and Jack's bags to one of the tents behind the hospital, telling him precisely which one.

"You must be Kate," the woman said with a smile. She had bright blue eyes, laugh lines near her eyes, and looked busy and cheerful. "I'm Pru, Prunella." Her accent was different from the one they'd heard in Johannesburg. "I'm from the Free State, we're mostly Dutch. We're so excited to see you." Kate hoped that was true of her father too. "Reed

will be out in a minute. He just finished his last surgery."
They had a generator at the hospital, which gave them the
electricity they needed. "Was the drive awful?" she asked,
and Kate smiled. It was an unexpectedly warm welcome,
more than she'd hoped for. Pru looked like she was Kate's
father's age, in her early sixties. And Kate knew she was a
doctor, from what her father had said in his emails. She was
a pediatrician, much needed in the area, where the infant
and child mortality rates were high, and malaria, TB, and
cholera were frequent.

"It was bumpy but fascinating," Kate answered. "We saw
a lot of animals on the way, and little villages. The driver
told us about the tribal wars."

"It's left over from the civil wars. They give us plenty of
business," Pru said cheerfully. Some of the squatting women
waved at Kate, and she waved back, just as a tall man came
out of the main building and hurried down the steps to meet
her. Without even trying, she could see a resemblance with
him. And she could see why her mother had been attracted
to him. Reed Phillips was a handsome man, although he
looked his age. He was serious and had a warm smile. She
noticed that he was observing her closely and saw the resemblance too. Kate had always thought she looked like her
maternal grandfather, but now she saw that she looked more
like Reed, much more than she looked like her mother or

sister. She was happy to see it, and she felt as though she'd found an anchor here, so far from home and in this very distant place, away from all the modern conveniences she took for granted every day. This was a whole different life, another world, entirely unfamiliar to her.

Reed stood looking down at Kate with a warm expression, but he didn't reach out to hug her. "Thank you for coming. It's a long way to come to meet a man who's never showed up for you. Would you like a tour of the hospital?" he asked her very directly. He didn't know what else to say to her, and it was the best he had to offer, to show her what he'd done with his life. He was proud of it and, as they walked into the building, just the two of them, while Jack stayed with Pru, Kate saw that everything was immaculate. Her driver had told them that Reed had saved his little girl a year before. She had appendicitis and he operated before it burst, but it could have killed her. There was no other medical care within a hundred miles, and once a month Doctors Without Borders came in by plane. If they needed to, Reed and Pru could contact them by radio, but the two doctors handled most of the emergencies themselves, and all of the simple surgeries. They had three nurses in residence, and had trained several of the locals as medics, who were very good at handling minor injuries with one of the nurses at their clinic every day. Reed explained to Kate that his mission was to teach as well as heal and operate, so that the locals could become more self-sufficient and use better hygiene. Pru vaccinated all the local children. They were supported by donors from all over the world.

Kate could see that it was a tidy, well-run little medical unit. The families of some of the patients stayed in the tents behind the hospital until their family members got well and could go home. "That's part of their culture," Reed explained to Kate. "They don't do well if they're separated from their families and the people they know." The local language was Changana, which he and Pru spoke fluently, and some Portuguese, the official national language, and Pru spoke Afrikaans, which was based on Dutch. "She grew up here on her parents' farm and went to medical school in England. And afterward she came back here to work for Doctors Without Borders, when I was working for them, which is how we met. We've been married for thirty years. Our son, Austin, is in medical school in London. He's twenty-five, the same age I was when I met your mother. She was very brave to have you on her own. I just wasn't ready to settle down." He went straight to the heart of the matter, which surprised Kate, as though he wanted her to know. She wondered if he felt guilty for abandoning her. "I didn't marry Pru until I was thirty-three, seven years after you were born. I couldn't have managed fatherhood and my internship and residency. I never had the guts to tell my family about you. They wouldn't have understood how something like that could happen. They were very straitlaced and old-fashioned. I grew up on a farm in Ohio. It was hard enough putting myself through medical school. I couldn't have taken on more. I knew I couldn't do it. I told Pru about you when we got married. She thought that I should contact you. She's suggested it often, but by then you were settled in your life, I knew your mother had gotten married, and I didn't want to interfere. I had given up my right to when you were born. It was the right thing to do, for me." He clearly had no regrets. He just wanted to tell her his side.

"I would have liked to hear from you," Kate said as they sat down, after the tour, in his office with the battered desk and swivel chair, like the one her grandfather had had in his office in Vermont. In some ways, they seemed similar. Her mother must have thought so too, except her grandfather was nicer, and warmer.

"I didn't know what to say to you," Reed said. "You can't explain to a child why you ran away. You're a woman now, I can talk to you. I couldn't then; even later. You were only a child." But even as a woman she had trouble understanding why he had given her up and never contacted her. His clear reasoning and explanation didn't justify it in her eyes. Even a birthday or Christmas card from him would have been nice, and appreciated, and would have taken so little effort on his part.

"Were you close to the man your mother married?" Reed was trying to ease his conscience, Kate could tell.

"I was. He was a good man. He was always very kind to me." She didn't tell him about her inheritance. It had nothing to do with him. And her mother's life was so completely different from his. They were like two people on two different planets, but Kate could see that Reed was a serious, sincere person, and genuinely trying to help people at his hospital. He had dedicated his life to it. He had had none of the comforts she'd grown up with or had at any time in her life. Her life at home would have been completely foreign to him, and her mother's even more so, after twenty-five years of wealth and luxury.

"Are you going to marry the man who's here with you?" he asked her, curious and trying to make up for lost time and understand her life and who she was.

Kate hesitated before she answered. "I don't know. I want to write a book. I've always wanted to. I've been blocked, and my psychiatrist thought it would help if I met you. You've always been the big unanswered question in my life, about why you left me and signed your rights away." She hadn't planned to ask him so soon, but they had jumped into the deep end very quickly. He had brought it all up immediately.

"I did it because I wanted to do what I'm doing here—just like you want to write your book—and I knew I couldn't if I stayed with your mother and you. I didn't want to work for your grandfather, which she suggested, or stay in the States. The need was greater here. I wanted to come to Africa one day. This was my life's dream. I couldn't give that up." Not even for Kate, or her mother.

"Are you glad you did?" she asked with tears in her eyes, and he nodded.

"I am. Very. But I'm not glad I gave you up. You pay a heavy price for leaving a child, much more than leaving a woman. I've never stopped thinking about you." It was comforting to hear that, even though he had put his dreams and career first. Pru stuck her head in the door then.

"Dinner is in ten minutes," she said with a smile. She had been entertaining Jack while Kate talked to her father. She didn't like all his answers, but they were real, and so was he. "Do you want to go to your tent and wash up a bit?" Pru asked Kate, and she and her father stood up and he exchanged a warm look with his wife. They seemed very well suited to each other. They were businesslike and efficient and seemed in perfect harmony. "We eat in the dining hall behind the hospital. I showed Jack where it is. He has certainly been reading up on the area. He knows more about it than I do." She looked amused.

"He loves projects like that. He's very thorough," Kate said with a smile, and followed them back to where Jack was waiting for her. They went to their tent together.

"I like Pru. She's a nice woman. How was it with your father?" Jack asked her, curious.

"It was good. I got some answers." Which was what she came for. She still had more questions, but they had come far for the first night. Kate wondered if Reed had loved her mother, but realized now that maybe she didn't need to know. They hadn't stayed together. And that was their life; she had her own. She still had to figure out how much Jack meant to her. She was never sure about that or whether or not she wanted to marry him. Sometimes he was so annoying, but at other times she was grateful for his company. At thirty-seven and forty-two, they both had to figure out what they wanted and if they had a future. She could never decide. Maybe she could do that here.

Dinner was simple, but satisfying, a mixture of European food and some of the local dishes. After that, Kate thanked her father and Pru, and she and Jack walked back to their tent. Her father and Pru lived in the little house, and Austin lived there with them when he was home. He had grown up there. They had a house in Johannesburg, where they would live one day when they retired and life became too hard in the bush. They rented it for now and were saving it for their later years. Austin would inherit it one day. They had their future all mapped out, and Kate's father had followed his plan. There had never been room in his life for her, not like there was with Andrew, who had made so much generous space for her. She wondered if she had room in her heart for both of them, though maybe Reed didn't belong there. He had never done anything to earn it. He had chosen not to be a father in her life. She didn't know if she could have made that decision to reject a child. She didn't think so. She was glad her mother hadn't. Reed was unapologetic for having chosen his career plans over her, and justified his choice. Kate wondered what kind of father he was to his son, if he put his career first with him too. Maybe that's who Reed was. He was doing good deeds for his patients in Africa, but he never had done any for her, not even a letter or a card.

The next day, on Saturday, Kate and Jack toured the area with one of the local boys in Pru's car, an open Jeep. He took them on the back roads where they could see more wildlife. They came back at lunchtime and had lunch with her father and Pru. Reed told her more about the work he was doing at the hospital. He had started a maternity program several years before. Kate admired his work, but she noticed that he never asked her about her book or what she wanted to write. Pru catered to him, and he was the king of his little fiefdom. Kate's adoptive father had been a much warmer and more empathetic man, and a better father than Reed would have been. They were related by blood, but that was all, and she wondered if it was enough, or if maybe blood didn't matter, and the heart mattered much more. She had never seen it that way before in her fantasies about Reed. She had dreamt of him as a warmer person and he wasn't. He cared more about medicine and his hospital than anything else.

They had dinner together on Saturday night too, and Jack expounded about the history of the tribal wars and the earlier civil war thirty years before in the area, based on the books he'd read about it. He had been accurate in his research, but his audience was bored. To him it was all theory. To them it was real. They played Scrabble after dinner, which they all enjoyed, and Pru won.

On Sunday, Reed went to Guijá to send some emails and get some supplies. He looked sober when he returned. The others were at lunch when he walked in. Pru could see something was wrong. "Was everything all right in town?" she asked him.

"I heard some shocking news. There was an attack on New York two days ago, terrorists like 9/11. They all but destroyed the Empire State Building, the new World Trade Center, and an enormous mall area with apartment buildings adjacent to it. Thousands were killed, and many more injured. All U.S. cities are under lockdown, the borders are closed, and the airports are shut down. Nothing can get in or out of the States right now. Have you heard from your mother?" Reed asked her.

Kate looked worried. "I don't get cell service here." Reed nodded and knew that was true.

"I'll drive you back to Guijá later, and you can try there or send her an email. I hope she's all right. I'm sure she is. Does she live close to any of the damaged buildings?" Kate shook her head, shocked by what he'd told them.

"She lives in midtown. She just moved in. Those buildings are all downtown. Did they say who did it?"

"It sounds like they don't know, or they're not saying. It's obviously foreign nationals."

As promised, Reed drove Kate back to Guijá that afternoon. Kate couldn't get a phone line, due to disturbances on the line in the area, but she was able to send an email, telling her mother she was fine, and hoped she was too. She tried to reach Felicity in France but couldn't get through to her either. It sounded like a replay of 9/11. She read the reports on the internet and was shocked at the descriptions and the photographs she saw of Friday night in New York. It was very unreal. The images were devastating, and it all seemed so far away right now, so surreal.

She talked to Jack about it that night. "Maybe we should go home," she said hesitantly.

"I thought you wanted to spend time with your father." He looked puzzled and disappointed. He was having a good time. And he liked Pru.

"I did, I do. We've had some good talks, but I don't want my mother alone in New York, and Felicity is in France. But they say the borders are closed. We can't go back until they open them, and the airports."

"That could last several weeks. We might as well stay here, since we've come this far." Africa felt like it was light-years from home. Jack was in no hurry to leave. He had an audience here and was enjoying showing off his knowledge of the local tribes.

They drove back to Guijá again on Monday to get more news. When Kate was able to use the Wi-Fi connection, she got an email from her mother saying she was fine. The reports of the dead and injured were heartbreaking. Kate cried when she read them. She announced at dinner that she should go back to New York as soon as the borders opened. She didn't want her mother to be alone. And what if there was another terrorist attack, and that had just been the opening salvo? That had been one of the primary fears of 9/11 too, although a second wave of attacks had never happened.

"I don't think they would attack again," Reed said, and Jack agreed.

"It sounds like they did enough damage to satisfy them

116

on Friday night, from what you read," Jack added. He wanted to stay. "If we do go back, we should go up to your place in Vermont. We'll be safer there."

"I'm not leaving my mother when I go back," Kate said firmly, wishing she could reach Felicity, but it seemed hopeless to try and contact her sister, or even her mother, by phone. The service was just too poor.

Kate was uneasy for the next several days. It was a long week until she read on the internet in Guijá that the borders were now open and planes were flying again. Kate had been in Tomanini for a week by then, and it seemed long enough. She had met her father and discovered that he was a hardworking, responsible, and respectable man, doing good work helping others, but she had fewer illusions about him now. He was a man, like any other, with his flaws, and you couldn't turn the clock back, to recapture all the lost years. He'd been happy to meet Kate, but he was far more interested in his own daily life than hers, and didn't try to hide it, or pretend otherwise. Pru catered to his narcissism, which suited him. New York was so far away, it was hard for him to relate to it. At the end of the week on Saturday they went to Guijá again, and booked a flight for Monday. On Sunday Jack and Kate made their way back to Johannesburg with Pru's car and a driver, and stayed at a hotel for the night. Jack went out to dinner with his cousin Chad alone, and Kate stayed in her room to try to contact her mother and sister. She was able to reach both. It had been a stressful week in New York, under lockdown, and Felicity was flying back from Paris on Monday too. Kate and Felicity agreed that they would all feel better once they were back in New York and they knew more about what was going on. But at least their mother was safe.

When Kate left her father's hospital on Sunday, she felt that she had been given the time she needed to at least understand who he was. She no longer had the regrets she had before about his giving up his parental rights to her. She had been well loved by her mother and grandfather, and then by the father who adopted her.

"Thank you for coming," Reed said to her politely, as though Kate had come to tea or for a weekend, and not halfway around the world to meet him and hear his side of the story. Pru hugged her and wished her a safe trip home. Reed hugged her too, but she realized now that he wasn't a warm person, or he could never have done what he had thirty-seven years before. He had kept his own goals in mind and stuck to them, and never looked back. He had no regrets about leaving her. It had been the right thing for him. What she had seen of him was enough to put her heart at rest at last. His rejection of her wasn't personal, he just didn't have it in him. Discovering that had freed her.

"I enjoyed it, didn't you?" Jack said, looking relaxed and pleased with the trip, after they drove away. "Do you think it will help your writing?" he asked her, and she nodded, thinking about it. It had done much more than that, for her personally.

"Yes, I do." She had come to find her father, and instead, she had found herself, which was more important.

"Do you think you'll come back?" he asked her, and she looked pensive, and shook her head. She no longer had a pressing desire to meet her half brother either. They weren't her family. They weren't even friends.

"I don't think so," she answered Jack. "I don't need to." She had learned all she needed to. She was free now. Reed wasn't her father. He never had been. He had given all that up thirty-seven years before. Now she was ready to give him up too. It was long overdue.

Chapter 6

By Sunday, two days after the bombing, they were no longer finding survivors. The explosions had been too powerful, and people had been buried for too long. The workers were only finding bodies in the rubble, so they no longer needed Kezia's medical skills at the bomb site. All the living victims had been removed and were in hospitals, many of them in intensive care units. The death toll continued to rise as more bodies were found, and as the most severely wounded died from internal injuries, severed limbs, or severe burns. Those who were less injured were released, although the majority were severely traumatized by what they'd experienced and seen, and were grieving the friends and loved ones they had lost, many of whom had been killed while standing right next to them. It was a horrendous attack, even more gruesome than 9/11. The country would be forever marked by it, as it had been before. The violation of being attacked on home turf made it that much worse, and no one felt safe now, as cities remained tense and vigilant, fearing additional attacks. But in the two days after the July Fourth explosions, nothing happened. What had already occurred was bad enough. The entire country was suffering from the trauma, people had nightmares and trouble sleeping, whether they had lost loved ones or not. The country remained under lockdown, and people were urged not to leave their homes.

Sam had gone back to the site at the World Trade Center on Sunday morning, but the authorities and official OES personnel had things under control, still excavating for bodies and clearing away rubble. There was little he could do, and he came home to find Kezia on her terrace on what should have been a glorious July day. Even the beautiful weather seemed like an affront now, with so much grief and loss at hand.

He peeked through the hedge that had become the link between their two apartments, for rapid easy access, like a secret passage, rather than separate lobbies and elevators for more formal access, and Kezia looked up, saw him, and smiled. In the past two days, Sam had become a familiar face and constant companion, forming a friendship that might have taken months to establish otherwise. She was happy to see him. It was comforting not to be alone, and she had been touched by his quick response and willingness to help in the crisis. He felt a civic and humane responsibility to his fellow New Yorkers and citizens, just because they were human beings. She gestured for him to sit on the deck chair next to her. She was glad she had them, although in broad daylight, the ravaged view of the Empire State Building made her heart ache every time she saw it, knowing how many people had died there, even though it had been a Friday night and offices were closed on the holiday. There had been a large crowd in the observatory, to watch the fireworks. People in the street had died when the structural debris rained down from the explosion and the flames engulfed them.

"How was it?" Kezia asked him. She was thinking of volunteering at one of the hospitals, but there would be more red tape and delay involved than lending a hand on the street right after it happened.

"They're doing a great job. It sounds corny but the last few days make you proud to be an American. They have it pretty much under control downtown. There wasn't much I could do in a nonofficial capacity."

"The last two days really made me miss nursing," she said as they lay on the deck chairs side by side. She felt as though she had always known him, and he acted as though they had.

"Would you ever go back?" Sam asked.

"I never thought so, but I'm wondering about that now. It reminded me of everything I loved about nursing. It makes you feel useful. My kids are grown up, and we sold my husband's company, which kept me busy for the last five years. I have nothing to do now, except shop, go to museums, and go out for lunch. If I take a refresher course, I could get a part-time job as a nurse practitioner, maybe at a clinic for inner-city kids, and give something back, instead of just indulging myself." She liked the idea, and he was impressed.

"You gave a lot back for the last two days." He had watched how kind and competent Kezia was, reassuring people in their pain and distress. Her hands had been covered with blood from all the hands she held, until someone gave her a pair of surgical gloves.

"What do you do between films?" she asked him. It was the first time she had referred to Sam's professional work. His stardom seemed like the least important thing about him, and he paid no attention to it either, or seemed not to. He was a very humble person.

"Most of the time, I hunt for scripts. It's not easy to find good ones. People send them to me. I read a lot of books to see what we could adapt. I'm very picky about the films I do." It showed, since Kezia had never seen him in a bad one, or one she didn't like. He had made few mistakes, if any. "I spend time with my son when he has time." Sam smiled as he said it. "He's a busy guy. He works hard, and he has a revolving door of girlfriends, but at his age, that's to be expected and it's acceptable, although I'm not always crazy about the woman of the hour. He likes the flashy ones, and some of the smart ones. He's a good-looking kid, and he's a magnet for overambitious, greedy women, who see him as a stepping stone to what they want. I hate that for him. I avoided it by getting married young, before I was successful. I came from a normal family. They did okay. My father had a good job as a lawyer, but he wasn't overly ambitious. We were comfortable, but he didn't make a lot of money. I grew up in Philadelphia, and went to Penn. My mother didn't work. We were three boys, and we were expected to do well in school. Both my brothers became lawyers and worked with my dad. I was the youngest, and one of them is retired now, the oldest. Our other brother died fairly young.

"I wanted to be an actor. The whole family thought I was nuts. After I graduated from Penn, I went to L.A., which is where I met my wife. I got lucky after I took some acting lessons. We were both lucky, but she had more talent. It was easier then. I don't even know most of the young actors now. They come and go faster than I can learn their names. The studios used to build careers then. They wanted real stars that people would be loyal to, and they were. If you worked hard, most of the time you could be successful, with some good decisions and a certain amount of luck and hard work. Nowadays, they're in and out of the business, and want to be stars overnight. I don't believe in overnight success. I believe in hard work, and after a lot of years and sweat and some tears, it pays off. That makes more sense." It did to Kezia too. "There are only a handful of actors I really admire who have genuine talent and work at it. My wife was a talented actress, more so than I am, as I said." Kezia was struck again and again by his humility and how down-to-earth he was. She was curious about his son and wondered if he was as genuine as his father. She felt sorry for Sam for the loss of his wife. He had clearly loved her a great deal and it sounded like a good marriage.

"My husband was a hard worker too," Kezia said about Andrew. "He didn't believe in easy success either, like all the young guys now who make billions at twenty-three and twenty-four with social media companies, and don't know how they got there. It's like winning the lottery."

"It's an amazing phenomenon of our times. I like it better the way it was. At least I know I earned it, and I made it honestly. I sleep better at night."

They lay side by side for a while, not talking, and Kezia

got them bottles of cold water, and he thanked her. It was comforting being together in a time of crisis. It would have been much harder without him, and Sam felt that way too about her.

"Have you heard from your daughters today?"

"Not yet. I'm sure they'll come home as soon as planes can fly again. They'll be nervous being so far away, but maybe they're safer where they are. The scary part of all this is that you feel so vulnerable, right here at home, waiting to be attacked again, and not sure if you will be." Sam nodded in agreement. He was worried about it too. He was relieved that his son was out of town with his girlfriend in the Berkshires.

"I thought we were under missile attack the other night," Sam said to her. "It was inconceivable to me that it was happening right here in New York, again, and worse than last time." The death toll was much higher now, and the entire country had been taken totally by surprise both times, now and on 9/11. "We weren't prepared for an attack of this magnitude on home turf."

Sam fell asleep on the deck chair for a while, and Kezia couldn't help noticing how handsome he was, but he didn't play on it or use it, or even seem aware of it, although "officially" he was a movie star. She still found it hard to believe that she had met him and that they were becoming friends now.

His cellphone woke him, and he answered it. He listened for a few minutes and said he would call back, then turned to Kezia. "That was Louise. She wants to know if we want to come to dinner tonight. Does that appeal to you? I don't mind making a salad at my place if you want to do that with me, if you're not in the mood to see her, or if you want to be on your own," he said casually. He clearly wanted to spend the evening with Kezia, and she liked the idea. They had nothing else to do. He was good company, and the entire city was closed. They couldn't even order a pizza or takeout, and a little distraction was comforting.

"I like her a lot, that would be nice," Kezia said, feeling relaxed and happy to spend the evening with him either way. He called Louise back and accepted for both of them. Kezia wasn't sure if that was his idea or Louise's, and if he had included her in an invitation meant for him.

"She said to wear whatever we have on. She always wears her black skirts and black T-shirts or blouses. It's sort of her uniform. I'll put on jeans." He was wearing shorts on the terrace, and she wasn't even wearing makeup and had barely combed her hair. She felt relaxed with him, and they had already seen each other at their worst, so it didn't matter.

They went to their own apartments at the end of the afternoon, to shower and put on whatever they were going to wear. Kezia reappeared in a white T-shirt, jeans, and gold sandals, with her hair brushed back in a ponytail and a freshly washed face with just a little lipstick. Putting on makeup seemed like too much effort in the situation they were in, and too festive. Sam was wearing a blue shirt, white jeans, and loafers, his dark hair still damp from the shower, but she noticed that he'd shaved.

When they got to Louise's apartment, Kezia was surprised to see that another couple was there. The man was about Sam and Kezia's age, somewhere in his late fifties, and the woman with him was very attractive, around forty years old, with well-cut, highlighted blonde hair. They seemed very subdued. Louise explained that the couple were her neighbors and they had become friends in the last few years. It became clear in the conversation that Greg Avery was a big film studio executive, and divided his time between New York and L.A. The woman with him was clearly his girlfriend. Paige Robbins was very quiet, and in talking to her, Kezia discovered that she was an executive for a major fashion brand and had a big job in marketing. She was very discreet about it and let Greg have center stage, which he took over with ease. He was charming and funny, and Louise whispered to Kezia when they went out to the kitchen to get dinner ready, "She's worth ten of him." Oddly, he seemed to pay no attention to Paige, or very little. He spoke mainly to Sam and

Louise, and Kezia enjoyed talking to Paige. She was interesting and well-traveled, knowledgeable on a number of subjects, and very indulgent of her partner, who talked mostly about his own success, in case they were unaware of it. Sam knew him, having met him several times, and wasn't overly impressed with him. Greg was the opposite of Sam, who never mentioned his movies or his stardom. The dynamics of the evening were interesting. Sam was much warmer and friendlier to Kezia, in a nice way, than Greg was with Paige. Louise made pasta carbonara and a big salad, with fruit for dessert. It was delicious and easy, with a lot of good French wine. It was a very pleasant evening, and Kezia was happy to have met Paige.

She and Sam talked about the evening on the way back upstairs. "Greg is always very full of himself," he commented. "I always wonder why Paige puts up with it. His wife is a real Hollywood wife, all done up in Chanel with lots of bling, showy and very tough."

"He's married?" Kezia was startled when he said it. That had never occurred to her. He and Paige appeared to be very much a couple, with history together.

"Very much so. I think he has three or four kids around my son's age. And his wife is kind of a showpiece in L.A. She's a big deal socially and lets everyone know who she is. She's the exact opposite of Paige, who is always very quiet and discreet. They've been together for quite a while, a few years anyway. I don't know why good women get stuck in situations like that. She deserves better, and he never seems that nice to her." It made Kezia sad to hear it. She had really liked Paige and had enjoyed their conversation during the evening.

"Maybe she doesn't think she deserves better," Kezia suggested. "And single men aren't that easy to meet at her age, or her job intimidates men. She's around the age of my daughter Kate, maybe a little older. And Kate hasn't picked a winner yet. She's thirty-seven."

"Relationships aren't easy. It's hard to find good ones," Sam said. "We married young, but when my wife died, I had every lonely, over-the-hill, ambitious actress in Hollywood calling me. It was really depressing. I was surprised how forward they were. I felt like I'd been thrown to the wolves. I ran like hell and stayed in New York. People leave me alone here."

"Is that what you want, to be left alone?" Kezia asked him.

"I did for the first year, after Audrey. I'm better now. But I want to pick who I spend time with, and not be hunted down by women I don't want to talk to. Anyway, I hope Paige doesn't stay with Greg forever. I don't think he'll ever leave his wife. She would cost him a fortune, at least several houses, the beach house in Malibu, and his plane," Sam said with a smile. It was a whole new world to Kezia, and familiar to him. "I'd like to meet your daughters when they come home," Sam said casually, when they sat on his terrace at the end of the evening. "They sound interesting and like nice women, if they're anything like you."

"They're very different from each other, and from me. Felicity is very young and has a booming career. Kate is very introverted, and has been trying to write a book for years. She's fourteen years older than Felicity. I wasn't married to her father, which matters to her. The man I married was wonderful to her and adopted her, but she has issues about her birth father, who chose to never be part of her life, and gave up his parental rights, by his own choice, when she was born. She's in Mozambique right now, to meet him for the first time. She surprised me with that right before she left. She tracked him down. I think it's something she's wanted to do for a long time. I hope she gets what she needs out of it."

"He's African?" He was intrigued by the details of her life that he was discovering, little by little, as she was discovering things about him. The puzzle pieces of themselves all spread out on a table with no secrets or apologies.

"He's American, but he lives there. He was with Doctors Without Borders for years, and now he has his own hospital in some remote area. She wanted to see it, and to meet him."

"Very interesting," he said.

"I'd like to meet your son too."

"He's away for the Fourth of July weekend with his current girlfriend. He's a good guy, I think you'll like him. And I'm sure he'd enjoy meeting your girls. We can do a pasta dinner some night." It sounded like fun to her, if the girls would come to meet Sam and his son, and Blake was always a warm, lively addition, Jack a lot less so, if he'd even come, but he'd get lost in the crowd.

Kezia and Sam sat on the terrace talking for a while, and then retreated to their own apartments. It had been a nice evening, in spite of the circumstances of the lockdown and the terrorist attack two days before. At least it was a distraction, and Kezia hoped she'd see Paige again sometime. She liked her, but Greg a lot less, now that she knew he was married. That didn't seem like a happy situation for Paige.

There were worse fates than getting stuck at the Hotel du Cap-Eden-Roc at Cap d'Antibes in France, except for the bill for an extended stay. In her glamorous life as a highly successful model, Felicity had been there several times and she loved it, and so did Blake. He did extremely well at his job, and made a great deal of money, so he could afford to take whatever woman he wanted to there, and he and Felicity had been there once before. It was the most divinely comfortable, elegant, luxurious hotel in the world, with exquisite suites, fabulous food, private cabanas where you could spend the entire day and even eat lunch without ever seeing another guest, lying on mattresses and deck chairs to get a tan, or lounging under a big umbrella while waiters served food and drinks. You could swim in the Mediterranean, or the infinity pool. There was a gym, beautiful gardens, and impeccable service. The main building looked like a château and was at the top of a little rise, and at the water's edge, with two restaurants, was the Eden-Roc part of the hotel, where Blake always requested the best suite. Andrew and Kezia had spent their honeymoon there and she had fond memories of it.

It had been a fabulous weekend until Felicity saw the headlines in the newspapers delivered to their room on Saturday, which showed the terrorist attack on New York, and the three buildings with the orange ball of the explosions above them. She had been worried about her mother ever since, and Blake had done his best to distract and reassure Felicity while she couldn't get through to her.

Kezia finally reached her daughter by email on Sunday evening in France, and Felicity was so relieved she cried. Blake sent his family an email too but had had no response yet.

The American guests at the hotel had been conferring all weekend. It was shocking news, and they were all frightened of what it meant, and if there would be subsequent attacks, in New York or other U.S. cities. And no one had been able to reach their relatives or friends in the States the day after the attack. Blake remembered perfectly when the Twin Towers had come down when he was fifteen, and now it was happening again. Felicity was born a year after 9/11, so it was history and not reality to her. The current attack was all too real.

It was incredible that the whole country was shut down and communication was nearly impossible. Every city, village, and town in America was closed in case of an attack, or even a war.

Once Felicity heard from her mother and knew she was all right, she felt better, but she still wanted to get home as soon as the borders were opened. She had tried to contact Kate on her cell too, and couldn't reach her in Africa, in the remote area where she was. Kate had warned them of that when she left. Felicity wondered if she even knew what had happened in New York. Maybe not.

Felicity and Blake stayed in the cabana Saturday and Sunday, and Blake quietly checked his computer for news. The president had spoken, the governor of New York, the State Department, and the secretary of defense, to assure people that they had no enemies about to launch a nuclear attack. The heads of the CIA and Homeland Security also held a press conference to assure the American public that they were using every possible intelligence resource to identify who had carried out the dastardly attack, and apprehend them, to bring them to justice. The police commissioner of New York City reminded everyone to stay in their homes. It was unnerving to think that the perpetrators were still out there somewhere and could do it again. But security was so tight in Manhattan, Blake strongly doubted that they could.

As the days ticked by interminably, Felicity was more and more eager to get home. Communication was sparse from Kezia, as they all waited for news, confined to their homes for their own safety. They were waiting for the other shoe to drop, if there was one.

To cheer up Felicity, Blake decided to move forward a plan he had for later that summer. He was hoping it would make her happy, and doing it earlier than planned made no difference, and would certainly distract her, in a good way.

He left her alone for a few hours on Monday morning, and told her he had work to do, while she went to the cabana, taking her computer with her, in case she heard from her mother. She had a big black and white Chanel beach bag with her, with whatever she needed for the day. Blake was back in two hours, satisfied with his mission. It hadn't taken him long. He had gone into Cannes, with a driver from the hotel to take him. The concierge was extremely helpful, although Blake knew where to go for what he wanted.

He was back before lunch, and they ordered salads and iced tea in the cabana. Blake lay on the sun bed next to Felicity and smiled. He knew he had made the right decision—he had already decided two months before. Everything about it felt right to him, although he thought she might be harder to convince. He hoped not, but if so, he had a long list of rational arguments, and one romantic one. He loved her, immeasurably.

"You look happy today." Felicity smiled at him as they waited for their lunch to arrive in the cabana.

"I am happy."

"Our country has been attacked by terrorists, thousands have died, someone may be about to declare war on us or attack us again, and you're happy. Explain that to me." She was in much better spirits since she'd heard from her mother and knew she was safe. Now it was a waiting game to get to go home.

"There are other things in life too," he said, rolling over on his side on his sun bed to see her more closely. He leaned over and kissed her, and as he did, he slipped a ring on her finger. She didn't look at it, but she thought it was a fun present. Blake was very generous with her and loved to buy her gifts. She lifted her hand to see it, and her eyes and mouth opened wide when she did.

"Oh my God! What's *that*?" She had never seen a diamond

so big, not even one of her mother's. Andrew had given Kezia some beautiful jewelry. "Is that real or for fun?" It was too big to be real. It was a twenty-carat cushion-cut diamond he had bought at Cartier that morning, much to their delight.

"It had better be real," Blake said with a lopsided grin, and kissed her again. She was holding her hand straight up while she did, as though it might fall off or melt if she didn't. It was an amazing hunk of ice and very elegant. "Will you marry me, Felicity Hobson?" he asked her officially, and she couldn't believe it was happening to her.

"Are you serious? I'm too young to wear a ring like this—no one will believe it's real. We're too young to get married," she said, "or I am at least," but with far less conviction than he had feared. He kissed her again, and she rolled onto his sun bed and kissed him more passionately, wearing only her bikini bottoms, like all the French women. "I love you, Blake. Do you really want to marry me? I don't even know how to cook."

"That's not a prerequisite. You're a wonderful person, you're fantastic to me and Alex, and I'm crazy nuts in love with you. I was going to ask you next month, so we could celebrate with him, but we can do that anyway. He'll be thrilled. He keeps asking me if we can keep you. Can we?" He looked at her with all his love for her in his eyes, and she nodded.

"Yes," Felicity whispered, and then said it louder, "Yes!" She wasn't marrying him for the gorgeous ring; it was a fun add-on, very fun. She was marrying him because she loved him, although she did feel a little too young, even a lot too young for marriage. But she could actually see being married to Blake for the rest of her life. "Can I keep modeling or will you make me stop?" She looked worried.

"Of course you can. I'm not going to 'make you' stop. That's your career and it's your decision. I'm very proud of you."

"And no babies yet," she said pointedly. "I really am too young for that."

"No babies yet," he echoed. "We have time. I want us to have fun together, and go at the pace you're comfortable with. And I want you to be my wife." She beamed when he said it, and they kissed again. She didn't tell her mother in an email. She wanted to tell her in person, or at least on the phone.

Felicity had her chance two days later, when she could finally get through to Kezia on her cell. Kezia said she was fine, and didn't mention Sam Stewart. She felt very private about their brand-new friendship. And maybe when the terrorist crisis was over, he'd disappear like a mirage. She didn't know him well enough to have any idea.

"Guess what, Mom?" Felicity sounded like a kid again and Kezia smiled. She was obviously happy with Blake in France.

"I don't know." She smiled at how childlike Felicity still

was at times. She was like a big exuberant puppy. Kezia loved that about her. "You're coming home tomorrow?"

"I wish," Felicity said with feeling. The borders were still closed. "We're *engaged*! Blake asked me to marry him."

"Oh, darling, you're still so young. At twenty-three, you're a baby."

"No, I'm not, I'm a grown-up, Mom. And he's only sixteen years older than I am. Andrew was twenty years older than you."

"But I was older than you are now when I married him."

"I'm happy, Mom, I love him." She sounded strong and sure.

"When are you thinking of doing it?" At least it was a happy subject, more so than a terrorist attack.

"We haven't talked about that yet. We're not in a hurry."

"Well, then I'm happy for you. I can't wait to give you a big hug—and congratulate Blake for me."

"I will, Mom," she replied, and then they hung up. Kezia winced thinking of Kate's reaction to it. Her baby sister was getting married. Kate was going to have a fit.

Chapter 7

The meeting took place in a warehouse in Brooklyn on Essex Street. There were renovated slums in the area, as well as gentrified apartment buildings and warehouses. They all straggled in after business hours. There was a side door and a freight elevator they all rode up in. And, once on the top floor, there were reinforced bulletproof security doors, and all the electronic devices they had in all their offices around the city. Six CIA agents and two FBI special agents had been brought in from Texas, to see what they could add.

They were moving quickly, and the deal had been struck with their informant, with the attorney general's approval. It was a highly sensitive operation, and one slip could blow it sky high. What played in favor of the government agencies was that all the members of the Enforcers were young. They had been involved in violent crime before, but never at this level, with a highly coordinated synchronized attack. Filo Banks had proven just how dangerous they were. The president wanted them in custody, and all forty-six of them alive, if possible, to be brought to justice as an example. With federal charges, the death penalty would apply. And the intel they were getting at the agencies was that the Enforcers were cocky and jubilant, having pulled it off.

It was unthinkable to every one of the forty-three agents in the room that the horror perpetrated on the Fourth of July had been conceived of and executed almost flawlessly by a group of Americans. There were no foreign nationals involved. No Middle East oil groups were financing it. No clandestines from a government the U.S. was helping to overthrow. No conspiracy to bring down a foreign government had backfired. These were red-blooded American boys, most of whom had served their country in the armed forces, who had plotted it carefully. All were criminals, and their leader was a misdirected genius gone mad. But the plot had worked, tragically. It was a strike at democracy from within that was a revolution in its infancy, a cancer in the very heart of America that had to be stopped. The Enforcers were ex-cons and vets whose minds were irreparably twisted from the action they had seen in wars that never should have been, in Iraq and Afghanistan. They were bright minds that should have been put to better use. It was a tragedy for the country and a symptom of a dangerous sickness at our core. Banks's army, the Enforcers, wanted anarchy instead of democracy and were willing to sacrifice innocents to achieve it.

Close to a hundred agents and computer data analysts and experts were working to make sure that they scraped the last of this poison out of the country's veins. The goal was to capture all forty-six men, take them alive, and see that they would stand trial. The Enforcers' plan had been almost flawless. The one fatal mistake they had made was that they had stayed in New York afterward and lingered for several days. The city had shut down so quickly, they hadn't been ready to make their exit. They had planned to hang around for a few days and make a silent escape in twos and threes back to Texas. But the lockdown had happened too quickly and they didn't want to stand out. So they stuck it out, in twelve rooms, divided between two huge convention hotels near Times Square.

Some of them had even cruised by the bomb sites wearing OES jackets and carrying clipboards, just to admire their handiwork at close range. They wanted to make sure that people were hurting as badly as the Enforcers had been hurt by the system and by the wars to which they'd been sent. Some of them came from good families who would be deeply ashamed once they knew what their sons had done. The Enforcers had trained diligently for two years for this event. They were anarchists to the core, hell-bent on tearing the heart out of American society, striking back at an enemy they couldn't even define. It was a mission built on hatred and revenge, and every single operative involved had to keep a cool head and not react to their own feelings about it. The cleanup and the capture were missions for consummate professionals.

Joe Delano, the senior agent in charge, was getting direct orders from the military, the Pentagon, the White House, and the heads of the CIA and FBI. Everything had to be minutely synchronized for success. No one could deviate from the plan by even seconds.

Five days after the lockdown began, before the airports and bridges opened, the Enforcers were going to split into groups of two and three and make their move to their exit plan, dressed as street cleaners and police officers, cab drivers, and subway engineers. Everyone had a role to play. And hour by hour, they would leave the two hotels. According to the informant's own sources, they had already disposed of most of their weapons, and the explosives, in both rivers within an hour of the attack while chaos reigned. They'd only kept enough weapons to make their escape. They were going to be driving cross-country in legitimate trucks meant to be delivering produce, which was still moving even during the lockdown. They were going to be spending a few weeks in New Mexico, Arkansas, and Oklahoma, and wind up back in Texas in time to resume training for their next mission, the attack on Washington, D.C., which had to be even more minutely synchronized than New York's. They had only just begun. They were going to have the whole country on its knees by September, in the single greatest power play the country had ever seen. Banks was already training more men for that.

The SWAT teams were waiting for the Enforcers when they left the two hotels. The agents knew the Enforcers' faces and their profiles, how they worked and how they moved. The first four were captured, one of them killing an FBI agent in the process, and the other three were shot and killed when they tried to escape.

The first hotel rapidly turned into a war zone, a melee of highly trained SWAT teams, operatives, and special agents, as it turned into open guerilla warfare, which had been the fallback plan Joe Delano hoped to avoid. They moved on the second hotel the moment violence erupted at the first one. Eight civilians were caught in the crossfire at the second hotel. None were killed, although two of them were severely injured. A maid was taken hostage and found in a closet unharmed later at the first hotel. She was traumatized but not injured.

The men of the Enforcers who had been in the military knew to fan out. Several of them ran out of the hotel toward the subway, and gunfire erupted as the FBI agents chased them down the tracks. Three of them and the agents jumped out of the way of an oncoming train, and one Enforcer and two FBI agents were killed. No agent was going to forget their objective. None of the Enforcers could be allowed to flee and strike again. It was a mission that could have only one of two outcomes: capture or death.

By nightfall, after a life-and-death chase, in cars, in trucks, and on foot, seven of the Enforcers had been apprehended and were alive and being held in a locked interrogation room in a federal building. Thirty-eight of the men who had blown up the buildings on the Fourth of July were dead. One was missing: Filo Banks, their leader, the cleverest of all. It wasn't what Washington had ordered, but it was the best the combined forces of the CIA and FBI and police SWAT teams could do. The Enforcers were too heavily armed and too skilled with their weapons to be overcome easily. And they fought to the death. The surviving seven would stand trial. Eleven federal agents had been injured, four had died, and two NYPD officers had been killed. In all, forty-four people died in the battle to catch the men who had carried out the Fourth of July attack.

When he left the second hotel, disguised as an engineer, Banks disappeared into the bowels of Penn Station, pursued by six federal agents. He was ultimately trapped between two oncoming trains, and all six agents shot him dead before the trains hit him. It was over.

Fresh teams of investigators were brought in to interrogate the survivors, who were shocked to have been apprehended, and suspected an informant. Their enemies had betrayed them, not their friends.

They were interrogated relentlessly for two days, in the depths of the Federal Building, in locked facilities. Then they were flown to Washington and put in holding pens at a maximum-security federal jail for further interrogation.

The seven surviving Enforcers were proud of what they'd done and showed no remorse. They saw themselves as heroes. The loss of thousands of lives meant nothing to them, and nor did their fallen brothers. It was a holy war to them. They had all seen so much death that it was a sacrifice they thought necessary, and were willing to make, even if it cost them their own lives. They were men with no souls, no regrets, no remorse, only their twisted mission and their blind faith in their leader, who was gone now.

The capture of the seven suspects, and the deaths of the others and of their leader, were announced to the public exactly one week after the men had blown up the three locations. Law enforcement had moved quickly. The informant was never mentioned.

America was in shock. No foreign government was involved, no foreign nationals who had snuck onto American soil. It was carried out by young men who had grown up in America, said they loved their country, had served in the armed forces, and had become bitter and twisted in wars that had warped their minds. They claimed to be heroes and martyrs to the cause of anarchy, led by a sick hero, who had led his men to their death, and killed thousands of innocent people in the process.

Sam and Kezia watched the news together that night and heard the mayor's and the governor's speeches telling the American public what had happened. Lives had been lost in order to save some of the attackers, so they could stand trial.

"God, I hate to think what this country is coming to, if our own kids are trying to blow up the country and want anarchy. What a tragedy for all of us."

"And all the people who died needlessly," Kezia added, and he nodded.

The entire state, and all the other states, came out of lockdown that night. It was all over in eight days, which was remarkable. It hadn't taken months, thanks to their informant, who got everything he wanted. There was no question that without him, the Enforcers might have escaped. He had been removed and flown to his new location by midnight that night. It was one of the cleanest operations the federal agencies had ever run. Everyone's heart had been in it, and failure was never an option. The operatives and agents who had been part of it were never identified or shown, for their own protection.

And in Kezia's case, it had been an opportunity to meet Sam and become friends.

Both Kate and Felicity flew home the next day. Felicity arrived first and went straight from the airport to see her mother, with Blake. Kezia was stunned by the size of the ring, but it was beautiful. Kezia met with them alone. Sam was busy in his own apartment, and Kezia wasn't ready to explain things to them yet, and neither was Sam. They wanted to protect what they had, in its early stages. Kezia hugged Felicity and Blake, and congratulated them. They were so happy they were glowing.

They left after a short time, and Kate arrived late that night. She called her mother from the cab on her way into town. She said she was exhausted and would come by in the morning. She claimed she was too tired to make sense. She and Felicity had both commented that the airport had been a nightmare, and probably would be for many days, trying to get travelers back on track to their destinations with an eight-day delay and backlog.

Kezia saved the big news for her until the next day.

When Kate came to see her mother at the penthouse the following morning, Kezia shared Felicity's news with her.

"Your sister's getting married," Kezia told her over a cup of strong coffee. Kate looked shocked.

"When?"

"They haven't set the date yet, but not too far away, I suspect." Kate listened to her but didn't comment for a minute.

"She's too young to get married," Kate said, trying to keep the anger out of her voice. Felicity always won all the prizes. She got whatever she wanted, and what Kate wanted too. Kate wasn't even sure if she wanted to marry Jack. But the last thing she wanted was to have to go through Felicity's big splashy social wedding, pretending to be a good sport about it, and feeling like a loser and an old maid. Kezia knew she was upset and had expected her to be, but maybe it would prod her to finally make up her mind about Jack, and even move on, if she had the courage to do it. "She told me she didn't want to get married the last time we talked about it," Kate said plaintively, as though her sister had betrayed her.

"I guess Blake changed her mind while they were stuck at the Hotel du Cap, waiting to come home."

"It won't last," Kate said cynically as they walked out onto her mother's terrace. She was silent for a long time, with tears in her eyes, when she saw the Empire State Building. It shocked Kezia every time she saw it too, and made her heart ache for the symbol so badly damaged.

"God, Mom, that must have been terrifying." Seeing it made it all too real.

"It was, and heartbreaking."

"What happened to your hedge?" Kate commented when she saw the narrow opening Sam had made by moving one of the sections the night of the explosions. "It looks like someone pushed it out of line, your gardener maybe."

"I met Sam Stewart that night. We watched the fires together." She had told the girls he lived there, but she'd never seen him until the night of the attack. And she hadn't told them she'd met him, until now. Kate looked surprised, but Kezia and Sam were neighbors, so it didn't seem special or unusual.

"What's he like?"

"Very human and unassuming and down-to-earth. I want to introduce you and Felicity to him."

"That'll be weird," Kate predicted with a smile. "Having

America's biggest movie star over for dinner. At least you weren't alone. I'm sorry you had to go through it, Mom."

Kezia nodded and they sat down. "How was your father?"

"Interesting," Kate said cautiously. "He's doing good work, but I understand better now why he bowed out and ran away. He's not a warm person. It's all about him. His hospital, his plans, his life. He did his best to bridge the gap with me. I like his wife. But he's very self-centered and all about the work he's doing at his hospital. I think that's all that matters to him. It made me realize how lucky I was to have Andrew." It was comforting to Kezia to hear it. She hoped that Kate would finally be able to let go of her fantasies about her biological father. If she did, the trip would have been worth it. And in spite of the stress of not being able to come back to the States for a week, and the long trip, Kezia thought she looked relaxed and peaceful.

Kate left a little while later and didn't mention Felicity's engagement again. Kezia knew it would rankle, but if it woke Kate up to the fact that she was wasting her time with Jack, then that would be a good thing too. Or that she really loved him. Either way, Kezia hoped that her late bloomer was finally blooming, or about to.

When Kate went home that afternoon, having done some errands after visiting her mother, she started writing and was happy with it. It felt great, like flying, and she knew exactly where she was going with it. The trip to Africa had worked its magic. She had come back a free woman, and an adult.

Chapter 8

When Jack came back to the apartment after having lunch with a friend, and doing some errands after their trip, Kate was in her home office with the door closed, writing. He had gone as close as he could to all three bomb sites, to observe the damage. It was overwhelming to see what a small group of crazed anarchists had done to their own people and country. And it had brought tears to his eyes too. He wanted to tell Kate what he'd seen but found the door to her office closed and, when he looked inside, she was sitting at her computer with an intense expression. She looked up when she heard him come in. He was about to sit down in a comfortable battered leather chair, but she held up a hand.

"I'm writing. I'll be out in a few minutes." He retreated

quietly, poured himself a drink, and sat down, remembering the images of the devastated buildings, thinking about all the lives that had been lost or irreparably damaged. He waited for Kate to join him, but minutes turned to hours, and he fell asleep on the couch with the TV on after his second drink.

Kate found him there at nine o'clock when she finally emerged, shocked to realize how late it was. But what she wanted to write had taken off like an express train and she'd lost all track of time. She sat down across from where Jack lay. A few minutes later, he woke up on his own. He looked disoriented for a minute, and then sat up and smiled.

"I'm really sorry. I had an idea today, and I got lost in the story," she told him.

"Your book?" he asked.

"A new one. About a woman who makes a journey to find herself, and all the things that happen to her along the way." It was interwoven with her motivations to meet her father, and the discoveries her journey had spawned in her. She wanted to get it down on paper while the feelings were fresh. "Are you hungry? I'm sorry it got so late." She wanted to go back and write some more after dinner, but didn't say that. It was after nine by then, and she was in full creative mode. She liked writing at night.

"I could eat something. What do we have?" he said as he stretched. He had slept for three hours, with the help of two glasses of scotch. He had waited for her to make dinner or order takeout. He never took the initiative to cook for them or for himself. He expected it to appear, like a baby bird waiting for its mother to bring home the worms.

"I went to the grocery store after I saw my mother today, but I didn't buy much. Some cold chicken, lettuce, the usual, nothing special. We can have cold chicken and a salad, if you want," she suggested. She had forgotten all about dinner while she was writing. She didn't like to cook.

"Sounds great," he said, and followed her into the kitchen. She glanced at him a few times while she got the meal together. She wished he had more energy about life, a deeper hunger, a greater passion. He was easy to get along with because he was neutral in his view of life. He waited for life to happen, and went along with what she did, but he never initiated anything. He was like the old expression "pushing a rope". He was bendable and flexible, with no strength or resistance of his own. It made him easy to live with, but not exciting. He took what life doled out to him, without taking a hand in it himself.

"How was your mother?" he asked her politely when they sat down to eat.

"She's okay. It must have been incredibly traumatic to be here that night. I saw the Empire State Building from her terrace. It's devastating."

"I saw it today, and went to the other sites too. It's unbelievable." He was quiet for a minute, thinking about it.

"We talked a little bit about Felicity getting engaged last week. It's ridiculous. She's much too young. He's already been married and knows what he's getting into at his age. He has a child, and wants more. I can't see her having a baby anytime soon, or giving up her modeling career."

"Do you think he wants her to?" Jack looked surprised. It hadn't occurred to him.

"He will eventually, if they decide to have more kids. She can't fly around the world all the time, doing photo shoots, with a bunch of kids and a husband at home. She'll never see them. At twenty-three, she has no idea what real life looks like." She paused then, took a breath, and decided to leap in. "What are you thinking about us these days?" she said to him, trying to sound casual about it. But her younger sister getting engaged had woken her up to her own age, and the reality that she and Jack had been drifting for four years. Things were no different from when he'd first moved in three years before. He was eking out a small living with freelance writing, tutoring jobs, and teaching the occasional workshop, and not having to pay rent or expenses living with her. He seemed to have no plan to do anything else. He was comfortable as he was, and the status quo in their relationship suited him.

"What do you mean?" He looked blank at her question. "What am I supposed to think? I'm very happy, Kate. Things always go smoothly with us." Because she never complained or expected anything from him. They were like old married people, or roommates with occasional sex thrown in, and it had become more occasional with the passing years. She made no demands on him on any front, mostly because she was never sure what she wanted herself, so it felt safest not to move at all. Meeting her father had changed something and subtly turned the dial. Kate wanted more out of life than just existing or drifting. She wanted to live life, to write a book and actually finish it, or give it up, or get a job, or get married to the right man, and have a child one day. At thirty-seven it was worth thinking about, and worth taking a more active role in her own life. Jack was passive about everything. He didn't want to make waves and risk what he had, and Kate was a great deal for him. "Is something wrong?" he asked her. He knew she was jealous of her sister and suspected that Felicity getting engaged had set her off. He wanted to duck and cover in the meantime.

"No, but sometimes it's good to know where we're headed, and not just let the ship drift with no direction."

"We have direction. You want to write a book, and it looks like you're getting started on it in earnest. That's huge!"

"I want more than a book to show for my life, Jack. That would be great, but it's not enough. I'm thirty-seven. Do we want to get married? And have kids? Or have kids and not get married? What's our plan? What do you see on the horizon for us?" She had never put it to him that bluntly, but she felt braver ever since the trip to Africa. Seeing her father had freed her to move forward, she felt more grown-up and adult, with needs of her own.

"Why do we need a plan? You know my income doesn't allow me to consider marriage, for the moment, and if I take a job, it will interfere with my freelance work, and stifle my writing. You've never been keen on marriage, you told me so yourself, right in the beginning. And I'm almost too old for kids now. I'm forty-two, and I can't see myself chasing a kid with a ball at fifty. Why is marriage so important?"

"Maybe because I'm getting older, and I don't want to make choices by not making them and regretting it one day. It's true, I never have been sure about marriage, but maybe I feel differently about it now. If I want to have kids, I need to think about it one of these days. You can always change your mind later about having kids. As a woman, I can't. I've always hated the image of a biological clock ticking loudly, like a time bomb waiting to go off, but maybe it's more real than I want to believe. I guess I want to know what you're thinking about us, before I wake up another four years from now and nothing has changed, and still not knowing what I want."

Jack was pensive for a moment and looked at Kate. "I love you. Isn't that enough?"

"I don't know," she said clearly, without apology. "Maybe not, after four years."

"We've only lived together for three," he pointed out, silently hating Felicity for upsetting the apple cart for him, by getting engaged at twenty-three. "What about if we get engaged?" he suggested, with what he thought was a stroke of genius. "That would make us more official," or seem that way, Kate thought.

"Will I be introducing you as my fiancé when I'm ninety?" she said, only half joking, but it did seem like an improvement of sorts. "I guess we could do that. It would make things more real. Would you want to plan a wedding and the whole deal?" She felt odd forcing the issue, and what he had said wasn't entirely reassuring, although it did mean he was planning for a future with her, if that was what she wanted. Everything always seemed so vague with him, like chasing mercury across the floor, or a greased marble egg, as her grandfather used to say.

"Why don't we just enjoy being engaged first? We don't have to rush into planning anything yet. I wouldn't want a big wedding anyway. Would you? I'm sure Felicity and Blake

161

will go crazy with that. That's not my style or yours. I'd be very happy with just a small ceremony at the church near us in Vermont, and our families there." He didn't have a lot of friends, and he and Kate had a small social circle, mainly made up of other would-be writers they had met at the workshops they attended in the summer. "I wouldn't want a big wedding," he said again, and she nodded. She'd never really thought about it before, and the picture he painted was very restrained, but she had to admit, it suited both them and the way they lived. "Does that make you feel better?" he said, as he leaned over and kissed her, and she smiled at him.

"I guess it does." It was some kind of forward movement, and commitment, which was what she was seeking. Progress, without which their relationship had begun to seem stale. Nothing ever changed. He hadn't mentioned any major career plans, and she knew he didn't have any. The status quo on that front suited him too, with him having minor jobs, and Kate paying for everything. It worked well for him, and she could afford it.

"So, we're engaged now," he said firmly, as though they had reached a major decision. She wasn't sure they had, but at least she knew that he'd marry her eventually, if that was what she wanted. He had seemed equally happy without any formal commitment, but he made it clear that he was amenable to marriage at some later date, with a very small Vermont wedding. It didn't feel like a proposal, and it certainly wasn't romantic, but he apparently intended to spend the future with her.

They went to bed that night and didn't make love. Nothing more was said about the engagement, and he said he had a headache as she got into bed. She wasn't entirely sure if he had just humored her, or if he actually wanted to marry her, or saw it as an obligation of some kind to maintain the status quo of their living arrangement. By the time she fell asleep, she had a headache too.

Kate spoke to her mother the next day, and mentioned their plans to her. "Jack and I got engaged last night," she said, sounding blasé about it, and Kezia was surprised.

"You did? So I'm going to be planning two weddings now?" The thought of it was daunting, if they both wanted real weddings, and it was obvious that Felicity and Blake did. They were all excited, and Felicity was already talking about the dress, and which designers' collections she wanted to look at. She wanted Kezia to come with her. They were talking about two or three hundred people at the wedding, maybe even four hundred. Blake had a huge number of friends and acquaintances. Felicity had friends from school, from work, from all her travel, photographers she was fond of, the editors of *Vogue* and *Harper's Bazaar*. The list was going to be endless. Kezia was already nervous about it, and now Kate wanted to get married too. Kezia was suspicious about how their engagement had happened. She was sure that Kate's sudden willingness to marry was in competition with her sister. In that sense, Kezia wasn't surprised at all. "How did that come about?" she questioned Kate.

"We were talking about it last night, and Jack wanted to get engaged," Kate said calmly. She didn't say that it had been a compromise position, as a slow prelude to marriage, or a proper proposal, which it wasn't.

"When are you thinking of doing the wedding?" Kezia asked, feeling panicked. Organizing two weddings at once was going to be an enormous undertaking, and she had no one to help her. She didn't have an assistant in New York. She had one in San Francisco when she lived there, because she had a social life, and served on several boards. She didn't need anyone in New York, until now. She wondered if she should hire one for the weddings.

"We're not in a hurry, and Jack doesn't want a big wedding," Kate said, and immediately calmed her mother's fears. Kezia's voice had suddenly gone high and squeaky at Kate's announcement.

"Is that what *you* want?" Kezia asked her. "Usually, it's the bride who decides what kind of wedding she wants, and most men go along with it, even if it's not their vision. Do you want a small wedding?" She was defending Kate's interests. She didn't sound excited about the engagement.

"I don't mind. He wants to do it in Vermont." It sounded sad to Kezia, but she didn't comment. It followed the lifestyle Kate had adopted for the past four years, and the bohemian, would-be writers' groups she and Jack met at writing workshops. It didn't sound exciting to Kezia, but she reminded herself that it wasn't her wedding. She still believed that the plan had been provoked by Kate's competitiveness with her sister, more than any profound desire to marry. And Kate didn't sound excited to be marrying Jack.

"Did he give you a ring?" Kezia inquired, although she didn't expect him to compete with Blake on that score. The ring Blake had given Felicity was unnecessarily large. Kate wouldn't expect something like that, and Jack wouldn't be able to afford it.

As her mother asked, Kate woke up to the fact that they hadn't even thought about it, and Kate knew Jack didn't have the money to pay for even a modest ring and she didn't want to buy one for herself.

"Not yet," she said to Kezia. "I'm sure he will. He's not much of a shopper, and he knows nothing about jewelry."

"Maybe he can get a pretty antique ring. They're usually

much less expensive. I'm sure he'll figure it out. Well, best wishes, darling," she said with a sigh. "Now I have two brides. Should we start shopping for a dress?"

"I don't even know when yet, or what time of year. Let's wait," Kate said.

"Felicity is thinking next spring, May or June, which seems a long way away, but it's less than a year from now, and the time will fly. We have to figure out a venue. I think the Frick museum would be nice."

"It'll cost you a fortune, Mom. They require extra security to protect the art. Someone I know got married there. Her father was in shock. I forget how much it was, but it was a lot."

"We'll see when we start looking at venues. It would certainly be beautiful, it's a lovely setting, right out of a movie set, and very elegant." It suited the couple. After the conversation, Kate realized that her lucky little sister had done it again. She always won. She had the star father, now she'd have the star husband, and their mother would give her a spectacular wedding. And Kate would seem like the poor cousin again, this time with a tiny wedding in Vermont, while Felicity made the big splash that suited who she was.

Before they hung up, Kezia had invited her to dinner, with Jack. She said she wanted to introduce her and Felicity to some new people she'd met in the building. She said they were all very interesting. She wanted to do it that week, maybe on the weekend. Kate said they were free, and she was curious about who her mother was going to invite. She had only lived there for two weeks, but a lot had happened. She wondered if Jack would go with her. He didn't like heights, but he liked meeting important people, which would probably override his fears.

The papers were full these days of the background stories of the seven surviving men who had carried out the terrorist attack in New York, and were part of the group of anarchists who had done a legendary amount of damage and killed thousands of their fellow Americans, supposedly to support a better way of life than the one they had, which was hard to listen to, and even harder to believe. And they had survived, while thirty-eight of their cohorts and their leader had died in their capture. They considered Filo Banks a martyr to their cause. Kezia still couldn't believe that the entire event had been created, built, and delivered by fellow Americans. They had each been assigned federal prosecutors. It had taken massive amounts of security at their arraignment to keep anyone from attacking them when they came in and out of court. They were easily the most hated people in the country at the moment, and the federal prosecutors' office was well aware that, without the help of their extremely vocal informant, previously a member of the Enforcers himself, they would never have been able to identify them. Had Filo Banks not betrayed and banished him, he would never have talked and would have remained one of them. Instead, he had come forward, exposed their plan and their future plans in Washington, D.C. He had gotten even with Banks.

The police and the guards in federal jail were also aware that any time the surviving seven men were exposed in any way, they were more than likely to be shot and killed. Just not on my watch, the federal prosecutor admitted to the police commissioner, Homeland Security, and the FBI. He didn't want to lose any more men than had already been lost to defend sick, vicious criminals like the Enforcers. The youngest of them, the nineteen-year-old computer genius, was one of the survivors. His brother had died. They all had rap sheets an arm long with burglaries, assaults, kidnapping, one with murder, others with drug-related charges, all manner of violence, involving firearms and explosives, and they had served in the military before turning to a life of crime. They were being held in confinement two to a cell in a maximum-security section of the federal jail in Washington, D.C., for interrogation and were due to be returned to New York, where they would ultimately be tried. Their lawyers were requesting a change of venue for the trial, claiming that there was nowhere in the state of New York, or the country, where they would be able to get a fair trial. The judge had not granted the change of venue at the arraignment. Everyone was talking about them, and the trial was set currently for the following May. There would doubtless be many continuances by the time it actually went to trial. If they were found guilty or pleaded, it was a death sentence trial. The charges were "causing death by using a weapon of mass destruction." In fact, no punishment would be adequate for what they had done and the lives they had taken, and the people they had severely maimed and injured and would survive. Many of the victims were still critically injured and dying.

When Kezia called Felicity to invite her to dinner with Blake, she mentioned Kate's engagement, and that she and Jack were coming too.

"That's weird," Felicity said when her mother told her about the engagement. "She always says she doesn't know if she wants to get married, or if she wants kids. And now she gets engaged as soon as I do. When's the wedding?"

"They haven't set the date, and they want a small family wedding in Vermont."

"That doesn't sound like much fun," Felicity commented.

"It's what Jack wants." Kezia was worried about both her daughters. One seemed to be marrying too young to a man with a jet-set life, a marriage which could turn out not to be solid, and the other one was marrying a man no one liked, and Kezia wasn't even sure how much Kate loved him. They never seemed like a warm, affectionate couple to her. Kate never seemed to be passionate about him. She was comfortable, which didn't seem like enough to Kezia. She thought Felicity had a better chance for success with Blake, despite her age, than Kate with Jack. But they had to make their own choices, and Kezia hoped they were the right ones. She had strong reservations about Jack. "What about dinner?" she asked Felicity. "Can you make it?"

"Sure, Mom, it sounds like fun. We don't have any plans yet. And I'm moving out to the Hamptons soon. Blake is going to try working from out there, and only coming into the city a couple of times a week." It sounded heavenly to Kezia. She confirmed the date with Felicity and hung up a minute later.

The others were easy to reach. Louise answered her phone and said she was free and delighted to come. Paige was equally so, and said Greg was still in town. After that, Kezia called Sam. She hadn't seen him in two days, and suspected he was very busy again now that the lockdown was over.

"How've you been?" He sounded happy to hear her. "I've missed you."

"I've been busy. Catching up with my girls. Both of them

are getting married. They just got engaged. Apparently, it's contagious." She had wondered if it would be, given Kate's long-standing jealousy of her sister.

She invited him to dinner, and he accepted too and sounded pleased. He had missed their nightly conversations on the terrace, and so had Kezia. Once her daughters got back to New York, she had spoken to them on the phone every day, and she still had a lot to do relating to her move and everything that would be arriving. All other life had stopped entirely right after the attack, during the lockdown, and was moving again now.

She realized that it was odd that she missed someone she barely knew, but the days they had spent together had been so intense and emotional, particularly the night of the attacks, that it felt strange when they went back to their own lives. He said he had just read a novel he liked and was exploring the possibility of buying the rights to it for a movie. What he did sounded a great deal more interesting than what she'd been doing. Ever since the attacks, she'd been considering the refresher course in current nursing practices and techniques she'd need if she wanted to start nursing again. It had been gnawing at her. He asked her if she'd done anything about checking out classes. He had been vastly impressed by her nursing abilities the night of the attacks.

"I haven't had time, I'm still busy with the move. But I'm

wondering if I've been out of it for too long. Maybe my nursing days are over." She had certainly thought they were, but now she wasn't so sure following her volunteer work after the attacks. Maybe it was just the drama and emotions that made her think she should go back to nursing.

"It's never too late to do something you love," he said, and she smiled. She liked his practical philosophies and his straightforward way of thinking. If you loved something, you should do it. She wondered if it really was as simple as that. "Thank you for inviting me to dinner." She could easily imagine that, as a major star, he was invited to countless exciting events much more enticing than a simple dinner on her terrace.

"I wanted you to meet my girls. Louise is coming too, and Greg and Paige." She was less excited about Greg coming than seeing Paige again. She had sounded happy to come.

"I'm looking forward to it," he said, and she smiled.

The night of the dinner, Kezia wore white linen slacks and a matching tunic. Her blonde hair was long down her back, and she had a tan from the days she and Sam had spent on the terrace together, when the city was shut down. She wore small diamond studs, which sparkled on her ears. Sam was the first to arrive and rang the doorbell like a proper guest, and Kezia smiled when she saw him.

"You could have come the back way, you know, by the terrace." He returned her smile and followed her into the nearly empty living room.

"I didn't want to shock your daughters, or presume anything." The doorbell rang shortly after, while Sam opened a bottle of wine for her. She'd had summer food sent in from a great restaurant. There was lobster salad and sushi, and an assortment of cold meals, and cold pasta salads, set up on a buffet table in the dining room, and she had enough chairs so they could all sit on the terrace. She had kept it very informal, but she knew the food would be good. There was French red and white wine.

She opened the door to Louise while Sam removed the cork to let the red wine breathe. Kezia had said dinner was casual, and Louise had worn white jeans and a white T-shirt, which was a change from her usual black skirts and jeans. Greg and Paige arrived a few minutes later. They were all happy to see each other, and the latest news about the terrorists who had attacked New York took up the first minutes of the conversation. The city was badly scarred and would be for a long time, and everyone was shocked by the men who had done it. Young Americans killing their own in the name of anarchy. Some of them heroes of the war in Iraq.

Felicity was the first of Kezia's daughters to arrive, with Blake. They were a breath of fresh air, like a summer breeze. Felicity looked spectacular in a short white summer dress, and she gravitated toward Sam with ease, and chatted with him about his latest film. He recognized her face from magazine covers, and they had a lively conversation about the book he had just read and wanted to buy. She had read it and loved it too, and Blake knew who Greg was and enjoyed talking to him, while Paige and Louise had a quiet conversation, and Kezia circulated in their midst making sure they all had wine. They were helping themselves, which Kezia had preferred to having waiters serving them. She answered the door when Kate and Jack arrived. Kate looked pretty in a pale blue sundress with her dark hair swept up in a loose bun. Jack was quick to interrupt Felicity's conversation with Sam and tried to dominate it immediately. He was so impressed by the guests, he paid no attention to the view or the fact that he was on the sixtieth floor. Sam was polite and went to help Kezia in order to escape him. He picked up one of the bottles of wine to do refills on the terrace.

"Thank you for helping." She smiled at him. He looked happy and as though he was having a good time.

"Your daughters are gorgeous, and fun to talk to. Felicity and I are both crazy about the book I told you about. She's a terrific young woman. What's her fiancé like? Do you approve?" he asked in an undertone.

"Yes, but she's too young to get married," Kezia said in a low voice no one could overhear.

"That's a very impressive sparkler on her left hand. I'd say he's very serious about her." Kezia nodded agreement.

"I wish he'd waited," she commented.

Sam made a point of talking to Kate after he refilled people's wine glasses, and found her interesting to talk to about her recent trip to Mozambique. He'd been on location to make a film there years before. He loved the people and the place. The conversation was lively all through dinner, and Louise had them laughing about a shoot she'd done recently with a famously irreverent but brilliant playwright. Despite the dark specter of the Empire State Building in the distance, they managed to talk about a multitude of subjects, and not the July Fourth attack for the entire evening. The subject finally came up again at the end of the night, when Sam mentioned that he and Kezia had volunteered at Hudson Yards together, and she had been amazing.

Both her daughters looked shocked when he said it.

"You went down there?" Kate said to her mother, and Kezia nodded.

"They put out a call for volunteers on the news channels, particularly medical, and I still have my license. We were both there all night." Sam didn't explain that he had carried body bags for hours, but he and Kezia exchanged a glance, thinking of it.

"You didn't tell us you did that," Kate said quietly, stunned by her mother.

Everyone stayed late and enjoyed the evening, and Sam left politely just before the others, down to the lobby and back up in his private elevator. Kezia talked to her daughters for a few more minutes and both of them said how much they liked him.

"You have to bring him out to Southampton, Mom," Felicity said. "He's really a nice guy. He just acts like a regular person."

He and Kate had talked about writing and her trip to Africa. Blake thought Louise was fascinating. The atmosphere had been warm and lively all night, and the girls thanked their mother when they left. After they were gone, Kezia wandered out to the terrace with her glass of wine, sat down on one of the deck chairs, and relaxed. The dinner had been a big success. It was the first time she had entertained in her new home. She was lying there thinking about it when Sam's voice came through the hedge divider.

"Everybody gone?" he asked, and she laughed.

"Yes, come on over." He squeezed through and came and sat down in the chair next to her.

"That was a great evening. Your daughters are terrific.

And Blake is a very enterprising guy. He's crazy about your daughter."

"I know, she's crazy about him too. Unfortunately, Jack isn't a prize, and now Kate's engaged to him."

"They don't seem as close as the other two," he said, trying to be moderate in his comment.

"I don't know why Kate hangs on to him, and now she's going to marry him. He's so full of himself. He drives me crazy." Sam didn't think Kate seemed enamored with Jack either. They had ignored each other for most of the evening, and there had been no visible signs of affection, whereas Blake and Felicity held hands and he kissed her several times.

"Maybe she won't go through with it," Sam commented.

"I hope not," Kezia said, and they lay looking up at the stars together, quiet for a few minutes.

"That's the best part of the evening." He smiled at her. "Being able to talk about it afterward." She smiled at him. She and Andrew had done that too. "I've missed that. Audrey used to fill me in on all the gossip of the evening after the guests left."

"It was a nice group tonight," Kezia said happily.

"Your daughters added all the youth and spice to it. Kate says she's writing a book."

"She's been doing that for years. Maybe this time she'll finish it."

"I told her she should call my agent. They have a literary section. If she's serious about it, she needs an agent." It touched Kezia that he had done that. They sat together for half an hour and then he got up to go back to his apartment. He looked sorry to leave when he said good night. "Would you have dinner with me on Friday?" he asked her hesitantly.

"I'd love that," she said, and he looked pleased, kissed her on the cheek, and then left, through the hedge, back to his apartment.

She left all the dishes and glasses for the cleaning crew the next day, undressed, and got into bed. She was thinking of Sam, and what a nice evening it had been, and doing the recap with him afterward. She loved talking to him and was looking forward to Friday night. In his apartment, Sam was smiling too. It was exactly the kind of night he enjoyed, a small gathering of good friends. Kezia was rapidly becoming his best friend, and he liked her daughters.

Chapter 9

Sam came to Kezia's front door again on Friday when he arrived to take her to dinner. He was wearing black slacks, and a black shirt with neither tie nor jacket. He was freshly shaven and looked like he had just stepped out of the shower. He looked like a proper date come to pick her up, which made her smile. She was wearing a short black summer dress, which showed her small waist and slim body. Her hair was in a neat blonde bun. They made a handsome couple as they left the building, and the doorman acknowledged them both. Sam had a driver waiting outside in a dark blue SUV, and they hopped in. They weren't going far, but the car gave them protection from prying eyes and paparazzi. She was suddenly reminded that he was a major star and that people recognized him no matter how discreet

and unassuming he was. She had even noticed it the night
of the attack, at Hudson Yards. People had recognized him
and then went back to what they were doing in the emergency, but in normal life, there were times when fans pursued
him. He did the best he could to stay below the radar, but it
was impossible to avoid having people recognize him all the
time. He was too big a star for that.

They stopped at a restaurant they'd never been to before
but had heard about. Felicity had mentioned it to her. The
food was Italian. It had a pretty garden, and the atmosphere
was friendly, chic, and informal. The head waiter greeted
Sam warmly and led them to a secluded table in the garden.
It felt like being in someone's home in Italy, and when the
food came, everything was fresh and delicious. It was nice
being outdoors on a warm night, and not thinking about
what had happened recently in New York. People had to
heal from the trauma of what they had been through, and
it would take time. Many were still not going out, and the
restaurant wasn't crowded that night. For most, it took
weeks to get a reservation there, but not for Sam. The restaurant was always full. They didn't fawn over Sam, as some
places did, which always made him so uncomfortable he
never went back. They were respectful and excited he was
there. He liked to go unnoticed in the crowd, and he led a
very private life.

Kezia commented on it at dinner, and he said he had never liked that aspect of stardom, of being conspicuous and on show all the time, with no private life.

"It was even harder when Audrey was alive. Everyone knew her, and she was notoriously kind to everyone who asked for an autograph. People wanted their photographs taken with her, and we'd get trapped for hours. My son hated it, so we always went to very remote places on vacation with him. We took him to Africa, which is how I knew the area where Kate just went. I made a movie there once. We went to Kruger National Park too. It's a beautiful part of the world. She said she's writing about it now." Kezia was startled that he knew that and she didn't. She was afraid to ask Kate about what she was writing. She didn't want her to think she was prying. Kate had always treated her writing as her private world.

"I think the trip was good for her," Kezia said quietly. "She seems happier since she came back. I thought it was from meeting her father. It seems to have freed her of her illusions about him, and then she and Jack got engaged as soon as she got home. I can't believe that both girls are getting married. By the way, Felicity moved out to the house she rented in Southampton the night after she came to dinner. Work is slow for her in the summer, especially in August. She asked me to come out for the day tomorrow, and she wanted me to invite you if you'd like to come." He didn't hesitate for a minute, and smiled immediately.

"I'd love it," he said enthusiastically, and then he cautiously asked her a question. "Could I be very rude, and ask if my son could come too? I'd love him to meet Felicity, although unfortunately I think he'd bring his girlfriend. Is that too much to impose on her? I'm happy to come alone if she'd prefer." He felt comfortable enough with Kezia to ask her, but he really wanted his son to meet her girls. He hadn't mentioned Kezia yet. It was very new. They had only recently met, and everyone in the city had been engrossed by the terrorist attack, so other subjects had fallen by the wayside in the past few weeks.

"Kate and Jack are coming out too. It would be fun for all of them to meet. I'll ask her," Kezia said, and took her phone out of her bag and wrote a rapid text message. The response was instantaneous from Felicity.

"Of course, Mom. Tell him to bring them. Sounds like fun." Kezia relayed the message to Sam, and he in turn texted his son, John, who also accepted with pleasure for himself and Caroline. He had told John that friends of his had invited him and his son for a day in the Hamptons. John told his father by text that he'd give him a ride if he wanted.

"Do you want to ride with us?" Sam offered Kezia.

"I'd love to, but I already told Kate I'd ride with them."

She didn't say it, but she would have preferred to ride with Sam and his son and girlfriend than to listen to Jack pontificate for two hours about the latest writing workshop he wanted to attend or had been to, or the short story he was working on.

"It's very nice of Felicity to have all of us," Sam said. "I really enjoyed talking to her, and I'm very pleased she liked the book that I mentioned so much. It validates my opinion, and she's a woman of a whole other generation. Audrey used to be my sounding board," he said, looking wistful for a minute. "You lose so much when you lose a person, so many things you took for granted. It's not easy to replace that special mix that each person brings to your life. I have to admit, I've never tried. I wouldn't even know how to start."

"I felt that way about Andrew too," Kezia said gently. "I just filled the void with helping to keep his firm alive, because it meant so much to him. But you can't replace a person with a company. I guess eventually you just learn to live without what you had, like an arm or a leg or something. Moving to New York was the right thing to do. It's put a huge shot of energy back in my life."

"And we gave you a hell of a welcome when you arrived. Blew up three major buildings in a terrorist attack," he said.

"That's more than I bargained for," she said ruefully with

a wry smile, "but the city seems to be healing from its wounds with incredible determination."

"New York is amazing that way. New Yorkers have tremendous resilience. They survived 9/11 and Hurricane Sandy, they bounce back from all kinds of hardships, and they stick together bravely when it matters, like they did this time. I'm proud of this city."

"I'm glad I moved here. And it's nice being close to my girls. I'm looking forward to meeting John." Sam had mentioned that he was in investments, so he'd have the finance world in common with Blake. Kate and Jack would hold up the intellectual side of the group, although Kate had broader interests than Jack and he talked about himself most of the time, and no one listened.

Sam and Kate were among the last to leave the restaurant. The driver took them home, and Kezia invited him for a drink on the terrace. She gave him the address of Felicity's house and suggested they get there by noon, before lunch. She was planning to get there earlier with Kate so they'd have some girl time before the guests arrived. Blake usually played tennis or golf on Saturday mornings, and Jack could take a walk on the beach. The three women would be more than he could cope with.

They chatted for a little while on the terrace, which felt

familiar to them now. It was their private meeting place, and a moment of respite for both of them, and companionship, which neither of them had. They had their children, and friends, but Kezia realized that she hadn't had a confidant since Andrew died, and Sam hadn't either since he had lost Audrey. It was nice to have that now, even in a new friend. He made her laugh with his somewhat acerbic satirical comments about Hollywood.

Sam left earlier than usual since they were getting up early the next day and would see each other at the beach.

He kissed her chastely on the cheek when he left, and then sent her a text when she was in bed.

"Sorry if I folded early, need my beauty sleep for the beach tomorrow. And my wits about me for your daughters." Beauty was one thing he didn't need to worry about. He was a very handsome man. He didn't take advantage of it, but he just was. He had the kind of effortless, healthy good looks that would last forever. He was blessed, but he had a fine mind as well, which Kezia liked even better. Andrew had had a brilliant mind and good looks too.

She texted him back, "Thank you for dinner. Glad you're coming to the beach tomorrow." Their exchanges had a touch of schoolyard flirtation to them, which she thought was sweet. He wasn't some wild Hollywood seducer, which would have scared her off immediately. He had been a happily married man for thirty-two years, with a family, which made a big difference. She wouldn't have asked him, but she was sure he'd been faithful to his wife, which was almost unheard of in Hollywood. She had been faithful to Andrew, and genuinely loved him. But he had been gone for five years now, and a little harmless flirtation didn't feel like an infidelity. It added a dash of hope and youth to her life, even though she was turning sixty in two months, which she preferred not to think about.

She woke up early the next morning to a brilliantly sunny day, got up and showered, read *The New York Times* online with a cup of coffee, and dressed for the beach in white jeans and a pink shirt and pink Chanel ballerinas. She was downstairs promptly at nine when Kate and Jack picked her up in their van, and Kezia got into the back seat.

"Good morning, everyone," she said cheerfully as they took off toward the Long Island Expressway on the way to Southampton. Kate commented that she'd been up late writing, and they chatted as Jack drove, lost in his own thoughts.

"Is she having guests or is it just us?" Kate asked her mother.

"She invited Sam Stewart and his son," Kezia said casually, and Kate raised an eyebrow, teasing her mother.

"Should I read anything into that, or are you just being neighborly?" Kate questioned her mother.

"Felicity is just being friendly, inviting them. I hope his son is nice. He's bringing his girlfriend."

"We can take a long walk on the beach if we don't like them," Kate said. Without intending to, Kezia glanced at her daughter's left hand, and there was still no ring on it. Jack hadn't given her an engagement ring yet. She looked away quickly, so Kate wouldn't notice. He obviously couldn't afford one, but hadn't given her a sentimental substitute either. Felicity's would have been hard for most people to compete with. As usual, Felicity got the big reward, and Kate got none. Kezia hoped she didn't mind.

They chatted most of the way to Southampton, and Kate told her more about their Africa trip. The territory around the hospital sounded really interesting and primitive. Kate had loved it, although she couldn't imagine going there again, even to see her father. She had gone to do what she needed, and seemed to have finally closed that chapter. Although the visit hadn't been unpleasant, Kezia could gather it hadn't been warm either. Reed's life was very different from hers.

As Kezia had hoped, they got to Felicity's rented house just after eleven. It was a big rambling New England–style house, freshly painted white, very handsomely remodeled, with dark green shutters, right on the beach. The cars were in the driveway: Blake's silver Ferrari and Felicity's red Mercedes. Kate's suburban-looking van seemed like a soccer mom car compared to her sister's jazzy sports car, but the difference in their age accounted for it too.

Felicity came out of the house as soon as they drove up. She was wearing very short pink shorts, white Chanel sandals, and a pink T-shirt, and Blake was wearing tennis clothes and was about to leave. He kissed Felicity before he did, kissed Kate and their mother hello, waved at Jack, got in his car with his racket, and drove off a minute later. Felicity had coffee waiting for them, and Jack grabbed a copy of *The New York Times* and headed for the back deck with a view of the ocean, while the three women sat in the kitchen. Both sisters were in a good mood, and Kezia enjoyed being with them, especially when there were no tensions between them. Engagement seemed to suit them both.

They were still talking and laughing when they heard a car in the driveway. They looked out the window and saw three very attractive people get out of an Escalade: Sam, John, who was the image of his father, twenty-four years younger, and a very pretty young woman with dark hair in a big fashionable straw hat, with huge dark glasses, a beige knit beach dress, and platform sandals Kezia recognized as Dior. She was dressed more for the south of France than the Hamptons, or for a more elegant gathering. Kate and Kezia exchanged a look when they saw her, and Felicity went out to greet them. They all saw John stare at her in amazement. He recognized her and hadn't realized they were spending the day with a supermodel. His girlfriend's eyes were riveted to the rock on Felicity's hand, which Felicity was oblivious to. She hugged Sam, smiled broadly at John, who stammered and felt tongue-tied at how beautiful she was, and introduced herself warmly to his girlfriend, Caroline, as Kate and Kezia came out to join them. Sam gave Kezia a hug and she smiled at him. The dynamics were interesting, and he was clearly enjoying them as he grinned at her. Felicity led them all out to the back deck, where Jack had fallen asleep with the newspaper in his hand. Kate nudged him gently and he revived with a start, and stood up to greet the other guests and introduce himself. He looked very impressed by Caroline, who was observing all the Hobson women closely. John had told her it would be casual, but she hadn't believed him. Even though she was attractive, she couldn't compete with Felicity's striking looks. No one could. The others were used to her. And Felicity was so innocent and modest, she never thought she was beautiful and believed she had a funny nose. She always said it was too small. Every inch of her was gorgeous.

Kate helped her bring mugs of coffee out for everyone, as Caroline glued herself to John, to distract him from Felicity, which wasn't working. Jack told Caroline how chic she looked, and Sam leaned against the deck fencing and smiled at Kezia. "I didn't warn them about Felicity," he said to Kezia in a soft voice. "I guess I should have. She takes your breath away when you first see her. She is definitely a knockout. Kate's beautiful, but in a much more subtle way."

"It's Felicity's job now. Men reacted to her even when she was a child. She doesn't care. She doesn't think about her looks, except when she's working." Felicity had masses of blonde hair that cascaded down her back, and John looked like he wanted to run his hands through it. He was trying to regain his composure as they all sat on the deck. Blake showed up a little while later, was happy to see Sam, and shook hands with John. He greeted Caroline. Jack was trying to monopolize her, and John didn't seem to care. As soon as he saw Blake put his arm around his fiancée and kiss her, normal focus returned to John's eyes and he got the picture.

"Did you miss me?" Blake said to her, holding her close.

"Horrendously. I cried the whole time you were gone," Felicity said, and kissed him back, while the others smiled and John looked resigned. He was sitting near Kate, who chatted with him, and they wound up talking about the night of the attack, since John said he lived fairly close to the World Trade Center but had been away for the weekend.

"I was in Africa," Kate said, and he asked where, and they discovered that he had been within a few miles of where she'd stayed at the hospital, and they talked about Africa after that, and the trip he'd taken there with his parents.

The group mixed and talked until lunchtime. They had sandwiches Felicity had bought at a fancy deli that morning, a big salad she'd made, potato chips, and assorted trimmings. She didn't waste time in the kitchen. Caroline was talking about her job at *Vogue,* as an assistant beauty editor, and she was waiting for a job in editorial. She was older than Felicity, who listened attentively. Caroline said she'd been on one of Felicity's cover shoots once, on a farm in Upstate New York, and Kezia could tell that Felicity didn't remember it, but pretended she did, to be polite.

Caroline was pretty, although not remarkable, and a fairly big presence for someone who didn't really have that much to offer, other than her looks, and the fact that she was very chic. No one in the group seemed to care, and John didn't either. Observing all of them, Kezia didn't have the feeling that John was in love with Caroline. She had more the vibe of a date than a woman he was in love with. Caroline was very interested in the fact that both sisters were engaged.

"Is *Vogue* covering your wedding?" she asked Felicity, who looked blank at the question.

"I don't know, I haven't thought about it. They'll probably

want to, but I don't know if we would," she said, and changed the subject. Kate said they hadn't chosen their date yet, to deflect from the subject.

After lunch, Jack suggested a walk on the beach and somehow roped Caroline into walking with him. Blake and Felicity said they were going to stay at the house to tidy up, though Kate suspected they had something else in mind, and she wound up walking with John since Jack and Caroline had gone ahead. Sam and Kezia brought up the rear. He smiled at her, and she laughed.

"They're fun to watch, aren't they? It's complicated being young," Sam commented. "Poor Caroline won't recover from today in a hurry. John couldn't keep his eyes off Felicity, who is obviously madly in love with her future husband, and Caroline got stuck with Kate's rather pedantic fiancé. I may be wrong, but I have this weird feeling that John and Kate would get along, if he can get his mind off the unobtainable younger sister," he said, enjoying all of it.

"Kate's older than he is, if that matters," Kezia said, amused at his analysis.

"Not by much," Sam persisted. "How old is she again?"

"Thirty-seven."

"They're only four years apart."

"Is he serious about Caroline?" Kezia asked. She liked John, he seemed like a straight shooter and a nice man, like his father. Honest, open and kind, as well as bright and successful.

"I think she has scared him off. She's hell-bent on marriage, and he's not. She's twenty-nine, the age at which some women start to panic if they don't have a lot going for them, and she doesn't. She's very ambitious, which usually turns him off. She wants to move in with him and has been pushing for it since they met. And he doesn't want to. Felicity's engagement ring must be driving her insane. Felicity has everything she wants. A good-looking, successful guy with a lot of money, a fancy car, and some very visible bling."

"John isn't exactly a slouch either. He's a prize too," she defended him, and Sam smiled. That pleased him. His son was all-important to him, and always had been. He only had the one child.

"He's not in Blake's leagues yet. He may be someday, but not yet." Blake was only six years older than John, and earned more money with a job at Goldman Sachs, but John was doing well too, for his age, at a small, ambitious, younger investment firm.

As they walked along, Kate was telling John about the book she was writing, and about the countless writing workshops she'd been to, how weird the people were who went to them, and that they had nearly scared her off writing forever. But she seemed very confident about what she was writing now. He liked her. She was almost as pretty as her sister, but in a quieter way, and she was smart and had a wry sense of humor.

"Your girlfriend seems to have a serious interest in weddings," she said to him, teasing him, and he laughed.

"Yeah, she put the Tiffany engagement ring catalogue in my briefcase two weeks before Valentine's Day. She's not subtle."

"What did you get her?" Kate liked him. He was funny and good company.

"A box of chocolates, and heart-shaped gold earrings, from Tiffany of course. I can take a hint as well as the next guy. Speaking of which, what's happening between your mother and my father, if you don't mind my asking? I think I missed a chapter here. The first I heard of her was today, on the way out here."

Kate looked amused. "They met the night of the terrorist attack. They're next-door neighbors. She just bought the other penthouse and moved here from San Francisco a week before the attack. And they're friends. It's pretty new." She told him all that she knew herself.

"He likes her, I can tell," John said.

"She likes him too. They're kind of cute. They're like two kids circling each other."

"He hasn't had a girlfriend since my mom died two years ago," John said. "He had a hard time getting over it."

"My father died five years ago. Mom just sold his business, so she felt free to move. I don't think she's dated seriously since he died. They had a great marriage."

"My parents did too. It sucks. They married really young, and look at all of us, we're all still single. I'm thirty-three, I don't know how old you are, but I don't even want to get married for years, in spite of Caroline's ambitions. They won't get her far with me. How old's your sister?"

"Twenty-three. She's too young to get married," Kate said.

"They'll probably be happy as hell, have five kids, and make it work. I think early marriages work best. By the time you're in your thirties, you have opinions, boundaries, a million preconceived ideas, and a trail of bad relationships tied to your tail like a string of tin cans, which makes it all harder."

"I never wanted to get married," Kate admitted, which seemed odd to tell him when they had only just met, but she felt like she knew him. "I had all those bad relationships you just mentioned, and I've been dating Jack for four years, and lived with him for three of them, and all of a sudden, it just seemed like we needed progress, or something different, or we'd die of boredom the way we were."

"I'm not sure that marriage is the antidote to boredom. Isn't that the cause of most of it?" he said, and she laughed.

"I'll let you know."

"When are you getting married?"

"We haven't set the date yet."

"Oh, that's a bad sign," he said, shaking his head, and Kate grinned as he picked up her left hand and pointed at it. "Where's the ring?"

"We haven't gotten around to it," she said, chuckling. If her mother had said the same things, she would have been furious.

"That's another bad sign. Do I sense cold feet here? His or yours?" John persisted.

"Previously mine. Maybe now his. Maybe both. I just felt that we needed some progress, so I prodded him a little. All of a sudden I could see myself calling him my boyfriend at my ninetieth birthday party. That would be embarrassing."

"Well, keep me posted on this. I want to hear about it when you get the ring and set the date. And keep me posted about my father too. He's being very closemouthed about this."

"I don't think there's a lot to tell at this point," she said. "My mom is very discreet too."

"I beg to differ, not about her discretion. They've known each other for a few weeks, and somebody masterminded a day at the beach so her kids and I could meet each other. Clever, huh?" Kate hadn't thought of it that way.

"I think this was Felicity's idea. She was just being friendly, and he wanted to bring you."

"Then it was his master plan! My father's a smart guy. If he wanted us to meet each other, he has something in mind." He looked at Kate then. "I'm glad he did. Partners in crime here, to share information?" he asked her, and held out his little finger to hook hers, and she laughed like a kid and linked fingers with him.

"Pinky swear!" she said, and they couldn't stop laughing, and then he raced her down the beach at full speed, and she almost beat him, but he won by a few inches and they collapsed on the sand, breathing hard. The others had turned back by then. "You cheated," she accused him.

"I did not! I ran faster than you."

"You got a head start!"

"Did not!" She took off running again and he followed her, and then they took a detour into the shallow waves. The cool ocean water felt good in the heat, after their run. They waded deeper into the water together and got out. Sam and Kezia were watching them from the beach, closer to the house.

"I think I'll make you a bet," Sam said with a broad grin. "I'm going to put my money on my boy to get that dead bore out of your hair and hers forever. I give him two months to do it, maybe even by Labor Day, for a hundred dollars." Kezia was grinning broadly.

"How do I bet if I want you to be right?"

"You just trust me. He's a smart kid. He knows a quality

woman when he sees one. And I think Miss Greedy's days are numbered."

"Will she take the dead bore with her?"

Sam turned to Kezia with a stern expression. "I like the occasional gentleman's bet when the odds are in my favor. I'm not a magician."

"Oh, sorry," she said as he put an arm around her shoulders in the late afternoon sun while they watched their children run toward them at a slow steady pace side by side. They looked nice together.

"Labor Day, you'll see."

"I'll take the bet," she said. "I hope I lose, and will we dance at their wedding, mother of the bride, father of the groom, all that?"

"Of course. And long before that, if you like." He took her hand, and they walked back to Felicity's summer rental.

Blake and Felicity looked suspiciously happy and cuddly when the others returned.

Blake manned the barbecue that night, and Sam helped him. They had barbecued ribs and hamburgers, cheeseburgers for those who wanted them, with mountains of potato chips, and store-bought mashed potatoes and corn on the cob. It was delicious and they all had a good time together. They were old friends by the time the visitors left at eleven that evening. Kezia volunteered as the designated driver in Kate's car, and Sam in John's. He winked at her as they got into their cars. Felicity hugged them, and Blake had enjoyed the evening too. They were sorry to see them all leave, and they promised to do it again soon. Caroline was absolutely glowing and could already see herself as part of the family, sure that the day had been a victory for her.

John hugged Kate before he got in his car and pointed to her ring finger again with a meaningful look, and she laughed. They were like brother and sister. She had always wanted a brother growing up.

Blake and Felicity waved as the two cars drove away, and a few minutes later, Kezia said to her passengers, "I had a really great day." Neither of them answered and she turned to look at them. They were both sound asleep. The wine Blake had served was exceptionally good. Kezia smiled, thinking of her walk on the beach with Sam, and how warm and pleasant it was being with him. She turned on the radio. She drove Kate and Jack all the way home, woke them up and dropped them off, parked the car for them, and then took a cab home.

She had just put on her nightgown and was brushing her teeth when she got a text from Sam. "Labor Day!" it said, and she laughed out loud, and then another: "I had a fantastic day today." She dried her hands to answer him, "Me too."

"Talk to you tomorrow," he wrote back, and she got into bed with the warm glow of a beautiful day well spent with her daughters and their friends, and Sam. It was the best day she'd had in years.

Chapter 10

The seven surviving members of the Enforcers were in the news again the next morning. They'd been transferred back to a federal jail in New York and had a hearing. The trial date had been set for May, but there were liable to be many delays and continuances before they went to trial. They were still being kept in isolation, in a secluded, undisclosed area of the federal jail, for their own protection. They were at risk of being killed by other inmates before they got to trial. It wouldn't have surprised anyone, and no one would have been sorry. Even a guard could do it, or let it happen. So many police officers had lost their lives at the bombing sites, and firefighters in the fires after the explosions, that everyone viewed the crime as horrific, and police and guards at the jail were hostile with them. Sam was particularly vehement about them, after all the body bags he'd moved that night.

After Kezia saw the news, she made the phone call she'd been debating about. She called NYU for their course for nurses returning to the workforce. There was a special program for nurse practitioners, and she asked for the brochure. There was a class starting in October, and she didn't know if it was too late to apply.

Once she'd made the call, she sat down and made lists of all the things she needed to do for Felicity's wedding. She ordered some books. The list she made was long, and then she made another list for Kate's smaller wedding in Vermont. But everything about that wedding was vague. The date, the venue. Would they want to get married in the snow, in winter, in the spring, or the summer? Kate was procrastinating about it, and she really needed to make up her mind. Thinking about it, Kezia smiled, remembering the bet Sam had made with her the day before, that John would steal her from Jack by Labor Day. Kezia was all for it, but she doubted she'd be that lucky, in spite of Sam's faith in his son to lure her away from her fiancé. Kate was stubborn and loyal, and Kezia was afraid that even if Kate suspected she was making a mistake, she'd marry Jack anyway. She very rarely changed her mind once she made a plan, and they had been dating for four years. It would take strength and courage to change course before the wedding. Kezia just couldn't imagine her doing that. Jack had his heels dug in, and his claws deep into her. Sam was going to be very disappointed on Labor Day, and so was she. But it was a nice dream. In the meantime, Kezia had to go along with the plan for Kate to marry Jack Turner, like it or not.

She called Kate that afternoon to see if they were any closer to picking a date or a venue, and Kate didn't answer. She was writing.

Sam called Kezia shortly after that.

"Can I interest you in dinner tonight, or am I calling too late? I'm sorry if I am. I got wrapped up in calls to the West Coast, and the time got away from me. Do you have plans?"

"I'd love to," she said simply. They agreed that he'd pick her up at eight, and they were going to a sushi restaurant nearby. It was fun discovering New York with him. She knew the city well from many visits, but he knew all kinds of small, out-of-the-way places she'd never heard of before. He had a list of restaurants where he was able to eat in peace and relax, and Kezia loved going to them with him. It was a new adventure every time they went out.

"I hate eating alone," he admitted to her as they went to the lobby in her elevator. He'd walked across on her terrace. "It's so lonely and no fun. I'd rather not eat. I lost twenty-five pounds after Audrey died."

"The same thing happened to me when Felicity left for New York, three months after Andrew died, and I was all by myself. I lost fifteen."

They ran into Paige Robbins in the lobby coming home from work. Kezia thought she looked sad, and when they stopped to chat with her, she mentioned that Greg was in L.A., which meant with his wife. Kezia felt sorry for her all over again, and they talked about it as they walked to the restaurant, which wasn't far away on Third Avenue. She marveled at how people didn't recognize Sam when he walked at a fast clip, his eyes down, wearing a baseball cap with jeans and a lightweight jacket. He looked like anyone else on the street until you saw his face. But no one noticed them as they slipped into the restaurant and sat in a back booth no one else wanted. It was perfect for them.

"I feel so sorry for Paige," Kezia said after they ordered. "I've been alone, and very lonely at times, but that's not the same thing as being unhappy with someone."

"I agree. But no one can get her out of it except her. She must be very much in love with him. And I can't see that either, because he doesn't seem like a nice guy."

"Some women fall in love with bad guys," she said matter-of-factly. "*Really* bad guys. I should take her to lunch sometime."

"It's crazy how complicated some relationships are. Even

look at our families. Your daughter looks bored every time Jack opens his mouth. How's that going to play out? Caroline is trying to put a noose around John's neck, and he doesn't even want to live with her. But he doesn't walk away either. And Paige is living with a guy part-time who's with his wife the other part. You and I both had good marriages, but our kids are willing to put up with second-rate relationships that won't make them happy in the long run. And they're smart. Kate is a bright woman, and John's a smart man. They're both with people they shouldn't give the time of day to. It drives me crazy sometimes when I see the women he goes out with."

"I feel the same way about Kate," she said. "I've been watching her pick the wrong man since she was in her teens, that's twenty years now. Her birth father abandoning her is not a sufficient excuse. Now she wants to marry one of those guys. At least John's not engaged to Caroline."

"No, but she could get pregnant. And he's decent enough to marry her if that happens. You just have to hope it all works out."

"I keep hoping she'll break the engagement with Jack, but I can't see that happening. She's stubborn."

"Here's to Labor Day," he said, toasting her with a glass of sake, and she laughed.

"Labor Day!" she agreed. And they turned to less stressful

subjects for the rest of the meal. She told him about ordering the brochure from NYU for the nursing program. He was very pleased for her, as it was a good start and a return to a path that had made her happy. He was all for it.

They made an early night of it. He had work to do, and Kezia was tired. They lingered on the terrace for a few minutes, and he surprised her when he took her in his arms as he said good night. He kissed her with a gentle flurry of his lips on hers, held her, and kissed her again. It was as gentle and tender as he was, and she had feelings for him she could never have imagined. It was like a whole new chapter of her life beginning, and a new road stretching out before them.

"You're an amazing woman, Kezia," he whispered to her. "I never thought I'd find someone like you now." She nodded, she felt the same way about him, and he kissed her with increasing passion. But neither of them wanted to rush anything. They wanted to savor each moment. This was only the beginning. "I hate leaving you when we say good night," he said in a husky voice.

She smiled at him. "Me too," she whispered. They stood outside, kissing for a long time, like two teenagers.

"I don't know how I got so lucky," he said.

"You deserve to be happy, Sam. You're a good man."

"You deserve to be happy too. I want to make you happy."

"You already do." They kissed for a last time, and he went back to his apartment, and she went into hers feeling like she was floating. She couldn't believe this was happening. If she hadn't had the courage to move to New York, she would never have known him. And what was she doing with a movie star? It was crazy, but crazy in a wonderful way. Sam was sitting in his office, thinking the same thing about her. Kezia lay on her bed, thinking about how gentle and loving his kisses had been. They both wanted more.

Jack tutored one of his students that night and came home at ten o'clock. He was tired and wanted a drink, and hadn't had dinner yet. The session had gone much later than planned. Kate had been writing and hadn't noticed.

"Is there anything to eat?" he asked her, expecting her to make dinner for him, but she wanted to go back to her book. It was really rolling, and she had better control over it than she'd ever had before. She didn't want to lose that.

"I don't know," she said vaguely. "I had a salad, there wasn't much in the fridge."

"There wouldn't be unless you buy it," he said, annoyed. Kate never felt that housework was her job. The daily woman who came in to clean during the week didn't buy groceries or cook. They bought takeout a lot, and Jack only cooked when he had no other choice.

"Why do I have to buy groceries?" Kate snapped at him. "Why can't you do it?"

"Because I write too." She didn't say that she paid for everything, so why should she have to buy the groceries too, but she thought it.

"My mother left me three messages today. She wants to know our wedding date. I don't know what to tell her," Kate said with an abrupt change of subject to an even more difficult issue.

"What's the hurry? Why do we have to pick a date? I thought we got engaged so we had a more official title. Not so we'd rush into marriage. I can't afford to get married, and you know it."

"You don't pay for anything now, that's not going to change when we get married. I don't expect you to. But we've lived together for three years. At some point, we have to decide if we're for real or not. I feel like a fraud. And if I want to have kids, we need to decide before I get any older."

"Do you want kids?" he asked her bluntly, and she hesitated before she answered.

"I don't know," she said honestly.

"Why don't you figure that out before you push us into a marriage neither of us wants and we don't need, just so we're 'respectable,' or because your sister is going to be married and you're not. This is all about her, isn't it?"

"No, it's about us," Kate said with an icy calm. "It's about you and me. I'm not going to drag you to the altar, Jack, or hold a gun to your head."

"But that's what you're doing, isn't it?"

"Is that what it feels like to you?"

"Yes, it does," he said, and poured himself a glass of whiskey, without rocks, and downed it in one long gulp.

"There's our answer then, isn't it? So what do I tell my mother? That you've changed your mind and we're not getting married?"

"This was your idea in the first place, after Felicity got engaged. You wanted to be engaged too. That was our compromise, and all of a sudden we have to pick a wedding date and a venue to keep your mother happy."

"She's trying to make us happy," Kate said quietly.

"Well, I'm not. Now you want to get married. Next you'll want a baby. Jesus, Kate, that's never been us. We're writers, both of us. We're creative people. We don't need marriage, or children. This is enough."

"What if it isn't? I never realized that you really don't want to get married."

"I'm forty-two years old. I don't need all that crap. What difference does being married make?"

"It makes a difference to me," she said clearly, and realized for the first time that it was true. It did make a difference to her. She did want what Felicity had. A guy who was crazy about her and couldn't wait to be married to her. Why couldn't she have that too? But Jack wasn't Blake and never would be, with or without a ring on her finger. Jack wanted her to support him forever and give nothing back. Why hadn't she seen that before? Why didn't she want to? She had spent her whole life waiting to meet her father, and the last four years waiting for Jack to grow up and he never would. But she wasn't ready to say it to him yet. It was bad enough that she knew it. And he knew it too. He knew what he wanted and what he didn't, and so did she.

He stormed out to the kitchen then and foraged in the refrigerator, and she went back to her office and closed the door. She had a sick feeling in her stomach. She couldn't hide from it anymore. She knew the truth. With or without a ring on her finger, what Jack had to give her wasn't enough.

That night, John Stewart and Caroline had been to an engagement party for a girl Caroline had gone to school with. She was twenty-nine, the same age as Caroline. She was an attorney, and she had just gotten engaged to a junior partner of the firm. She had her whole future mapped out. One day they would both be partners. They would make a good living, they would be married and have children, move to the suburbs and commute to work. They would need both their incomes to be able to afford kids. It sounded like a death sentence to John. He was happy for them since that was what they wanted. But it wasn't what he wanted, and surely not now. Not for a long time, if ever.

As always, when they went to engagement parties or weddings, Caroline started pushing him afterward. He had heard about her biological clock ticking so often that he felt like Captain Hook in *Peter Pan*. He had never misled her. He had told her right from the beginning that marriage wasn't on his radar, and wouldn't be for a long time. Women never believed him. It had happened before, and it kept happening. He hadn't dated a single woman yet who made him want to get married, and the more they pushed, the more he wanted to run in the opposite direction. Engagement parties didn't fill him with longing. They filled him with dread. He was faithful to the women in his life. But he wanted a relationship, not a wife. He knew that when he finally did want a wife, if he ever did, she wouldn't be like Caroline. She seemed like a predator to him, and she wanted to eat him alive. He had nightmares about it sometimes. He knew now that he had been foolish to think she'd back off, that she'd listen to him and believe him when he said that marriage wasn't on his agenda, and wouldn't be for a long time.

She started in on him as soon as they left the party, which hadn't been fun. Caroline had a good time; him not so much.

They went to his apartment afterward, which was a mistake he recognized as soon as they got to his place.

"When are you going to let me move in?" she said plaintively.

"Caroline, we talked about this when we started dating. I don't want to live with anyone."

"It's been eight months," she said, and he realized that she'd had a lot to drink, more than he'd thought, which always made her aggressive.

"That's right, it's been eight months, not eight years. And I haven't changed my mind. I don't want you to move in. I'm young, I'm immature, I'm selfish, I need my own space. I don't want to live with anyone for the next several years." He knew that if she moved in, she'd never leave. She'd hound him until she wore him down, and he'd wind up married to a woman he didn't want and should never have dated. And somewhere along the line she'd get pregnant.

"I'm twenty-nine, my eggs are getting old."

"Oh my God, you're a baby."

"I'm almost thirty." He closed his eyes for a minute, and then he looked at her. She was beautiful and sexy. He had fun with her, when she wasn't hounding him. But it wasn't enough. It just wasn't worth it. He hated starting again, but he knew he had to. They had played out whatever they had, and it was going to be agony from now on.

"I can't do this anymore, Caroline. I'm sorry. I don't want to feel like an asshole because I don't want you to move in, and I don't want to get married, no matter how many weddings or engagement parties you take me to. It's not contagious, and I'm still the guy you started dating who told you the truth right away. I'm done. We don't want the same things. You need a man who's going to get your eggs to the altar in record time, before they fry or boil or do whatever they do. I'm not your guy, and by the time I would be, you'll have three kids, a dog, and a house in the suburbs. I can't do that, at least not now."

"Are you breaking up with me?" she asked with a look of outrage. She wasn't sad, she was furious.

"I'm not the guy you want. We need to stop now, before this gets nasty. We had fun. I think we've done it. You need someone else to take you all the way to what you want."

"Can I spend the night?" He shook his head. He knew that if she did, there was a good chance she'd try to get pregnant.

"I'll take you home," he said politely.

"You're a bastard," she said. But at least she couldn't say he had lied to her. He hadn't. He never did. She was young enough that he thought it would be okay. Twenty-nine was young to be as desperate as she was. All of her girlfriends had been getting married in the last year. He should have known. "You're a shit." He didn't respond and handed her

her jacket. She snatched it out of his hand and walked to the door. He opened the door and followed her out. She was just drunk enough that he couldn't let her go home alone.

They walked out of the building, and he hailed a cab and got in with her. He wanted this to be over now before it got uglier. She didn't live far, and when they got to her building, she asked him to come upstairs, and he wouldn't.

"I'm sorry," he said as gently as he could, as the doorman opened the door for her, and John got back in the cab. He watched her walk inside and she turned and looked at him with fury. He wondered if she was right, if he was a bastard, or if there was something wrong with him. But he knew that what was wrong, and stupid of him, was that he had spent eight months with her when he didn't love her.

He went back to his apartment and thought about her. He wasn't sorry, and he didn't regret what he'd done. But he felt stupid and selfish anyway. What was the answer? Stop dating until he met the woman of his dreams? Give it all up until he felt ready to settle down? Date older women? Younger ones who didn't care about marriage yet? But they didn't interest him much.

He picked up his phone and texted his father. "Lunch tomorrow?" The answer came back quickly. Sam was still awake.

"I'm sorry, son, I can't. I have meetings all day. Are you okay?"

"Fine. No problem. Will text you later this week. Good night." He realized he didn't want to talk to his father about it anyway. He was a grown man.

He went to bed a little while later, and lay there for a long time, thinking about Caroline. He should have stopped seeing her a long time before, or never gotten involved with her at all. Once he admitted it to himself, he fell asleep.

Chapter 11

When John woke up, he felt like he'd been beaten the night before. He knew he had been. He hadn't even had that much to drink. He wasn't sorry for breaking up with Caroline, he just hated that it had turned ugly in the end. He would rather have parted friends, as he usually did. They had had some good times. But in the end, it was all about what she wanted, and her schemes. She wanted to move in, get married, and have a baby, and he didn't want any of those things, not now and not with her. She was the wrong woman for him. He knew that ultimately he wanted to find someone like his mother, someone gentle and kind, who wanted the same things he did, not a girl with ulterior motives, who knew exactly what she wanted right from the beginning, whether he wanted the same things or not.

He hated it when things ended badly. But it had been fairly predictable with Caroline. He just hadn't wanted to see it. His father had warned him several times. And he was always right.

John had an odd thought when he got to the office, and didn't know if it was the right thing to do. She seemed like someone he could talk to, as a friend. He hardly knew her, and he wasn't trying to date her. He just wanted to talk. He called Kate Hobson, and then felt like a loser when he did. She picked up and sounded surprised.

"Did you get the ring yet?" he asked her. She laughed at the question.

"No." She was startled to hear from him, and she thought he sounded sick, but she didn't know him well enough to be sure.

"I'm feeling sorry for myself. Do you want to have lunch with me?"

"Sure. Okay. Something wrong?"

"Yes and no. I broke up with Caroline."

"Oh dear. I take it she didn't get the ring she wanted either."

"That would be correct. I overstayed. It was predictable."

"You're probably right about that." It had been obvious that Caroline had serious designs on John, and that she wasn't going to give up. But Kate didn't say that to him. "Are you sorry you broke up?"

"No. It was going to get worse. I think I got out on the last warning bell. Now she thinks I'm a shit."

"Were you?" she asked him bluntly.

"No."

"Did you lie to her?"

"No."

"Then you're clean." He liked talking to Kate and felt better.

"What about you? How's the fiancé?"

"We had a fight last night too. It must have been a full moon." Or the wrong people, but he didn't say that to her.

"Where do you want to have lunch? La Grenouille or the deli near my office?" he asked her.

"The deli. I love La Grenouille to celebrate, but we can talk better without six waiters serving us. What time?"

"One o'clock?" She agreed and he told her where to meet him. When he hung up, he felt better. She said he was clean and he knew he was. She was the perfect sister.

When John met Kate for lunch, she was wearing jeans and a striped T-shirt and ballerinas. Her hair was pulled back. He smiled when he saw her. She looked fresh and young, and sympathetic.

They ordered lunch, and he told her what had happened and what led up to it, that Caroline had tried to badger him into letting her move in, the ultimate goal being marriage. Kate looked serious when he said it, and John saw the expression on her face.

"What's wrong? Did I do something wrong?" She had been supportive until then. They hardly knew each other, but they felt like old friends from another lifetime, and she was so easy to talk to.

"Maybe I did something wrong," she said, answering his question. "Maybe that's what I'm doing to Jack. Badgering him into marriage. I just wanted some kind of progress in the relationship. Everything feels stagnant, nothing changes with him."

"Do you love him?" he asked her, and she thought about it.

"Yes. Sometimes. Not always. Most of the time. He's a good writer." John stared at her when she answered.

"Please don't tell me that you're marrying him because he's a good writer."

"No, of course not. But I respect his talent."

"Great. Buy his book when he writes one, don't marry him."

"I want to marry him because we've invested four years and lived together for three of them. That's a big investment of time. You don't just throw that away."

"You do, if it's the wrong person."

"He's not, or I wouldn't have stayed with him."

"Maybe you would have. Do you usually admit it if you make a mistake?"

"Not if I can help it," she said with a grin.

"If you invest in a company, and it fails and loses money, do you keep pouring money and time into it, or do you cut your losses and shut it down?"

"I'd probably stick with it for a while, but if it keeps failing, I'd probably close before it takes me down with it."

"That's a reasonable answer. And how long has it been? Four years, and the guy hasn't coughed up a ring yet, doesn't want to set a date, and you're telling me you have to badger him to marry you. How much fun does that sound like?"

"It's not," she admitted to him more easily than she would have to her mother or sister. There was a confessional feeling to it. Two strangers confessing to each other. Except he didn't feel like a stranger, he felt like a friend, and so did she to him, which was why he had called her. "It hasn't been fun for a while. I thought getting married would change that," Kate said.

"It would. It would make it worse. Marriage is a magnifier. And what do you get out of it?" John asked her.

"Companionship, someone to talk to. He's supportive of my writing. I'm not lonely, or alone."

"He's not the only guy on the planet," he said, and then John decided to take a risk and be fully honest with her.

"You could do a lot better. He's not exactly a ton of fun, and you look bored with him."

"Isn't that what marriage is? Boring most of the time, with occasional good moments?" she asked him.

"I sure hope not. My parents didn't look bored. They were crazy about each other. I think they had fun. How much fun do you have with Jack?" She didn't answer. She didn't expect to have fun with Jack.

"We're not here to talk about me. We're here to talk about you and your breakup," she said pointedly.

"Your relationship is more interesting. You still have one. I don't. So there's nothing to talk about on my side."

"Do you think you'll miss her?" Kate asked him, curious.

"Maybe. At first. But probably not for long. That sounds awful but it's true. I never thought of her as long-term." Kate was wondering how much she'd miss Jack if she broke up with him.

They didn't solve any major problems over lunch, but it was comforting talking to each other.

She walked John back to his office, then took a cab to her apartment, and went to her office to work on her book. But John's questions resonated in her head all afternoon. She wondered if he was right, and Jack was a mistake. But whether he was or not, Jack didn't want to set a wedding date and she had to explain that to her mother. And herself.

While Kate was having lunch with John Stewart, Kezia was having lunch with Paige Robbins. She had called her after they ran into her in the lobby. Paige was surprised and pleased, and they met at a restaurant close to Paige's office. She rarely went out for lunch and usually ate at her desk. She got more work done that way.

Her office was close to Hudson Yards, and when Kezia got out of the cab, she looked up at the ravaged buildings in the once-beautiful new development. They were tearing down the buildings that had been the most damaged. It was too dangerous to leave them, and the mall had been closed since the attack, and would be for the next year. They were going to build a memorial to the thousands of people who had died. More had succumbed to their injuries in the weeks following. It was a tragedy of epic proportions. There had been countless meetings, in New York and in cities around the country, about how to increase security measures and ensure that nothing like it could ever happen again. They had sought to protect American soil from foreign enemies since 9/11, but no one had ever expected such a devastating betrayal from their own. That Americans would seek to destroy the fiber of their own country and injure fellow citizens was beyond belief or comprehension. It had disheartened the entire country and the wound ran deep, in addition to the loss of life.

It reminded Kezia, as it always did now, of the night she had met Sam and the work they had done together, laboring through the night with their hearts breaking. It had brought new people into her life too: Sam, Louise, Sam's son, and now Paige. Kezia could see in her a deeply sad woman, tied to a selfish man who didn't value her, and it saddened her to see it.

Paige looked chic and cheerful when they met at the restaurant. She was wearing a navy-blue linen Chanel suit. She was beautiful, but one could sense that Paige no longer knew it. She was ten minutes late and apologized profusely. Kezia was waiting patiently for her at the table when Paige sat down with her.

"I'm so sorry. I had a conference call that ran late, and I couldn't get off. I couldn't even text you. We were on video."

"Don't worry, I'm not working, you are. I've got time." They ordered and Paige slowly relaxed and unwound, and by the time they were halfway through lunch, she felt at ease with Kezia. They'd been talking about Louise and how remarkable she was. Her photographs of the July Fourth bombing were in magazines all over the world by then. Despite the grisly circumstances, the photos were beautiful, and captured the raw emotions of that night. Paige looked at Kezia then.

"I suppose someone has told you by now that Greg is

married. It's not a secret, but it's always awkward when we meet someone new. I figured Louise must have told you."

"She didn't. She's very discreet. Sam did. That can't be easy for you."

"It isn't. We've been together for five years. His kids were still young then, and I thought that if I waited long enough, he'd extricate himself. He said he would, but he didn't. The youngest is starting college in September, and it's clear that it's never going to be any different. You kind of get used to it. He still spends all the holidays with them. They rent a house in the south of France in August every year. He'll be there in a week or two. He's coming back to New York for a few days and he'll leave from here." Paige's eyes were bottomless pools of pain as she said it.

"And what will you do?" Kezia asked her.

Paige smiled a wintry smile. "Work. It's depressing to travel alone. Greg and I go to the Caribbean every year before Christmas. His boat is there for the winter, and we spend a week on it, before his wife and the kids arrive," which meant that the crew knew it too, which was humiliating for her. She lived in the shadows. "I've invested five years of my life with him. You don't throw that kind of commitment away. It's too late to do anything else. I feel too old to have kids now, and at forty-two, you're not in high demand on the marriage market. Men want women half my age, and there are plenty of them. I kind of missed the boat on finding a husband and having kids. I have my work." She looked brave as she said it, and it made Kezia's heart ache for her.

"It's never too late. You don't know what could happen if you were open to it, Paige. I've been a widow for five years, and didn't even consider dating again. I thought my husband was the only man on earth for me. I gave up the idea of finding any other partner when he died. I'm turning sixty in September, and now I'm rethinking it. You don't have to be alone if you don't want to be, and you don't have to take the leftovers from Greg's table. He's got a sweet deal: his wife, his family, and you, on his terms." She was a little nervous about being so honest with her, but Kezia thought someone had to be. Paige was letting life pass her by, and Greg thought he was king of the world, with two women at his beck and call. She assumed his wife was too.

"He's really doing it for his kids," Paige defended him.

"And himself. It works for him, I assume. They're not kids anymore if the youngest is going to college. It's not fair to you." Paige had the saddest eyes she'd ever seen. She was paying a high price for Greg's self-indulgence and cowardice, which was how Kezia viewed it. "And you probably work crazy hours because you're alone."

Paige smiled. "Guilty as charged. I work most weekends because I have nothing else to do. And it's good for my job."

"What about joining a tennis club, or golf? You'd meet other men there. Or even other women, who might introduce you to someone. People tried to fix me up when my husband died. I wasn't ready, but the theory was good. I just didn't think anyone would measure up to him."

"And now you do?" Paige was intrigued by what she was saying, but not convinced.

"Now I realize that there are good people out there. Even if only as friends. I've really enjoyed meeting you, Louise, and Sam. I'd never have met you if I hadn't moved to New York. And the time was right. We sold my husband's business, so I seized the opportunity, and my kids are here." Kezia was nearly twenty years older than Paige, but she was fully alive and excited about life. Something in Paige had died. "And even if I don't find another partner, I've been married and have kids. You have a lot of life left to live, filled with things you haven't done yet. Don't let Greg rob you of that. Greg is my age, and he's had his life too. You haven't. Believe me, at forty-two, it's not over. You've got wonderful years ahead of you. Don't waste them."

"Louise says that too," Paige said softly.

"She's more alive than I am, and she's nearly eighty-nine," Kezia reminded her. "I wish I had her energy and spirit."

"You do. I felt it the minute I met you. I admire you. And you don't look your age."

"I do to me," Kezia said with a grin. "Some days are better than others. It really made a difference moving here. I was dying and didn't know it, after Andrew died. That whole part of my life that I loved so much was over. And now a whole new chapter is starting."

"Sam?" Paige asked her with a small smile.

"Maybe. We're friends. It's too soon to know. And everything has been so upside down here and upsetting for everyone since the July Fourth attack. Sometimes good things happen even in a time of crisis. You get to know people faster. But I have to admit, an event like that shakes your faith in the human race and reminds you of your own mortality, and how everything can be cut short in a minute. Don't waste a second of your life, Paige. You'll regret it one day. I never thought I'd be a widow at fifty-five or move to New York at sixty. And now I'm thinking of going back to school, and nursing again. That night woke me up to how precious life is, and how brief. But it's also too long for you to be waiting for a man who's having his cake and eating it too. I'm sure you love him, or you wouldn't be doing this, but you deserve better than you're getting. I'm sorry to be so outspoken. That may be the only benefit of being the age I am. But you're only five years older than my oldest daughter."

"My mom died ten years ago. I think she would have said the same things. I wish I had your courage and energy."

"You do. You just have to use them. You're letting someone else control your life, to his advantage and not yours."

"It's not easy for him either," Paige said, "being torn between two women." Kezia wasn't convinced that Greg was "torn." He seemed very comfortable with the arrangement, from what she'd seen.

"Maybe we could do something some weekend when you're alone, have dinner or go to a movie," Kezia suggested.

"I'd love that," Paige said gratefully, and looked at her watch. "I have to get back to the office. I have another conference call in twenty minutes."

Kezia paid for lunch—although Paige tried to—they hugged on the sidewalk, and Paige rushed back to her office. Kezia wondered if their lunch would make a difference. Paige was obviously deeply in love with Greg, but it was easy for someone else to see that the relationship wasn't going anywhere, except where Greg wanted it to. Kezia hated to see it. Paige was a lovely woman and deserved so much better. Kezia disliked him even more after spending time with Paige and hearing her story. It was no different than that of any other woman in love with a married man. So few of them ever got their man, and Kezia was sure that Paige wouldn't, and that Paige knew it too. She clearly no longer had any hope that Greg would leave his wife, even now, with an empty nest.

Kezia had time and it was a beautiful, sunny day, with a slight breeze, so she walked the twenty blocks home from lunch. She sat down at her desk when she got back to answer some emails, several of them from her decorator, when Kate finally returned her calls.

"Where've you been? I was getting worried." Kezia made an effort not to sound annoyed.

"I was writing. I don't like to interrupt the flow when it's going well." It was a weak excuse.

"I know you hate my bugging you, but I'm calling again about the date. It seems like a long way off, but it isn't. You know how booked up the inns get in Vermont in the winter, and even in the spring. What kind of time frame are you and Jack thinking?" Kate sighed and hoped her mother didn't hear it. She did. This was the call Kate had been dreading and avoiding. Jack wasn't making things easy for her, and Kezia liked to be organized. Kate didn't have her mother's precise view of time, or propensity for doing things well in advance. It was how Kezia's life ran smoothly. Felicity was much more like their mother. And neither of them had Jack to deal with.

"I know you want to know, Mom, but Jack has been swamped. We're going to a workshop in August, and he's teaching a class there for a week. He's trying to get ready for it. And he's been working on an essay he wants to try to sell to *The New Yorker*, which is a big deal. It's hard to get him to focus on something months away. He just doesn't want to make plans yet. He has no idea what we'll be doing this winter or next spring. I've asked him." And pushed him, and shoved him, and begged him, to no avail, like the fight they'd had the night before. It always turned nasty when he was pushed, if it was something he didn't want to do.

"Your wedding is a big deal, Kate. I hope he thinks so too. And it's more important than a workshop or *The New Yorker*."

"I know." But he didn't, Kate knew.

"Do you have any idea of time frame? Season?"

"No. And he won't discuss it with me, so your pushing me won't make any difference," Kate said, sounding stressed.

"And that's okay with you?" Kezia asked her, trying not to sound irritated. It was obvious that Kate was stressed about it.

"It has to be," Kate responded. "That's how he is. He doesn't like to be pushed or pinned down."

"He's a lucky guy. So what do I do?"

"You wait until I tell you we have a date, whenever that is."

"If it's short notice, you may not get one of the venues you'd like."

"Then we'll go somewhere else."

"We can't even look for a dress if we don't know what season."

231

"I know, Mom." Kate was getting depressed, listening to her. It was everything she had said to Jack the night before.

"Felicity and I are going to start looking for dresses next week when she comes into the city. December is just around the corner. We thought of Paris, but the fittings would be too complicated, so we're going to look here."

"Great. I won't need a big wedding gown like hers, for a small wedding in Vermont." Kezia felt sad for Kate. She was getting everything second-rate, starting with the groom. And Felicity was having all the fun, and she made it easy, and so did Blake. "I'll call you if I know anything, Mom. In the meantime, have fun with Felicity." At least it would keep her mother busy, Kate thought when she hung up. She thought about it all afternoon, and didn't feel like writing anymore.

She called John to see how he was feeling. He sounded better.

"I've felt better ever since our lunch. I got a nasty email from Caroline, which actually made me feel less guilty. She blames me that all her schemes didn't work, when I told her all along that she couldn't move in and I'm not interested in marriage. How are you? You don't sound so good."

"My mother is pressing me about the wedding date. I wish we'd never said we were engaged. It's just a big headache, and Jack doesn't want to know. It was just a bone he threw me. So now I feel stupid and humiliated."

"He sounds like the perfect guy to marry," John said, and she laughed.

"Yeah. Exactly."

"I have a better idea. Why don't you let me take you to dinner next week and cheer you up? I promise, I won't press you for a wedding date, just know that you can't move in with me. You need to have some fun. We'll go someplace loud and trendy so we can shout at each other, and there's no risk of intimacy." She laughed. He was a terrific new friend. She never had dinner with other men, and hadn't since she'd been living with Jack, but John was harmless, and clearly friend material and nothing more. And it couldn't hurt.

"Okay. Sounds good."

"You can tell me all about your book, and help me pick out new candidates on dating sites."

"That's disgusting. You can do that yourself. Is that how you met Caroline?"

"Sort of. I saw her online, and then I met her at a party. I was drunk, so I have an excuse for my poor judgment."

"She was pretty, and she dressed well, so you didn't get it too wrong."

"Yeah, except she comes equipped with a wedding dress, and she's hearing challenged, since I told her I wasn't interested in marriage, and now she's calling me a liar. She's a nasty piece of work." His father had warned him of that too.

It was written all over her. Kate thought so too when Caroline came to the Hamptons. They agreed on the following Monday night for dinner at a restaurant Kate liked. It was the best night for her because Jack had back-to-back tutoring students and probably wouldn't even realize she'd gone out, or care. She felt dishonest, but John was right. She needed cheering up, which seemed to justify it. It wasn't a date. John was a friend. Kate had liked talking to him ever since their walk on the beach in Southampton. He was playful but intelligent, had a good sense of humor, was serious about certain subjects, and was just a down-to-earth, unpretentious person, although he had a good job and his father was a big star. He didn't trade on who his father was, and the advice he gave her was reasonable. He was a welcome addition to her life.

Kezia told Sam that night about her lunch with Paige. She was getting a rotten deal from Greg Avery, with his double life.

"A lot of guys do that in Hollywood. A lot of them don't even bother to do it in another city, they have both women in L.A."

"I feel sorry for her," Kezia said. "It sounds like she's isolated herself for him. She thinks she's too old, at forty-two, to meet someone else, find a husband, or have kids, so she stays with him. It's really depressing, and I think she is depressed. I wish I could do something to help her."

"She has to help herself," he said wisely, and he looked at Kezia seriously for a moment. He wasn't sure if it was too soon, but he wanted to ask her something. He didn't want to be premature, nor wait too long and settle into friendship. She could see he had something on his mind.

He finally got up the courage to ask her while they sat on the couch, with his arm around her, after dinner. He looked very serious, and she didn't know what was on his mind.

"Kezia, would you consider going away with me for a few days, a weekend or whenever? I thought we could stay at some small hotel. We don't have to go far."

She looked at him in surprise. "Can you do that? What if someone calls the paparazzi?"

"Then we'll deal with it. We're both adults, unmarried, we have a right to do what we want." She smiled at him and he kissed her. "I didn't want to just spring it on you, or woo you into bed here. It would be good to get away for a few days." The atmosphere in New York was still heavy after the attack. The city was recovering, but the many deaths had left their mark on everyone.

"I'd love to go away with you," she said softly. And as soon as she said it, she thought of how long it had been since she'd been with a man, not since Andrew. The prospect was a little scary and exciting, and Sam had the same concern.

"I haven't been with anyone since Audrey . . . except once,

and it was a huge mistake, eight months after she died. It was too soon, and the whole thing was awful."

Kezia felt like a kid again as she smiled at him. "Whatever happens happens," she said philosophically, and she kissed him. "We'll figure it out."

"I have a pretty good memory," he said, and she laughed, but for her there was the whole added element that she was about to go to bed with America's biggest movie star. She couldn't think of anything more daunting. Who could have thought that she would fall in love at sixty after the worst terrorist attack in history? Life was certainly unpredictable, and exciting. Sam held her in his arms and she could feel his heart beating. He was just as scared and excited as she was, but, as Kezia said, they would figure it out.

Chapter 12

Before Kezia went away for her romantic weekend, she took Felicity shopping for a bridal gown. It was a major mother-daughter event, and Felicity wanted her older sister there as well. Kezia had thought of it, but hadn't wanted to suggest it unless Felicity did. They had appointments with three major designers. Felicity knew their work and had modeled for them before. They were very excited that Felicity Hobson was coming in to try on wedding gowns. She knew what she had in mind. A dress in heavy satin, since the wedding would be in December, with a long train and a traditional cathedral veil. She wanted the gown to be classic but spectacular and, with Felicity wearing it, it would be. In every show she modeled in, particularly the Paris haute couture shows, they had her wear the wedding gown. Now she was choosing one for herself. She could hardly wait, and Kezia was touched by how excited she was. And that she asked Kate to come too. It would also give Kate a chance to see what was available, although she was looking for a much simpler gown than her sister, for her country New England wedding.

Both Felicity and Kezia texted Kate the time of the appointments and the addresses, and Kate did everything she could to avoid them. She told them she was busy, had appointments she couldn't change, was writing, was coming down with a cold, had to help Jack with a workshop he was preparing. Nothing worked. They wouldn't let her off the hook and Kezia finally called her.

"Why are you being so difficult? It means a lot to your sister for you to be there. It's not too much to ask. She looks up to you, you're her big sister. You should be there."

"I've got a lot to do, Mom, and she knows a lot more about wedding dresses than I do. She wears them all the time."

"This is different. This is for her wedding. You're her maid of honor. She's not having any bridesmaids. She doesn't want anyone to see it except the two of us. Can't you make the effort for her?" Her mother made Kate feel selfish and self-indulgent, and dragging her feet all the way, she agreed to go. She didn't want to see Felicity in her grand wedding gown, bubbling over with excitement, when she couldn't even get Jack to pick a date. Her own wedding was beginning to seem more and more remote, which she didn't want to tell them, so, grudgingly, she agreed to go.

She took a cab uptown on the appointed morning, to see Oscar de la Renta gowns. Many of them were lacy and fabulous. Felicity chose the ones she wanted to try while Kate and Kezia stood by, waiting. She emerged from the dressing room with all the tiny buttons fastened down the back, the train stretched behind her for at least ten feet. She looked breathtaking, and Kezia had tears in her eyes as she looked at her, and Kate felt wooden as she smiled and said all the appropriate things to her sister.

They spent an hour there while she tried on different gowns and veils. She looked more and more beautiful in each one.

"I want Blake to be blown away when he sees me," Felicity said to her sister.

"He will be," Kate reassured her as she wondered what she'd look like in her own dress, at the small country wedding Jack said he wanted.

Felicity hadn't found exactly what she had in mind, and they went to see the gowns at Carolina Herrera, where Felicity tried all her favorites. The second appointment took even longer. And at noon they moved on to the studio of a new, unknown designer whose designs Felicity had seen and liked. She'd modeled one in *Vogue* and loved it.

Their newest creation was exactly what she had said she wanted. It was a heavy satin gown, with long sleeves and bare shoulders. Felicity's tall, perfect body looked regal in the ivory gown, with a train that stretched across the room, and a long lace panel behind her. It had a complicated system to loop it up for the reception so she could dance, and an elegant matching headpiece encrusted with tiny pearls, which sat on her blonde hair, with the veil attached. She looked truly spectacular in it as she beamed at her mother and sister. Kate was sure that *Vogue* would cover the splashy wedding her family was planning, with celebrities and socialites and politicians present. Between the two of them, they knew everyone. And Kate could easily envision the hundreds of guests fawning over Felicity. It was going to be a circus, but Felicity had thrown herself into it after her initial hesitation. Blake's son, Alex, was going to be the ring bearer, and Kate her only attendant. Kezia had already decided she was going to wear midnight blue and had found the dress, by an English designer who was making it to order for her.

Kezia had already ordered the save-the-dates and the invitations. The save-the-dates were going out that week so they could get on their guests' December calendars. The wedding was going to be held at the Frick museum, as Blake and Felicity had hoped. Kezia had scheduled appointments in

September with two caterers and three wedding bakers. The details were endless, and their comments swirled around Kate until she thought she would faint and had to sit down. It was all too much for her. It made her glad that Jack didn't want a big wedding, or maybe none at all. And Felicity's unbridled ecstasy made it even harder to stomach. Kate could feel her resentment of her younger sister bubble up in her like lava in a volcano, and she couldn't stand another minute of it.

Kezia could see that something was wrong and went to her while Felicity chatted with the designer. She was the most beautiful bride any of them had ever seen, which was neither surprising nor unexpected, and she knew just how to move and turn in it to best show the design of the dress.

"Are you all right?" Kezia asked Kate quietly as Kate shook her head.

"No, I'm not," she said, looking at Felicity in all her glory. But there was an innocence to her, like a child on Christmas. This was the preview of what she hoped would be her happiest moment. "There's something ghoulish about this," Kate said, and everyone in the room looked shocked. She looked straight at Felicity when she spoke. "Do you have any idea how many thousands of people died in this city a few weeks ago, or were maimed for life?" Felicity looked crushed as she said it. "And you're dancing around and preening in your wedding gown as though none of it ever happened. It's obscene. Who cares about your wedding and how many layers of crinoline will be under the train, or how many yards of lace trailing behind you? How can you stand there looking like that, talking about the invitations and the cake, the caterer and which photographer, and what band will be playing? We're dancing on those people's graves and making their deaths meaningless. We're on to the next big black-tie party. It's a travesty," she said angrily. Felicity was crying, and Kezia looked daggers at Kate.

"Stop it! Why are you doing this? Just to hurt your sister because she's happy and you're jealous of her? You have to spoil it for her, and steal her joy, so she can be as bitter and angry as you are. You have no reason to be angry, you have everything she does and more. Wearing sackcloth and ashes or refusing to pick a wedding date won't bring those people back to life or change what happened. I was on my knees on the ground with them that night. I saw them. I held their hands while they died. *This* is the antidote to that. This is what living is about, living joy and being happy to make the most of life while we have it. If you need to mourn those people, and we all do, do it on your own time. Don't use it as an excuse to spoil this moment for your sister." Kezia was furious with Kate, and put her arms around Felicity to comfort her.

Kate's face was ashen. She didn't even know why she'd said it, but their mother was right. She had wanted to spoil the moment for Felicity because she was so unhappy herself, and Jack was being such a jerk and had disappointed her so totally. He couldn't even get a ring out of a Cracker Jack box to put on her finger or pick a date to marry her. She wanted Felicity to be as miserable as she was. Kate knew she'd made a mistake trying to force him into some kind of commitment, which he had done nothing but resist ever since he had agreed to it. Unlike Blake, who was over-the-moon happy that he was marrying Felicity. Kate had just done everything she could to spoil it.

"I'm sorry," Kate said in a choked voice. "You look beautiful," she said to Felicity with tears welling up in her own eyes. "You're going to be a beautiful bride."

With her characteristic generosity, Felicity reached out and hugged her sister, and they held each other tight as they both cried, and Kate told her again how sorry she was.

"I'm sorry I was a shit. I don't know what happened. I was overwhelmed. You didn't kill those people. And Mom's right, we have to go on living, and you have a right to your big fancy wedding."

"Do you think it's in bad taste, Mom?" Felicity looked over her shoulder at her mother.

"No, I do not," Kezia said emphatically. "The wedding will

be five months after the attack. We didn't lose anyone in our family, thank God, and your father would want you to have the most beautiful wedding. And everyone will be happy to celebrate with you. Now take off the dress, and let's go have lunch." Kezia felt as though she had gone over Niagara Falls in a barrel, and Felicity disappeared to the dressing room to take off the dress, as Kezia spoke to Kate in a low voice with a stern expression.

"I don't know what's happening with you, but you need to deal with it before you hurt people and can't repair it. That outburst was completely inappropriate, and you spoiled this moment for her. She doesn't deserve that. She would never do it to you. She's an innocent here, and what you did is uncalled for. You tried to make her feel guilty for her wedding and her joy." Tears welled up in Kate's eyes.

"I know, Mom, you're right. I'm sorry. She was so happy that it made me crazy."

"Whatever is going on with you and Jack, you'd better fix it, before you cause irreparable damage, to yourself as well as others." It was the most intentionally vicious attack Kezia had ever seen and she was devastated that Kate had done it to Felicity.

Felicity emerged from the dressing room looking as beautiful and fresh as always. Her childlike naiveté was what was most touching about her. She was more than willing to forgive her sister for her appalling behavior. "Where are we having lunch?" she said sweetly, and smiled at them both. The last thing Kate wanted was to have lunch, but she knew she had to now. She needed to do something to make up for her outburst.

They left the studio after they placed the order for the dress, and Kezia reassured Felicity ten times that it was not disrespectful to the people who had died in the Enforcers' attack on the Fourth of July.

They went to Harry Cipriani at the Sherry-Netherland hotel for lunch, which was fortunately loud enough that it was impossible to broach any serious subject. Kate looked morbidly depressed and barely ate. Kezia tried to calm down and picked at a salad, and Felicity attempted to keep everyone happy, and said that Blake's son would be arriving soon and that they were excited about it.

After lunch, Felicity and Kezia went to Cartier for a final check of the invitations. Today was their wedding errand day, and Kate left them and went home to her apartment.

Jack was working on his essay for *The New Yorker* when she walked in, and Kate collapsed on the couch and looked at him. Sometimes when she did, he looked like a stranger to her. She thought of John Stewart asking if she loved him. Right now, she was not so sure, and there was never a simple answer to that question, and she knew there should be.

"What have you been up to?" he asked her casually.

"Buying wedding dresses," she said simply.

"For our wedding?" He looked instantly panicked.

"No. Felicity's. And I lost my shit at my sister and went nuts because I'm so stressed about us. If you don't want to get married, don't. But don't jerk me around, tell me we're engaged, and then refuse to pick a date or buy me even a token engagement ring."

"You know I can't afford one."

"I don't care if it's wood or plastic. It's a symbol."

"Of something I don't believe in, and you never did either, and now every time I see you for five minutes you want to pin me down for a wedding date."

"I don't want to pin you down, or drag you, or force you. If you don't want to marry me, then don't, and say so."

"I don't want to," he said grudgingly, "but I will if you insist, and if it's a prerequisite."

"For what? Your easy life at my expense?"

"The life of a writer is never easy," he said grandly.

"Then write something, so you have an excuse, and stop complaining about it. If you don't love me, then why are you with me?"

"I love you. That doesn't mean I have to marry you," he said stubbornly.

"No, you don't. And I don't either. It seems like it was a bad idea."

"I agree," he said, looking relieved, not understanding the implications of what he had just said, or the possible end result. She was beginning to realize that John Stewart might be right. Maybe the whole last four years had been a bad idea, and she had refused to face it. "We get along, and we're good companions, when you're not acting crazy about a wedding. We could have a very pleasant old age together." What he said was so pathetic it was laughable. She left the room so she didn't have to answer him. He was his own worst enemy, and she had some serious thinking to do. The last four years had suddenly become an affront to her dignity, her heart, and her self-esteem.

When she came out of her office several hours later, he was gone. He had tutoring, and he didn't come home until she was asleep. And he had left the apartment when she got up in the morning. She was relieved not to see him.

She tried to put a brave face on it when she met John for dinner that night, but he saw right through it.

"Wow, how are you?" he asked when she met him at the restaurant. She was happy to see him, but her spirits were in the tank and he could see that she was upset. He looked much better than he had at lunch the day after he broke up with Caroline. He'd been looking forward to dinner. They ordered wine and he waited for Kate to tell him what was going on. They had somehow inadvertently become confidantes. She felt comfortable telling him anything and being herself with him.

"I think I'm losing my mind," she said after the first sip of wine.

"How so?" He was happy to see her, no matter how down she was.

"I went berserk at my sister yesterday and launched a nuclear attack on her when we went to try on wedding gowns."

"Yours too?" he asked.

"No, hers. She looked incredible and I had some kind of jealous fit and was a total shit to her, and she's the last person who I should do that to. She's sweet to everyone. She forgave me, but I didn't deserve it. And I think you were right about the last four years. I don't know what the hell I was thinking. Jack and I had a huge fight about the wedding again. He doesn't want to get married, he never did. I think I forced him. I'm not even sure why. Maybe I thought if we got married, it would turn us into a couple, which we're not. He sees us as companions for our golden years. He doesn't want to get married, and I don't either now. I don't know what I'll tell my mother. This whole relationship has been a huge mistake since the beginning. I think I was just lonely and wanted someone to talk to, so I paid his bills. I don't think we even like each other. I always felt lesser than because

Felicity is so spectacular, and my birth father abandoned me. Now I feel better about myself, and it's like waking up and wondering what the hell I'm doing here. And even more to the point, what the hell is *he* doing here?"

"At least you're waking up," John said calmly.

"And I've wasted four years of my life. I'm thirty-seven years old and I'm living with a loser who won't even marry me."

"Thank your lucky stars for that," he said.

"I was never sure I wanted to get married anyway, but all of a sudden it matters, and I'm feeling old, and it's ridiculous that he wants to say we're engaged but doesn't want to get married."

To tease her, John made a point of looking at her hand to make sure there was no ring. "Ah, I see he hasn't made it to Tiffany yet."

"I just feel stupid. This should have ended years ago, or never started."

"That's how I felt about Caroline," John said.

"Is she still contacting you?" Kate asked after they ordered dinner.

"Only the occasional nasty text. They're shorter than her emails." Kate laughed.

They talked about other things then, and she felt better being out and having dinner with him. He was so easy to talk to, and they got along so well. Everything wasn't all about him, and he was interested in the book she was writing.

Halfway through dinner, he asked her if she knew what was happening between his father and her mother.

"She doesn't talk to me about it," Kate said. "I think they're a little bit like kids with a crush on each other."

"My father is very private about his life," John said. They talked about his job investing for his clients, which sounded interesting and busy. He had a lot of responsibility for someone his age. Kate was four years older than he was, but at times he was very mature in his view of life. He said his father was his best friend, and she envied him that. She explained to him about her birth father, and the impact being rejected at birth had always had on her, and that meeting him had been interesting but somewhat disappointing. He had dedicated his life to good causes, but he wasn't a warm person, had few, if any, regrets about abandoning her, and had never reached out. She had a deeper appreciation for her adoptive father now, having met her birth father. And she was close to her mother, but not as close as John was to Sam.

Kate realized now that her life had been dominated by Jack for four years. She wondered if he had even stifled her writing, insisting that they go to every workshop. She'd been tired of them for the past two years, and the book she was working on was going well.

The evening went by too quickly, and at the end of the meal, he asked her what she was going to do now.

"About Jack?"

He nodded.

"He made himself pretty clear last night. It's not what I want. Married or not. I have to tell him. I feel more like his landlady than his girlfriend. I'm tired of bolstering him and propping him up about his talent, and burying mine, if I have any. I'd like to find out. What are you going to do without Caroline?"

"I have some ideas," he said vaguely. "I need to be more careful. Women like her are dangerous. They have high, unrealistic expectations, and they don't let go easily. I felt trapped most of the time I was with her. I dodged a bullet by not letting her move in with me. I thought I could keep the situation under control, but that's risky. She was always fighting for more ground, ignoring what I said, and overrunning my boundaries."

"I have to talk to Jack. It's funny, our pseudo engagement is what finally broke our relationship."

"So you're not engaged anymore?" he asked her with a smile, and she held up her naked hand in answer.

"I guess I never was."

"That's good news," he said, and she wondered what he meant by that. "And then what?"

Danielle Steel

"I breathe, I write, Felicity invited me to visit them in the Hamptons. Blake's little boy will be with them in August."

"Can I go with you sometime, for the day, I mean?" he said cautiously, and she laughed.

"I'd like that, 'for the day.' Of course. You can bring your new girlfriend, when you find one." She had a feeling it wouldn't take him long. He was very attractive and fun to be with.

"Would you ever go out with me?" he asked her, feeling like a teenager when he did, and she looked confused for a minute.

"You mean as a date?"

"Yeah, I would have asked you out if you weren't engaged to Jack when I met you."

"You would not." She laughed at him. "Your eyes almost fell out of your head when you saw Felicity. I saw you."

"That's just window shopping. Besides, she really is engaged and she's crazy about Blake."

"Yes, she is. I thought at first that she's too young to get married, but they're good together, and he takes care of her and protects her."

"It's not about age, it's about how you are together. I had fun with you that day," he said, remembering their day at the beach.

"I'm too old for you," she said, and brushed off his

252

suggestion, although she thought he was very appealing. But she didn't think it was an option. "I'm four years older than you are. You need someone younger."

"No, I don't. Young girls bore me. I want a grownup in my life. But not one who's trying to take over my life. Four years is nothing. And, besides, we're practically related. Our parents are dating each other," John said to her.

"We don't know that for sure, we're guessing. They like each other."

"I like you too," John said openly, "if you get rid of that creep you're not engaged to."

"Good to know," she said as they left the table and walked out of the restaurant. They walked slowly in the direction of her apartment, which wasn't far. They stood outside her building for a few minutes. She was thinking about what he had said to her and wondering if he was serious.

"I am," he said, reading her mind. He could see on her face what she was thinking. "I meant what I said," he told her, and brushed her lips with his when he said good night. It was almost a kiss, but not quite. She let herself into the building then, and waved as the door closed, wondering what she had just done. She had almost let him kiss her. She would never have let him do that if she was still in love with Jack. Whatever happened now, or didn't, she knew she had to end it with Jack. It was over, and had been for a long time.

She just hadn't wanted to face it. She didn't even feel sad at the thought of breaking up with him.

She let herself into the apartment and was surprised to see him sitting on the couch, with a drink in his hand, watching TV.

"What are you doing here?" she asked him.

"Where were you?" he asked her, his eyes still on the TV screen.

"Out. We have to talk." She sat down on the couch next to him, and he glanced at her.

"My last student canceled so I came home," he explained, and she realized that he never kissed her hello or goodbye anymore, and hadn't in a long time. They hadn't made love in a couple of months. He wrote at night, and she was an early riser, so the time they spent in bed together, they were usually both sleeping.

"You need to move out," she said in a soft voice.

"Why? Because I don't want to marry you? Is this a ploy to force my hand?" He looked amused as he said it. He didn't take her seriously, but she meant it.

"It's not a ploy. I don't want to force your hand. I just think we're done. There's not enough in this relationship to keep us together."

"Are you that desperate to be married?" He looked surprised, but not very upset.

"Desperate? No. If I want kids, I should think about it. You hate the idea of marriage. If you don't want to get married at forty-two, I think it's a safe bet you never will. There's no glue in this relationship to keep us together. We can't go to writing workshops forever. You need to move out," she said calmly, and he looked at her. It finally dawned on him that she was serious.

"I can't move out. I can't afford an apartment."

"That's not a reason to stay here. You don't love me, and I don't think I love you anymore." She tried to keep it as low-key as possible, she didn't want to fight with him.

"I do love you, and you can't just kick me out because I didn't buy you an engagement ring."

"You told me last night that you didn't want to get married and I was forcing you. I'm not forcing you, and the door is open. We're done, or at least I am." He had pushed her too far and presumed too much.

"Okay, so I'll marry you," he said grudgingly.

"That's no longer an option," she said clearly. "Find a place to stay. You can't stay here. I'm sorry." She got up and walked into her bedroom. He was sitting on the couch, staring at the TV in shock. He called after her.

"And how am I supposed to pay rent?"

"You paid rent before you met me, you can do it again. Get a job, tutor more students, teach some workshops."

"What about my writing?" He was incensed.

"You'll figure it out." He had taken without giving back, and it had taken her four years to notice how little she was getting from him, and the last straw was that he barely wanted to be engaged and didn't love her enough to marry her. That said it all. Except if it meant losing free rent. She came out of her bedroom in her pajamas and looked at him.

"I'll sleep in my office tonight. You need to find someplace else to stay tomorrow. You can pack your things next week when I'm out, when the cleaner is here." He stood up and stared at her then. The entire procedure had been bloodless, but he could see that she meant every word.

"Why are you being such a bitch to me?"

"I'm tired of you taking advantage of me, and not appreciating me. You've had a free ride, in every possible way, for a long time. I'm done." She walked into her office and locked the door. There was a small settee she could sleep on, but she wasn't willing to share her apartment with him after that night. She knew that he had friends he could stay with. She didn't feel sorry for him. He approached her office door and spoke to her through the door.

"Will you pay my rent?" he asked her as she shook her head.

"No, I won't," she called back to him.

"I'm still willing to marry you," he answered back, but he forgot to say "I love you."

"I'm not willing to marry you. Good night, Jack," she said, and heard him walk away a minute later, and then she heard her bedroom door slam.

The next morning when she got up, she saw that he had packed a bag, one of her suitcases. But she'd rather lose a bag than her freedom or her life. She knew she had made the right decision, just as John Stewart had with Caroline. Some people just didn't deserve to be in one's life. They were takers, not givers.

She hung around to make sure he didn't take anything else when he left. His sense of entitlement knew no bounds. He was gone by eleven o'clock that morning. He didn't tell her where he went and she didn't ask him. He didn't say goodbye, say he was sorry, or tell her he loved her. She knew now that he didn't. She was a convenience in his life, a bank and nothing more.

She had the locks changed that afternoon, so he couldn't let himself in, or get in when she was out. She went for a long walk that afternoon and felt proud of what she'd done. She didn't think she'd miss him, but if she did, she knew she'd get over it. Four years had gone down the tubes, but better four than ten or twenty, or the rest of her life.

Chapter 13

Sam had found a little hotel on Long Island, next to a long white sandy beach. There were four rooms in the hotel and they served no meals. He made the reservation under another name he used when he traveled, and he was wearing a baseball cap and dark glasses when they checked in. There was total privacy and they didn't see anyone else at the hotel. They must have been out, she thought to herself. There were enough restaurants in the vicinity that they could go out to eat. It wasn't luxurious, but he had wanted them to have the time alone without the world or fans or paparazzi intruding on them. So he chose a small, remote, little-known hotel.

Kezia was wearing a big floppy straw hat when they checked in. Sam apologized for the lack of luxury, but it was the only way for them to be anonymous. Even if he had rented a house for them, in the end someone would have found out. This way, only he and Kezia knew. And they weren't even far from home. They were just outside New York. It had taken them an hour and a half to get there.

As soon as they dropped off their bags and checked in, Sam drove them to the beach. They parked the car and got out and took a long walk down the white sand.

They'd worn bathing suits under their clothes, and they left their shorts and shirts under a rock and went swimming. He'd brought a beach towel, and when they came out of the water, he spread it out and they lay down side by side, lying in the sun and snuggling close to each other. He turned to look at her and kissed her. It was exactly what they'd wanted, and they lay on the towel and dozed, and talked to each other when they woke up.

"This is perfect," she said to him, and he nodded. There were clouds that looked like little cotton balls in the bright blue sky, and when they'd had their fill of the beach, they went back to the room, their skin still warm from the sun. He kissed her again, this time with more passion, and pressed himself against her. He was aching for her, and she for him, and then as though they had always been together, he peeled off her bathing suit and dropped his, and they climbed into the bed and made love. It was exactly as they had hoped it would be, as if it had always been, as time and history melted away. He was a passionate, generous lover, and she was overwhelmed with tenderness for him. Afterward they lay spent and smiled at each other.

"I love you," she whispered to him, and he pressed her against him and wanted her again, and they made love for a second time.

"I love you more than I can tell you," he whispered, and ran his fingers down her body, and they fell asleep and woke up at eight o'clock that night.

He held her again before they got out of bed. "Are you hungry?" she whispered to him.

"Starving," he answered, and she laughed.

They showered together in the small bathroom and got dressed. She loved the fact that they hadn't tried to hide in some big, luxurious hotel. This was their own private world for the next two days. It was a solemn ritual between them, and the beginning of a new adventure.

The first restaurant they found was a hamburger joint with a bar and a pool table. The hamburgers were delicious, and Sam felt better after he'd eaten.

"What are we going to say to our children?" she asked him as they shared a basket of French fries.

"Do we have to say anything? They'll figure it out eventually. Unless you want to tell your daughters. I've never had to say anything to John. There's been nothing to say until now. We talk about his love affairs, not mine." He smiled at her and leaned over to kiss her. "You are amazing!" he whispered to her, and she looked shy.

"You're pretty amazing yourself," she whispered back. It was still odd to think that he was a movie star and he was in love with her, when he could have had any woman in the world.

They went to bed early that night and woke up early in the morning. They went for a long walk on the beach before breakfast at a coffee shop. The town looked like a throwback to the 1950s, when it had probably been popular with summer residents, and had been somewhat forgotten in the years since then.

Their two days there were magical, and they were sorry to leave. They had made precious memories together.

When they got back to her apartment, he grinned at her as he carried her suitcase in for her. "If you'll forgive me for asking, your place or mine?" She laughed.

"Whatever you prefer. Maybe yours. You have furniture, I don't, but you can send me home anytime you want."

"I want to wake up in the morning with you," he said. She loved that idea. And there was a locked door between their two apartments, in the hall. Sam had the maintenance crew come up and unlock it, and he opened the door and blocked it open. "Now we can go back and forth without climbing through the hedge." The door had been put there in case someone bought both apartments and joined them as a single penthouse. Sam had already bought his when she bought hers.

They spent the night at home in his supremely comfortable bedroom. They had a giant screen to watch movies, and comfortable furniture to lounge on. She dressed in her own apartment and kept her clothes there. They each had double the space they had before.

"It'll be fun when my furniture comes," she said, looking around. "We can really spread out then and entertain on whichever side we want." Her furniture was more formal, and his was more relaxed. The combined apartment served all their needs, more like a house.

"If I ever come home and find the door locked between the two apartments, I'll know I'm in trouble," he said, and she couldn't imagine that happening.

Kate called her that night, and Kezia was lying on Sam's bed while she talked to her, thinking that it was a good thing they weren't using FaceTime, or Kate would have seen immediately what was happening. She liked Sam's idea of letting their relationship "emerge gently," rather than announcing their unofficial union and possibly dealing with a reaction. They had no set plans for the future. They just wanted to live it and see how it all worked. This was new territory for both of them after long first marriages. There would inevitably be things to adjust to that they couldn't foresee now, but hopefully not too many. They had an unusually harmonious relationship, and were both easygoing. And it was fun being together. Adding sex to the mix had made things even better, more so than they had expected or hoped for with new partners. It added another layer to the relationship, and greater depth.

When Kate called her mother, Kezia had just gotten out of the shower and was wearing Sam's bathrobe. He was lying next to her, looking intolerably sexy.

"I just wanted to let you know, Mom, there's been a change," Kate said to her. All of Jack's things were gone by then. He had picked them up when Kate was out and the cleaning person was there. Kate had made a point of being gone so she didn't have to see him. She didn't feel ready to do that yet, and he was still furious at being made to leave the apartment. He said he was living on a friend's couch, which didn't change her mind.

"Have you two finally figured out a date or a venue?" Kezia said, feeling relaxed about it after the heavenly two days she and Sam had just spent together. She was determined not to be upset by anything Kate told her.

"Actually, no," Kate said just as calmly. "There isn't going to be a wedding. We broke up this week. I'm fine. I just wanted to let you know, so you don't need to stress about the wedding. There won't be one."

Kezia frowned as she listened. "Darling, I'm sorry. Are you very upset?" She didn't like Jack, but four years was a long time, and it was going to be a big change for Kate. Kezia wondered which one of them had pulled the plug on the relationship, but didn't ask. "I hope it wasn't too traumatic, nor dramatic."

"It wasn't, for me anyway. I just realized that it's been wrong for a long time and I didn't want to face it. I guess I didn't want to be alone, or admit I made a mistake way back at the beginning. We never had the same goals. I thought we did, because of the writing, but the rest was too different. I put all the effort in, he didn't. And he really didn't want to get married. It wasn't my intention, but I forced his hand, and it's better to know that now. I don't think he would ever have decided on a date or a place." Kezia was surprised how tranquil Kate sounded about it. It had obviously been the right decision.

"Did he give you a hard time about it? There was no violence?"

"No, Mom, of course not, he's not crazy. He wasn't happy, because he doesn't like paying rent, but he had three years of a free ride. I figured that was enough."

"I think you made the right decision," Kezia said, enormously relieved.

"I know you never liked him. I kind of missed the signs of when to jump off, but it was the right decision for me now."

"You're very brave and very smart. Some people stick with the wrong decision all their life. This way you can meet the right person one day, and marry and have kids, if that's what you want. Or not, if you don't."

"It's a little late now, at thirty-seven."

"No, it's not," Kezia said firmly. "You have time to meet 'the one,' and even have a family. It's never too late to find the right person, and certainly not at your age." It made Kezia think of Paige, who had waited even longer and was still with the wrong man.

"Anyway, I'm proud of you, I know it can't have been easy."

"It was easier than I thought it would be. It was the right thing. If you don't mind, don't tell Felicity, I'll tell her myself. But I wanted you to know first, so you don't worry about the wedding. This way, you only have Felicity's to deal with."

"And next time, it will be you. You still have to pick a maid-of-honor dress, by the way. I'm sorry to bring that up now, if the subject is painful."

"It isn't. I think I was lucky to escape." Kate was echoing

John Stewart's words, but she thought they were true and John was right.

She hadn't told him yet. She wanted to tell her mother first. "I'll tell Felicity in the next couple of days, and then you two can gossip all you want." She laughed. There was nothing her family liked more than a good gossip.

"Of course," Kezia reassured her. "It's up to you when you tell her. Thank you for telling me." They hung up a minute later and Sam raised an eyebrow.

"What was that about?"

"Kate broke up with Jack. The engagement is canceled, and he moved out."

He gave her a knowing look. "I know you're pleased." She had complained a lot about him, and Sam agreed.

"I'm happy he's out of her life because I think he was the wrong guy, but I'm sad for her if she's upset or hurting. She sounded pretty good actually. I'm surprised. Well, at least the rest of us won't have to put up with him anymore," she said. But she felt sorry for Kate, if she had loved him.

"I wonder if my son had anything to do with this," he said with a mysterious expression. "Do you remember, I predicted that John would have her 'fiancé' on the run by Labor Day? Maybe I'm right."

"I doubt it. Kate and John hardly know each other. They only met that once at Felicity's house in the Hamptons."

"You never know, they may have been seeing each other since then. He had a strange light in his eye when he met her, after their walk on the beach."

"Would John tell you if he's been seeing her?" Kezia asked him, curious now too.

"Maybe, but I doubt it. If it's just a casual fling, he would. But if it's anything serious, he'd keep it to himself till he's sure."

"I think my girls work on that theory too. At these ages, they don't like telling us too much." She smiled at him then. "It's kind of fun having kids the same age. We'll have to do another picnic day. Maybe Felicity will invite us all again."

"If she does, then they'll know about us for sure. You can't hide happiness. Will they mind?"

"No, they'll be happy for me. But I don't think I would tell them right away. It's still a little soon, and I am their mother after all. I have to at least pretend to have morals and decorum."

"Morals, yes. But decorum after the past two days would really be too bad," he teased her, and slipped a hand into the bathrobe she was wearing. He kissed her and pulled off the robe gently, and they made love again.

After Kate told her mother about the breakup, she decided to call and tell Felicity. She was relieved too.

"I hope you meet a good one now." It was more than a little disconcerting how happy her family was that Jack was gone. Both her mother and sister could barely conceal their relief and delight.

And after that, Kate made a clean sweep of it and texted John. She wrote him simply, "Done. He moved out. I'm a free woman." It wasn't an invitation, just an announcement. She knew he'd be relieved for her too. Her phone rang two minutes later. It was John.

"Congratulations! Do you want to come out and celebrate, or are you in deep mourning?"

"Neither one. It is what it is. A mistake I made that has now been corrected."

"I salute your excellent correction. Was it very bad?"

"My mother wanted to know if it was violent." She laughed.

"Was it? Did he go nuts?"

"No, it was all very civil. He was pissed because it's the end of free rent for him from me. He's staying on someone's couch."

"I can't think of a better place for him."

"Unfortunately, neither can I. It was long overdue. You helped me to make the decision. And now I have to start all over again. Like the game of Chutes and Ladders. I go all the way back to the beginning."

"Try not to be too sad. You did the right thing. I'm proud of you, Kate."

"Me too," she said. They hung up and she turned on the TV. She was watching a show when the buzzer from downstairs rang, and she went to the intercom to answer it. The voice said there was a delivery of a package for her. She buzzed them in and went to the door to collect the package and saw John bounding up the stairs, with a bottle of champagne in one hand. She grinned when she saw him.

"What are you doing here?" she asked him, as he came through the front door and kissed her on the cheek.

"I figured you could use some champagne to cheer you up." But she didn't look upset to him. She looked surprisingly well. "I can always drink it if you don't want it." He followed her into the kitchen, where she got two champagne glasses out, and he poured the already chilled champagne into them. She took a sip, and it was very fine champagne and delicious. He looked serious for a minute. "I know it's incredibly rude of me to just show up, but I wanted to make sure you're okay. You actually look pretty good." Her bookshelves were half empty, Jack had taken all his books. The wall was bare where he took a painting he owned, which she didn't like anyway, and she wanted to move some things around, but she looked relaxed and pretty in jeans and a white blouse, and he sat down to drink the champagne with her. "I won't stay long," he promised, but he was happy to see her. And he had her laughing at his stories with the second glass. She relaxed and told him that it was strange that, after four years, she didn't even miss Jack, and she had no regrets.

"My mother and sister must be dancing in the streets tonight. You know, it's weird, all my life I've wanted to meet my birth father. I had all these illusions about him, about what a cool guy he must be. And I finally met him, and he wasn't. He's smart and dedicated, and doing good things with his work in Africa, but he seemed like a very selfish guy. Seeing him changed something for me. When I got back, I started writing again, better than I have before. All the bullshit I put up with from Jack didn't seem tolerable anymore. I realized that I deserved better, from my father, from Jack, from any man in my life. What I got from them just wasn't good enough. I'm glad I went to Africa, it freed me, and gave me self-confidence to expect more from the men in my life. It was kind of an epiphany," she said, as she poured herself a third glass. And John poured himself a third too, which emptied the bottle.

"I felt that way about Caroline too. I was tired of the takers and the schemers and women who expect everything and give nothing back." He looked at her when he said it and leaned over and kissed her. It seemed like the most natural thing in the world as she put her arms around him and he gently felt under her blouse. They forgot the champagne and devoured each other like two starving people, desperate for connection and tenderness, and love. They made love on the couch and in her bed, with a passion that neither of them had felt before, and when it was over they were entwined tightly and clung to each other.

"Oh my God," he moaned, "Kate, I'm sorry, I've wanted you so badly ever since the day I met you . . . I'm sorry . . . are you mad at me?" He was hoarse with desire for her, and nothing would sate him except more of her.

"Desperately . . . I'm furious with you." She kissed him and matched his passion with her own. And afterward, still holding each other, they fell sound asleep. They stayed that way, wrapped together closely, until the sun woke them the next day. Their faces were inches apart as John looked at her. He had a headache, but he didn't care. The night he had spent with her was unforgettable and worth whatever he had to suffer for it now. He didn't want her to have regrets.

"I think I have a brain tumor," she whispered.

"It's the champagne," he whispered back. "I didn't mean to take advantage of you. I was just going to drink the champagne with you and leave, but I couldn't once I saw you."

"I wouldn't have let you leave. I wanted you too," she admitted. And they made love again before they left her bed.

"I think I'm addicted to you," he said afterward, trying to

catch his breath. She was breathless too. They finally made it out of bed, she made coffee, and they had something to eat, and he stood looking at her, naked in her kitchen. She was beautiful and totally at ease with him. "I'm so glad you broke up with him."

"Yeah. Me too." She grinned. She looked around, her body as spectacular as his, in all her naked splendor. He couldn't take his eyes off her. "I hate this apartment. I think I want to move."

"You can move in with me," he said.

"It's a little soon, don't you think? Maybe in a while."

"We'd never get out of bed. I might have to give up my job."

"Good idea," she said, and they kissed again. They spent the day discovering each other, it was a weekend and they had time, and then went for a walk in Central Park. It was too depressing staying downtown, in plain view of the mangled buildings from the July Fourth attack. Uptown, everything looked normal, the park was green, and children were playing while their parents watched. The world looked bright and new. They stopped walking and he put his arms around her and kissed her and felt like the luckiest man in the world. She suddenly had everything she wanted, and a man she knew she could love. All she'd had to do was let go of the wrong one, and the right one walked into her life.

Chapter 14

Six weeks after the Enforcers' savage attack on New York, there was a midnight candlelight memorial mass at Saint Patrick's Cathedral on Fifth Avenue. All of Fifth Avenue was blocked off and two million people attended, with those who couldn't fit into the cathedral holding candles outside. People filled the streets from Fifty-seventh Street all the way downtown to the Washington Square Arch. There had never been anything like it. There was a healing quality to it, as people sang and hugged each other. The hymns from the mass were amplified outside and two million people sang "Amazing Grace" and listened to Beethoven's "Ode to Joy" and "We Shall Overcome" sung by a gospel choir from Harlem. Mariah Carey sang the national anthem, and Barbra

Streisand "America the Beautiful." A Broadway cast sang "New York, New York."

Kezia had never been as moved in her life as she clung to Sam's hand, and he put an arm around her and held her tight. Their love had been born on the worst night the country had ever known, and something beautiful had come from it. People cried and sang, and the names of the dead were read. There were battalions of firefighters and police in formation on the street with other first responders. In their hearts, they each vowed to rebuild the city and remember the dead. The archbishop reminded them all that love was the answer to death and pain and suffering, and that every person who had died was in the arms of God now, smiling down at them, and that it was their mission now to rebuild and heal the city as a shining beacon of love that no one could destroy. He spoke of resurrection and rebirth in the time of sorrow. And everyone there that night came away uplifted and filled with the hope of better days ahead. Sam looked down at Kezia. Tears ran down their cheeks as they remembered that night and held hands.

"I love you so much," he said to her as he held her.

"I love you too," she said, thinking of the first time she saw him peeking through the hedge. So much had happened since then, all good things after such terrible ones. And they had both found a new life they had never expected to find, and new love, not to replace the loves they had known before, but to lead them on a new path and honor the old one.

They left the crowd on Fifth Avenue at three in the morning, and walked home. At least half the crowd stayed until sunrise, and visited the church in orderly lines to light candles for the dead and injured. It was an incredible night, and Sam and Kezia fell into bed exhausted but feeling blessed by what they'd experienced.

They woke up late, and Kezia made breakfast while they talked about the night before. It had been extraordinary. Kezia hoped that someone had recorded the music. She had never heard anything like it. The whole night had been uplifting and part of the healing process.

"You know, I was thinking. We used to go to a dude ranch in Wyoming when Johnny was a little kid. It's a beautiful, peaceful place, and after all this trauma, I'd love to go with you. I haven't been in a long time. It's very comfortable. Do you like to ride?" he asked her.

"I do."

"You don't have to if you don't want to. You can fish or hike, or just relax. It's at the foot of the Grand Tetons. I have to start preproduction on a film in September, and I know you want to be here when all your furniture comes at the end of the month. But we've got a couple of weeks now. Why don't we just get away, it will be a good balance to all the trauma of the summer and get us ready for the fall."

"I'd love that," Kezia said, enjoying too how thoughtful he was. It sounded like just what they needed. It had been a deeply emotional six weeks that had jarred them all. And they were lucky enough to be able to get away. Felicity and Blake and Alex were living a healthy beach life in the Hamptons, and Kate was planning to spend some time with them.

"I'll have my assistant set it up tomorrow," Sam said. It sounded heavenly to Kezia. New York was struggling to its feet again, but there was a tension in the city, a residue of fear, and there were so many broken hearts, it was impossible to get away from it completely while in the city. The dude ranch sounded like an ideal respite before they got busy in September. Kezia was waiting to hear any day if she had been accepted into the refresher nursing course at NYU for late September. They had a rolling enrollment so you could apply at any time.

The next day, Sam told her it was all arranged. They were leaving in two days, and staying at the ranch for nine days. She'd be back just in time to receive all her new and old goods for the apartment.

She packed that night and bought a few things the next

day. The night before she left, she called both her daughters. She never went away without telling them where she was going and how to reach her in an emergency if they couldn't get hold of her on her cellphone.

She called Felicity in the Hamptons. She had just gotten back from the beach with Blake and Alex. They'd been building sandcastles. Kezia told her simply that she was going away. She could have done it by text or email, but she thought that this time it might need some explanation.

Sam wasn't worried about John. He said his assistant could always find him if his son had a problem or needed something.

"A dude ranch?" Felicity sounded surprised. "That sounds like fun. What made you think of that?"

"I figured a quick vacation would do me good before the installation."

"How did you find out about the ranch?" Felicity could easily imagine her mother going to Paris, London, or the south of France, but not a dude ranch.

"Sam has been there before. I'm going with him," Kezia said serenely, expecting a reaction, but there was none. Felicity was so open and easy it didn't occur to her to challenge her mother, question it, or object. She respected her too much to do so.

"That sounds like a great plan, Mom, thanks for letting

me know." Kezia said she'd text her the information. "And, Mom," Felicity added, "I'm happy for you. Have a great time."

"Thank you, darling. Take care. I'll see you in a couple of weeks."

"Don't forget Labor Day weekend with us out here. And of course, Sam too." They had accepted him with ease into their midst. Kezia was grateful for that. It would have been painful if they objected for some reason, or didn't like him. He was hard not to like, and he liked them too.

She called Kate next and gave her the same information, and Kate hesitated for an instant before she reacted. "That's pretty cool, Mom. And different for you. Is it serious with Sam?"

"I think so. It seems that way. It's been a wonderful thing for both of us, an unexpected gift. I guess it's never too late to find happiness again after all," she said, and Kate laughed. She sounded happy too. And Kezia was glad. She'd been worried about her after the recent breakup with Jack.

"I think you're right," Kate said easily. "Have a great time, Mom. See you at Felicity's for Labor Day."

"I'll be at the apartment before that, setting everything up, if you're around."

"I'm going up to Vermont for a few days. I'm putting the cabin on the market. The place always depressed me, and it's too small. Jack loved it, I didn't. I want to get rid of it."

"That sounds like a good idea. See you in the Hamptons, then." The conversation had been peaceful and easy.

She had just hung up after speaking with Kate, marveling at how accepting her daughters were of Sam, when the doorman called her and asked if Paige Robbins could come up. She and Sam were leaving the next day at dawn.

She hadn't seen Paige since their lunch.

"I came to say goodbye," Paige said, smiling warmly as Kezia asked her to come in. Sam was in his own apartment, looking for an extra pair of cowboy boots he couldn't find.

"How did you know we're leaving?" Kezia said, surprised. She hadn't even been able to tell Louise about the trip. She was in India for a month, on a shoot. "We're going to Wyoming tomorrow." Paige looked startled.

"Actually, I came to say goodbye because I'm leaving. I'm moving out of the building tomorrow," she said with a meaningful look. "You inspired me, after our lunch. It's time."

"Is Greg still away?" Kezia asked her, and Paige nodded. She looked serious, but calm.

"I'm moving out while he's gone. I should have done it a long time ago. I rented a small apartment downtown. I'll get it set up when I come back. And I'm spending two weeks in Portofino and Capri. I've never done a trip like that by myself. It's time for a new chapter, as you said, Kezia. You were right. I'll see you when I get back. Let's do lunch again. And have a great time in Wyoming." They hugged each other, and Kezia was proud of her. She knew how hard it must be after five years to finally give up on Greg and move on. She hoped Paige stuck with it when she got back. But moving out of the apartment was a big step. And the trip to Italy would be fun for her.

Paige left a minute later, and Kezia went to pack her toiletries.

"Found them!" Sam said victoriously, holding up a pair of ancient, battered cowboy boots. "I've had them since I was nineteen and worked on a ranch one summer."

"They're gorgeous," she said. She had riding boots, but they were on a truck heading east with all her other belongings, and she was planning to buy a pair of cowboy boots in Wyoming.

She told him about Paige then, that she was moving out of Greg's apartment.

"That's a good thing," Sam said. "She needs to get away from him. Have you heard from Louise, by the way?"

"I got a postcard from her a few days ago. She sounds fine." She was truly amazing, working and traveling around the world at eighty-nine.

They left first thing the next morning, and got to the ranch in the early afternoon with the time difference. It was as beautiful as Sam had said, with the majestic Grand Tetons towering over them. They had their own cabin. The ranch was subtly luxurious, but rustic enough in appearance to be charming. There was a large staff to attend to the guests. The morning after Kezia and Sam arrived, they went on a sunrise ride, on two solid, steadfast horses that were easy to ride and sure-footed. Their guide took them on beautiful trails, past shimmering lakes and fields of wildflowers.

It was a romantic interlude and a rest they both needed. It was almost like a honeymoon. Kezia and Sam spent peaceful hours together, reading, fishing, hiking, and swimming in a lake, and they rode every day. The trauma that they had experienced in New York seemed remote, in the wholesome atmosphere of the ranch. It was everything Sam had promised and more. They were sad to leave at the end of nine days, but they both had work to do when they got home.

"Thank you for a beautiful trip," she said to him on the flight home. "I'd love to go there again."

"We can go back any time you want," he promised.

Their open-door policy at home between the two apartments worked wonderfully. She had all her belongings in her apartment, and he had his on his side, but they circulated freely between the two as though it was one exceptionally big one, and she loved watching movies on the huge screen in his bedroom. They spent most nights in his bed, and were happy together.

Two days after they got back from Wyoming, the trucks arrived with all her belongings. Her wardrobe, furniture, and art, and boxes of small treasures, files, and papers. All of her new upholstered furniture was delivered, and everything she'd bought. Chandeliers, sconces, light fixtures, new kitchen equipment, rugs. An army of installers arrived, the curtain hangers, the decorator with her fleet of assistants. They filled her apartment with bodies, boxes, drills, ladders. Kezia stood back to watch the constant activity. The rugs were already down when Sam came to observe it with her. The component parts were very elegant, and dressier than his more casual, masculine, mostly black-and-white and very sleek Italian leather furniture. The theme of his living room was modern. Her living room was a nice counterpoint, more feminine, and it suited her, and when the curtains were up, they looked fabulous. The art went up last, and he liked most of it. Her bedroom furniture and curtains came from her old house, and were fine antiques and extremely elegant. Oddly, the two apartments provided contrast and added depth to each other, just as Kezia and Sam did. Together, it was even more of a showplace than either one alone.

It took three days to install everything with an enormous crew, and on the Friday night of Labor Day weekend, Kezia stood back and was thrilled with the result, and Sam came to admire it with her. Her apartment looked truly gorgeous.

"Wow, you did a fantastic job," he said to her. He had watched her direct where to hang every painting, had placed every object herself, moved furniture around, changed the angle of things to make the groups more inviting. She had a knack for decorating, and her constant eye on it and good taste had brought about a fantastic result. Even the decorator and the installers were impressed, and so was Sam.

"I can't wait to entertain here," she said happily. "We should give a dinner party in the fall." Her acceptance to NYU had been confirmed while they were in Wyoming. She was starting a six-month course at the beginning of October, and after that she wanted to join a practice part-time as a nurse practitioner. He was very proud of her. And he was in the process of overseeing two new scripts and starting preproduction on a film. They were both going to have a lot to do in September, but the life they were sharing now added joy to every project they did, every plan, every moment they spent together.

They left for Southampton on Saturday morning, after Kezia stood quietly and admired the apartment again before they left. Sam came to put an arm around her, and smiled at how pleased she was with the end result. It was fun to do. She loved decorating her home, and she was good at it.

Sam was asking her about her art on the drive out to the Hamptons. He loved collecting art too and had some beautiful pieces by well-known artists, like Robert Indiana and Ed Ruscha.

She was looking forward to spending the weekend with her daughters. And she was eager to see Kate and make sure she was doing well.

Kate had called Felicity the day before and asked if she could bring a friend, and Felicity was such a good sport, she said she could. They had plenty of bedrooms in their big rambling rented house. Kate hadn't told her sister who the friend was, and Felicity was curious about who she was bringing. Obviously not Jack. She hadn't had time to tell her mother that Kate was bringing a guest, but it didn't really matter. They had room, and it would be nice for Kate. Felicity was curious if she had a new man. It was unlikely so soon, but you never knew.

Kezia and Sam arrived before Kate, and it gave her time to catch up with Felicity, who'd been having fun with Alex, and they had a nanny with him. Blake was serving champagne, and Felicity was busy in the kitchen. The men were going to man the barbecue again that night. They'd heard that the security in the city was going to be tremendous, at every monument and federal building, outside hotels and additional iconic buildings, like Rockefeller Center and the Chrysler Building. The entire police force was working, and the National Guard was in evidence. They were taking no chances with the holiday this time, and the Fourth of July would never be the same again.

Everyone was sitting on the deck when Kate arrived in a big silver SUV. Felicity thought the car looked vaguely familiar, but she couldn't see who was driving, and as they arrived with a case of wine, Felicity realized that it was Sam's son, John. Sam spotted him too and caught Kezia's eye. He walked over to her and whispered, "You owe me a hundred dollars! I won the bet. Look who Kate just arrived with."

Kezia turned and saw John and laughed. "Felicity probably invited him for the weekend, and they drove out together so they weren't alone for the ride," Kezia countered.

"Don't try to make excuses. Pay up! Jack got pushed aside and she wound up with my son."

"Very funny!" Kezia was making fun of Sam as Kate and John arrived on the deck. John handed Blake the case of wine and he was delighted. Looking a little sheepish, John put an arm around Kate's shoulders and smiled at the others.

"It's nice to see you all again," John said as Kate giggled and looked very pretty in a pink sundress. She looked young and happy, and so did John. He kept his arm around her shoulders, and it was obvious that they were together, and not as friends. They had that kind of tangible intimacy one sees between couples in love. Kezia looked at Kate in surprise, and then back at Sam in amazement.

"Now, how did you pull that off?" she said to Sam in an undertone the others couldn't hear. She was delighted if he was right.

"I know my son, and I saw the way he looked at her the last time we were all here together. And I'm damn happy not to see him with some little gold digger trying to drag him to the altar or holding him hostage! I'm glad we don't have Caroline with us this time," he whispered.

"Or Jack," Kezia added. Everything had changed in a very short time, in Kezia's life as well, and Sam's.

Felicity whispered to her sister as they went to get a pitcher of iced tea in the kitchen. "Are you with John now?"

Kate smiled at her sister and nodded. "I am."

"How did that happen?"

"We started out as friends and confidantes, after we met here. And then things developed after Jack left. I didn't have any idea it would happen, it just did."

"Are you happy?" Felicity asked her. She couldn't think of a better outcome for both of them, and for their mother with Sam. What had started out as a disastrous summer, steeped in catastrophe and tragedy, had turned out surprisingly well. Felicity was genuinely happy for them.

"I'm divinely happy," Kate answered her question.

John and Kate took a quick walk down the beach before lunch, while the others all talked about what a surprise it was that they had wound up together.

And John and Kate were laughing about it on their walk.

"Well, that went over pretty well," he said, and leaned over and kissed her as the others watched them from the deck, and Kezia handed Sam five twenty-dollar bills from her purse.

"Thank you very much. You're an honest woman."

"I always pay my debts, and this is one bet I'm delighted to lose. I have no idea how it happened, but I'm grateful to the fates that it did. So now we have two Stewart men among us." Kezia beamed at him, and he kissed her.

"You'll find us very hard to get rid of," he said to her.

"I have no intention of trying to get rid of you," she said, and cuddled next to him under his wing, and a few minutes later Kate and John joined them again, and Blake handed them each a glass of champagne, and raised his glass.

"To the amazing, beautiful, and remarkable Hobson women, and the three men who are lucky enough to have them in their lives and love them. Long life, and many years of happiness, and good times for all of us!" They all raised their glasses as John pulled Kate close to him, and Sam and Kezia held hands and smiled at their children.

Danielle Steel

It had been a summer of change, healing, and victory, and
the discovery that it was never too late for dreams to be born
again.

UPSIDE DOWN

Oscar-winning actress Ardith Law is a Hollywood icon. While her long-time partner is away filming, Josh Gray, an actor waiting for his big break, is employed as Ardith's assistant at her Bel Air home. When tragedy strikes, he becomes an invaluable support, stirring up conflicting feelings in Ardith for this younger man.

In New York, Ardith's daughter Morgan is swept off her feet by Ben Ryan, one of the country's most famous TV news reporters. Though two decades her senior, she falls headlong for his charms. But, when a blackmail scheme puts his career – and their relationship – on the line, she doesn't know where to turn.

It's time for both women to find a way to follow their hearts – because finding true happiness with the right partner has nothing to do with age.

Read on for an extract . . .

Chapter 1

The line of limousines snaked down the driveway of the Beverly Hilton hotel at a snail's pace to drop off stars and starlets, producers, directors, ingénues, the famous and the infamous and the unknowns and wannabes, desperate to be seen at one of Hollywood's most glittering annual events, the Golden Globe Awards. The greatly respected award was second only to the Academy Awards. At sixty-two, Ardith Law, one of Hollywood's biggest stars for the past forty years, had won three Golden Globes so far. And she had two of the Academy's coveted Oscars to her credit as well. This was an evening she never missed, as much to pay her respects to her fellow actors as to be seen herself. It was one of those things one had to do. It was expected, and you had to keep your face out there if you wanted to continue to get work, and your face had to look damn good or you'd better not show up!

Ardith was known for the variety and depth of the roles she accepted, and the quality of the movies she starred in. Occasionally, she took a small, unusual part if it intrigued her, which happened from time to time, but as a rule, she only took major starring roles. She was an extraordinary actress with a huge talent and a well-deserved reputation. She was picky about the parts she took. She wanted to be in movies with depth and merit, which weren't always easy to find after a certain age. She looked exceptionally good at sixty-two, was still beautiful, and unlike nearly every actress in Hollywood, she had had no "work" done. She preferred to keep her own natural face and left it to the makeup artists on set to correct whatever needed attention. And she was never afraid to take an important part if it aged her beyond her actual years.

Ardith wanted roles with substance that stretched her to the limits of her abilities. She turned down most of the easy parts. Although, for the past two years, there had been no offers. No one dared to cast her in minor roles, and producers knew that her agent, Joe Ricci, would turn them down before the offers even got to her. But once she turned sixty, there had been no appropriate parts for her. She read scripts constantly, looking for the right roles, but hadn't seen any she wanted to play. Her high standards and perfectionism on set had won her the reputation of being difficult or a diva, which wasn't entirely true. She was an extremely dedicated actress and demanded a lot of herself and everyone she worked with. So now and then, when others fell short, forty years of the best parts available and producers who would do almost anything to keep her happy had led to rare but memorable outbursts that supported the notion that she was a diva. She was above all a consummate professional, and a star to her very core. It wasn't about ego, but more about wanting to be the absolute best she could be in every role, at all times. She hated working with lazy actors, and she hated stupidity and phonies. She was true to herself and her high standards in every way. She was an honest woman, and a great actress more than a diva, no matter what people said who didn't really know her. Her career was vital to her sense of well-being and purpose. She had missed working for the past two years but preferred it to accepting roles in second-rate movies. She was waiting for the right film to come along, and she knew that eventually it would. In the meantime, she read every book and script she could lay her hands on.

Her personal life had always taken a back seat to her career, and it still did. She had one daughter from an eight-year marriage that began in her twenties. She had been married to one of Hollywood's biggest producers, John

Walker. They had been a powerful pair and had made several movies together, which had been legendary box-office successes and enhanced both their careers. It had been a tumultuous but creative match, which also produced their only daughter, Morgan, who was now thirty-eight years old and a plastic surgeon in New York.

Morgan had avoided the Hollywood scene all her life, and chose medicine as an exciting, satisfying alternative. It suited her. She was a partner in a successful practice of plastic surgeons, with two senior partners who had worked together for years. One was close to retirement, the other was in full swing, and Morgan was the only woman they had ever invited to join the partnership. One of the senior partners also taught at Columbia medical school. They set the bar high.

Ardith wished now that she had spent more time with Morgan when she was younger, but her own career had been white-hot then, and she was too often away on location and away from Morgan, and didn't deny it. Ardith had missed all the important moments and landmarks in Morgan's life, the school plays, her first prom, her first heartbreak, many birthdays, and it was impossible to catch up. She felt guilty about it now but there was no way to make up for it, or relive the past. Once Morgan was an adult, the two women were very different. Morgan respected her mother's career but had never enjoyed it, and the differences in their personalities and respective careers were hard to bridge now. They spoke often, out of duty and respect, but agreed on very little. Morgan had few memories of her father, who had died when she was seven. There had been scandal around her father's death, which had troubled her for years.

John Walker had died in a tragic helicopter accident, which was even more traumatic for Ardith because he was killed with the young woman he was rumored to be having an affair with at the time, a budding actress who was appearing in one of his movies and whose career he was shepherding. She was twenty-two, and Ardith was thirty-one then. The letters she found after John's death with his protégée confirmed her fears and suspicions about their involvement. Ardith had never forgiven him for it. The press had turned his death into a lurid event. Morgan knew the story once she was older, and had harbored illusions about him anyway. His films remained as tributes to him, but his reputation as a womanizer lasted after his death. Ardith knew it wasn't his first affair by any means and had said as much to Morgan. He could never resist the actresses in his films. Ardith had never married again and had no regrets that she hadn't. It was an experience she never wanted to repeat, as she had no desire to be married to another cheater and she didn't want more children. Morgan was enough to deal with on her own, and their relationship had never been easy, and less and less so when Morgan grew up. She'd been rebellious in her teens, and angry about the parents she didn't have. Ardith readily admitted that although she loved her daughter, motherhood wasn't her strong suit. Morgan agreed. Ardith hadn't been prepared for how much she had needed to give a child, especially after her father died. They occasionally had a good time together, but they didn't see each other often anymore. Ardith had the time to give her now, but Morgan didn't have the interest or the availability. She was busy with her career as a physician in New York, and her mother was proud of her, but Ardith still had her own life as a star in L.A. Morgan was single at thirty-eight and said she didn't have time for a husband and children, or even dating. Her work and her patients were her priorities. In some ways she was like her mother—her career came first. And the tables had turned. Ardith hadn't made enough time for her when she was a child, and now Morgan made no effort for her. It was a cycle they couldn't seem to break, and Ardith had accepted the fact that it was too late and they would never be close. They existed on the periphery of each other's lives. And living on opposite coasts, they saw too little of each other to heal the damage of the past. They had the occasional nice dinner together, and then Morgan flew back to New York, and they didn't see each other for months.

For the past twelve years, Ardith had found comfortable

companionship with William West, who was almost as big a star as she was. He had been a readily identifiable hero over a fifty-year career, even longer than Ardith's. He had never won an Oscar, and hadn't taken the challenging roles she had, but audiences loved him. He took parts that endeared him to his fans. Since he wasn't as demanding about the parts he played, he worked more often than Ardith, and still did one or two pictures a year. He was leaving in two days for England on location, playing a worthwhile role, although he was no longer the romantic lead. At seventy-eight, he was healthy and energetic and wanted to continue working, even in slightly less important parts. He had no desire to retire.

Ardith always said that the sixteen-year age difference between them didn't bother her. When they'd gotten together, she was fifty and he was sixty-six, still a handsome man, and a star. They had their careers in common, and he was kind, attentive, and good company. He had slowed down a little in the past few years, but other than the handful of pills and vitamins she handed him every day to keep him healthy, he was in surprisingly good condition for his age. No one knew what would come later, but for now he was doing fine and still working. He hadn't been as wise with money as she was. He had never commanded the salaries she did and was grateful to be living in her home in Bel Air for the past ten years. He contributed a small amount to expenses, but Ardith didn't expect anything from him. He had been married and divorced twice, to actresses both times, had only stayed married briefly, and had no children, which kept things simple. He had always been friendly to Morgan, but she was already doing her residency at Columbia by the time he and Ardith got together, so Morgan's relationship with him was cordial but superficial. She had no complaints against him, he was friendly and polite and good to her mother, and he had appeared much too late to be a father figure to her. She said she had no need for one, and she found him somewhat narcissistic, like most actors, more concerned with his own looks, projects, and problems than anyone else's. Ardith was used to it and didn't mind, and they were each the longest relationship either of them had ever had. After twelve years, they had become a legendary Hollywood couple, and were always seen together. It wasn't a great love affair and never had been, but it was companionship for both of them. They had each other and weren't alone or lonely.

When the car finally stopped in front of the Hilton, Ardith stepped out of the car in a long sleek black satin gown, which molded her impeccably maintained figure. She had a white fox wrap on her shoulders, was wearing a diamond necklace and earrings she had borrowed from Van Cleef & Arpels, and her blonde hair was combed in a smooth, elegant bun. She looked dazzling, and the press went wild when they saw her, flashing her picture, shouting her name, waving to catch her attention as Bill West stepped out behind her in an impeccable tuxedo. She smiled and waved like royalty at the mass of photographers and the fans hovering near them at the edge of the crowd, and she and Bill glided smoothly inside to make their way down the red carpet before the dinner and award ceremony began. Once Ardith and Bill were in a room or a crowd, all eyes were on them. Most people assumed that they were married by now, but they weren't, and she still had no desire to be. She said there was no reason for it, although Bill reminded her from time to time that he would prefer it, but he was of a previous generation. And she always pointed out that at this point marriage wouldn't change anything. They had lived together for ten out of twelve years, and there was no additional benefit to marriage, except emotional reassurance she didn't need. Ardith was a strong, self-sufficient woman and preferred her life that way.

Bill had beaten prostate cancer five years before, which had left him healthy and cancer-free but unable to perform sexually, which she accepted. She was young to give up sex, but it was a sacrifice she made for him. The relationship they had suited her, and him as well. She couldn't imagine meeting someone else now and having to adjust to a new man. She had had enough men in her life and was satisfied to have

Bill West be the last one. They were both Hollywood icons and thought to be the perfect couple. In some ways, being with a man his age aged her, and in others it made her feel young. They seemed right together in everyone's eyes, including their own. He was the perfect supporting actor to her, the star.

They spent half an hour going down the red carpet, then made their way to their table, where they would have dinner and watch the awards. The Golden Globes were important and often predicted how the Oscars would go two months later. Ardith and Bill were seated at a table of comparably major stars, and the TV cameras sought them out constantly. They would be under close scrutiny all night, and Bill had already told Ardith he wanted to go home right after the awards and skip the after-parties. He still had a lot to do before he left for England two days later, and he didn't want to stay out late, although she would have enjoyed it. She didn't want to go to the parties without him, so she planned to leave with him.

Ardith and Bill both accurately predicted who would win that night, and approved of the foreign press's choices, and after making their way back through the photographers, they escaped without attending any of the parties and were back at Ardith's house in Bel Air before midnight. Ardith had already packed most of what Bill would need in England, but he kept adding to it, afraid she had forgotten something. She was going to pack his various medications in his brief-case, with notes about what to take when. He fell asleep with his arm around her that night, with Oscar, Ardith's tiny white toy poodle, on the bed next to her. She took him everywhere, which Bill had objected to at first, but he finally got used to him. Ardith claimed the dog was her soulmate, and his constant presence was non-negotiable.

Ardith was an early riser and was already at the breakfast table the next day when Bill appeared in a navy cashmere dressing gown with navy satin lapels. She looked up and smiled when she saw him. She read the *Los Angeles Times, The New York Times,* and *The Wall Street Journal* every day. She had an insatiable hunger for knowing about the world around her, more so than Bill, who read *Variety* for news of the film industry, which was all that really interested him. He said that he left Ardith in charge of world news, and was sure she'd let him know if the stock market crashed or a war broke out, and she promised she would.

"Did you sleep well?" she asked him, as she did every morning, with a tender look.

"I did." He smiled at her. "I hate to leave you for two months," he said wistfully, as she poured him a cup of coffee. But he had no desire to retire either. He enjoyed his work

Danielle Steel

and loved going on location. It made him feel busy and alive, and important. "I had an email from the producer this morning. Your assistant starts tomorrow, when I leave." As part of his contract, and to induce him to go on location for two months, the producers would provide an assistant to help Ardith with all the small tasks Bill did for her. He worried about her being alone for so long with no one to help her and felt mildly guilty leaving. He was still a bankable name and to keep him happy, the producers agreed to provide Ardith the assistant, she had guessed probably a young actress they knew well who wasn't currently working and needed the money. And she was grateful for whatever help an assistant would give her. She was expecting a female assistant. She had a housekeeper who came daily during the week, and left dinner for them if they weren't going out. Ardith often drove herself around town, but used drivers too. She drove Bill when he had appointments, or he took an Uber. She thought an assistant might be superfluous, but Bill wanted her to accept it. It was free and an add-on to his contract, which his agent had negotiated. It was a perk for her to share, so she agreed somewhat hesitantly. Since it wasn't Ardith's contract, they didn't offer her the opportunity to interview whoever they hired. She was mildly worried that an unknown assistant might be more of an annoyance than a help, but she could always fire her if she didn't like her, and it made Bill feel as though he had done something special for her, so she hadn't argued about it.

"Did they tell you anything about her?" Ardith asked, as she poured skim milk into a bowl of cereal for him. She watched his diet more carefully than he did. He would have preferred bacon and fried eggs, which she didn't allow him. There was a responsibility that went with being with a man his age. She was as much a nurse as a girlfriend.

"No, they didn't," he said about the assistant. "I'm sure she'll be very nice. You can send Oscar to the groomer with her," he said, a task which he personally didn't like. Oscar had never been overly fond of Bill. Oscar knew who his friends were. Bill wasn't a "dog person" and Oscar knew it.

"I don't mind taking him," Ardith said breezily.

"What are you hearing from Morgan these days?" he asked her. He was impressed by Morgan's medical career. Even though they weren't close, Ardith frequently asked her for medical advice, which Morgan was loath to give her. Ardith checked on all of Bill's medications with her daughter, to be sure there weren't dangerous side effects the doctors hadn't informed him of.

"Nothing much. All Morgan does is work," she answered his question.

"No man in her life?" He was sorry she hadn't met someone by now, at thirty-eight. He thought she should make some effort in that direction, as she wasn't getting any younger if she wanted a husband and a child. Bill had old-school views on every subject, particularly women and relationships.

"She says she doesn't have time," Ardith said. She had stopped reminding her daughter of it herself. It was up to Morgan if she wanted marriage and kids. It didn't look like it so far, and she loved her work. Morgan had never been very interested in marriage. "She's thinking about going to Vietnam this fall, to work on a special project, pro bono, helping kids with burns. It sounds awful, but noble."

"She's a good girl," Bill said admiringly, and left the table a short time later to finish packing. Ardith drove him all over town to do last-minute errands, and they were both exhausted that night when they went to bed. He had to leave the house at six A.M., as the producers were having him picked up for a nine A.M. flight to London. He was getting VIP treatment all the way, due to his age and status.

The alarm went off at five, and he was ready to leave when the car arrived. He looked lovingly at Ardith as they stood in the doorway, she in her nightgown, and Bill elegantly dressed for the trip.

He looked every inch a movie star, in a dark gray suit, blue shirt, and navy tie, with a well-cut navy overcoat, and a hat that made him look very dashing. He was excited to be going to work on a film for two months, and to have a good role, but he was sorry to leave her. She had promised to visit him in three weeks, and she was looking forward to some time alone while he was gone. She was planning to spend a night in New York on the way, to visit Morgan if her daughter had time. The plan wasn't definite yet. Morgan didn't make plans far in advance and said she was swamped at work.

"Try to behave while you're gone," Ardith teased Bill. "Don't fall in love with the star."

"You too," he said, and kissed her. He had more to worry about than she did, but they were faithful to each other. She stood waving from the doorway as the car pulled away, and she envied him for a minute. She would have liked to be leaving to work on a film on location, and hoped she would be one of these days, for the right movie. It made Bill feel useful and engaged to be working. He had three suitcases for his elegant suits, and a fourth one just for shoes. He had friends in London he planned to see when they had breaks, and he wouldn't be on set every day. The role wasn't too physically demanding, unlike the projects Ardith usually signed on for, which required months of preparation. His career had never been as demanding as hers. He was the only actor she'd ever been involved with who wasn't jealous of her and didn't punish her for her success, which was one of the reasons their relationship worked so well. He had never been resentful of her fame. Bill was easygoing, comfortable with who he was, satisfied with the degree of success he'd achieved, and didn't want more than that. Unlike Ardith, who had always pushed herself hard, physically and mentally, with the roles she took, always wanting to achieve more. It was why she had won two Oscars and he hadn't, and he didn't mind that either. At seventy-eight, he was just happy to still be in the game and to have work at all. He had never been as ambitious or driven as she was. They were a good fit that way.

She went back to bed, thinking about him after he left, happy for him that he would be working. It was an impressive cast, which would be fun, and a famous director whom Bill had worked with before.

She fell asleep, woke up two hours later, showered, and put on a green face mask she didn't like applying when Bill was at home. It made her look like the witch in *The Wizard of Oz*. Then she sat down to breakfast with the papers she read every day. She was halfway through the *Los Angeles Times* when there was the sound of an explosion outside, or some kind of major disturbance. She looked up in surprise, peeked through the blinds of the kitchen window, and saw an enormous motorcycle head straight for the house and spin around with a spray of gravel. The biker riding it looked like Darth Vader or a Hell's Angel, in a helmet with a black shield that concealed his face, a black motorcycle jacket, torn jeans, and biker boots, and he sat staring at the house for a minute, looking as though he was going to kill someone if he got inside. Benicia, the housekeeper, came running up to Ardith, looking terrified.

"He looks like a Hell's Angel, should I call the police?" she whispered, while Ardith tried to evaluate the situation and just how dangerous the biker was. He looked like a rough customer. Oscar was barking frantically from the noise the biker had already made with the Harley.

"Where are the panic buttons?" Ardith asked, whispering too. The rider looked menacing as he slowly got off the enormous motorcycle. You heard about guys like him, who broke into homes or held people at gunpoint while they robbed them in broad daylight.

Benicia took a panic button out of a drawer and handed it to Ardith, as she continued to watch him, wondering if he was armed or going to break a window to enter the house. It had never happened before. She didn't like guns and didn't keep one in the house, although Bill thought she should, for an event such as this. Burglars and criminals in the Los Angeles area were known to be pretty bold. Ardith was holding the panic button in her hand, about to press it, while watching what the fearsome-looking biker was going to do. He took the helmet off, and she saw that he was unshaven, with a face covered in beard stubble, and had longish hair that looked as though it hadn't seen a comb in months. He had a powerful build, and she had visions of him tying them up while he robbed the house. He didn't look like a drug addict, more like a thug. He was in good shape, with broad shoulders. He walked away from the kitchen windows, strode up the front steps, and rang the doorbell, which wasn't what she expected at all. Or maybe robbers were just that brazen now, they rang the front doorbell, grabbed you, and tied you up. She hit the panic button as soon as he rang the bell and tiptoed to the front door to get a better look at him through the peephole. He was just standing there, and she knew the police would arrive in less than ten minutes. Ardith told Benicia to stay in the kitchen—she didn't want her house-keeper getting hurt—and stood on the opposite side of the front door, wondering what to do before the police arrived. Bill had been gone for exactly three hours and they were under attack. She remembered then that he had told *Variety* that he was leaving town for two months on location, which she didn't like. Not that he would be any match for the hoodlum on their front steps, who was built like a body-builder and looked about thirty years old, if that, probably younger.

"Who is it?" Ardith shouted through the door, curious what he'd say, and trying to sound fierce herself. Her throat was dry, and she was shaking, but the adrenaline rush of fear made her brave.

"It's Josh Gray. Ms. Law's assistant," he said, sounding much meeker than Ardith as she let out a gasp and felt her knees go weak.

"You're *what*?" She unlocked and pulled open the door and stared at him, in her bathrobe and bare feet, with her hair piled on top of her head, and her face green with the forgotten face mask. She and the fierce-looking alleged assistant stared at each other in disbelief.

"I'm her new assistant . . . your new assistant," he said, hesitantly, assuming she was Ardith Law. "I'm supposed to start this morning. Mr. West's producer sent me."

"And you came to work looking like *that*?" she said with blatant disapproval. "I thought you were going to break into the house and kill us. And you're supposed to be a woman."

"Sorry, they sent me. For two months." Oscar the toy poodle ran into the hall from the kitchen and barked frantically at the man. Ardith could hear sirens in the distance, and in less than a minute, two squad cars arrived and four officers ran toward them with guns drawn, as Josh Gray looked panicked.

"Hands in the air," the police shouted at him, as one of them pushed him to the ground and he lay facedown on the lawn. Ardith looked embarrassed.

"I'm sorry," she said to the officers, as two of them stared at her. "It was a misunderstanding. I thought it was a break-in, but it was just my assistant coming to work." She tried to look starlike and sound charming and casual, as Josh looked up at them from the ground in shock, and she caught a glimpse of herself in the hall mirror and saw the green face mask she had forgotten. "Oh my God. I'm really sorry." The police withdrew quickly, and Josh got to his feet and stared at her. She was unrecognizable with the green goo on her face, but she was obviously Ardith Law. It was a hell of an introduction to his new boss, and he hadn't wanted the job anyway. Josh was an actor, out of work, his next movie had just been canceled so Bill's producer on the film assigned him to Ardith as an assistant for two months, which Josh had been dreading.

He had read about her reputation as a diva and had no desire to be her cabana boy for two months, but he was being paid to do it and he needed the money, since the sci-fi movie he'd been hired to do hadn't happened. But this was a lot worse than a bad movie. He was forty-one years old and had been acting in second-rate movies for the last ten years, and waiting on tables. He was still hoping for his big break, and it hadn't happened yet. Ardith Law was clearly not it.

"Come in," she said to him sternly, "before the whole neighborhood sees us." She picked up Oscar, Josh walked

312

into the front hall, and she shut the door hard behind him. "What are you doing coming to work on that *thing*? You'll terrify the whole neighborhood. I thought you were a Hell's Angel."

"So you called the police?" He was still stunned at what had happened.

"You look dangerous. And why didn't they send a woman?"

"I think they were going to, but she got a part on some teen vampire movie, so you got me instead. The sci-fi movie I was supposed to do got canceled so I was free. I have a friend in the producer's office. He set me up for the job."

"Great. You look like Darth Vader. You can't come to work on that thing," she told him as he followed her into the kitchen, and Benicia stared at them both, unable to understand why Ardith had invited their attacker into the house.

"I don't have a car," he said politely, wondering if she was crazy, or just weird with the green face.

"Take an Uber. My neighbors will kill me for that racket. I can give you a car to drive while you're at work."

"What exactly am I going to be doing?" he asked, looking worried. "They said you needed an assistant while Mr. West is away."

"Exactly. You can take the dog to the groomer, pick up packages, do errands for me. Whatever I need," but having a male assistant was going to be a problem. He couldn't come into the room when she was undressed or take orders while she was in the bathtub. He wasn't what she wanted at all, and they had never told Bill they might send a man. He was almost useless to her.

"I'm not a trained bodyguard," he warned her.

"I don't need one. Or I didn't until you showed up. You scared poor Benicia to death," she scolded him. "And you have to come to work decently dressed, you can't run around town looking like a Hell's Angel. Do you have a jacket, like a blazer or something?"

He nodded. "Do you want me to wear a suit and tie?" he asked dismally.

"No, a proper shirt, clean untorn jeans, and a jacket will be fine, and real shoes or running shoes, no axe murderer boots." She looked at him with disapproval. "Do you like dogs?"

"I've never had one." Oscar was still barking, and Josh didn't look enthused at the prospect. "Does he bite?"

"Only people he doesn't like," Ardith said curtly. "He weighs three pounds. You don't need to worry about him." As she said it, Oscar bared his fangs and looked more like a rabid guinea pig than a dog. Josh looked miserable.

"Do you want me to go home and change?" She considered it, still in her green face, which she had forgotten again while berating him. He had upset them all, even the dog.

"You're fine for today. Try not to scare us to death

tomorrow." He nodded, still remembering when he had been lying facedown on the lawn minutes before, with two armed LAPD officers pointing their guns at him. "I'll get dressed. You can run me into Beverly Hills to do some errands, that way I won't have to park."

"Fine." He nodded, still stunned by the first moments of his new job. The next eight weeks seemed frightening, given what he'd seen so far. A crazed mouse of a dog, a boss with a green face, armed police forcing him down on her front lawn. If he could have hit his own panic button, he would have. This was a lot worse than he had feared. She wasn't a diva, she was insane, and he was stuck with her for the next eight weeks. A drink to calm his nerves would have been appealing, and then maybe she'd fire him and he wouldn't have to deal with her for the next two months. But for now, he was on the hook, because his damn movie had been canceled and he had to be an errand boy to a lunatic. He wanted to run screaming out the door, but he knew he couldn't. He needed the money to pay his rent. Benicia looked at him suspiciously as he sat down at the kitchen table and waited for Ardith to reappear so he could drive her somewhere. As far as Josh was concerned, she needed an exorcist, not an assistant, and as he waited, he reached down to pet the frenzied toy poodle, who bared his fangs at him again, aspiring to be Cujo.

"Be nice," Josh whispered to him. "I'm not liking this any more than you are. I promise not to bother you if you don't bite me. Deal?" Oscar hesitated for a minute, stared Josh in the eye, uncurled his lips, and marched off to find his mistress, while Josh wondered what the production company would do to him if he quit on the first day. It was very tempting, and he reflected on whether he'd need a tetanus shot if Oscar bit him. This was definitely a high-stress job, and not at all what he'd expected. But how much worse could it get? At least the cops didn't shoot him, but he couldn't bring his Harley to work, and he had to dress to cater to her. It was possibly the worst job he'd ever had, and diva didn't begin to describe it. A diva with a green face and a savage toy poodle. He couldn't wait to get home, smoke a joint, and have a martini. It was going to be a very, very long eight weeks working for Ms. Ardith Law!

If you enjoyed

NEVER
TOO LATE

you'll love these other titles by
Danielle Steel

THE BALL AT VERSAILLES

A life-changing night . . .

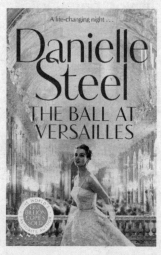

1958. The Palace of Versailles is hosting
an event that will go down in history. It is a
glamorous dusk-to-dawn ball, where a select group
of debutantes will be presented to international
society and royalty. And for four young women, all
with something to prove, it is an event they will
never forget. An exclusive invitation, a trip to Paris
and one spectacular, showstopping night will
change their lives for ever . . .

SECOND ACT

The courage to begin again . . .

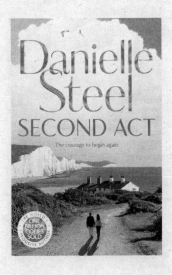

When Andy Westfield, the head of a
prestigious movie studio, unexpectedly
loses his job, he takes a break from Los
Angeles and rents a luxurious home on
the south coast of England. There he meets
local woman Violet Smith. Violet leaves the
manuscript of her unfinished novel lying
around one day and Andy is captivated by
the story that begs to be adapted for the big
screen. Could this be the miracle they've
both been looking for?

HAPPINESS

Happiness is a choice . . .

When Sabrina Brooks learns that she is
the sole heir to a historic manor house in
Hampshire, she is forced to cross the Atlantic
and see the property for herself. Sabrina
learns about her family history – and the
secrets her father kept from her. She starts to
fall in love with the manor and its beautiful
gardens. And she cannot help but enjoy the
company of the devastatingly handsome but
complicated lawyer who acts as her tour
guide . . .

PALAZZO

Dreams do come true . . .

After a tragic accident, Cosima Saverio
assumes leadership of her family's haute
couture Italian leather brand at just twenty-
three. Success comes at a cost, and her needs
are always secondary . . . until she meets
Olivier Bayard, the founder of France's most
successful ready-to-wear handbag company.

But, as her brother's gambling addiction
spirals out of control, Cosima is forced to
make an impossible choice. Is there a way to
rescue everything she has fought for – before
it goes up in flames?

Danielle Steel

Have you liked Danielle Steel on Facebook?

Be the first to know about Danielle's latest books,
access exclusive competitions and stay in touch
with news about Danielle.

www.facebook.com/DanielleSteelOfficial